A
GAMBLER'S
JURY

ALSO BY VICTOR METHOS

An Invisible Client

Neon Lawyer Series

The Neon Lawyer
Mercy

A GAMBLER'S JURY

VICTOR METHOS

THOMAS & MERCER

Published by Thomas & Mercer, Seattle

www.apub.com

Amazon, the Amazon logo, and Thomas & Mercer are trademarks of Amazon.com, Inc., or its affiliates.

ISBN-13: 9781503949041 (hardcover)
ISBN-10: 1503949044 (hardcover)
ISBN-13: 9781542046398 (paperback)
ISBN-10: 1542046394 (paperback)

Cover design by Jae Song

Printed in the United States of America

First Edition

For my father. Hope you're dancing among the stars, Dad.

If you are neutral in situations of injustice, you have chosen the side of the oppressor.

—*Desmond Tutu*

1

It was all fun and games until I showed up to court so hungover that my head felt like it was going to explode.

I caught a reflection of myself walking into the Salt Lake City courtroom and I didn't look good: like a haggard metalhead after a drug binge. A haggard metalhead after a drug binge who'd just woken up behind a bar with a bowl of Cap'n Crunch in her face. I don't know what a bar was doing with Cap'n Crunch, but I can't imagine the Cap'n would've been proud of whatever it was.

I was wearing jeans and, I realized then, a sports coat that wasn't mine. Apparently I had grabbed a man's coat on the way out of the bar.

The sunglasses over my eyes and unlit cigarette dangling from my lips didn't help my image as a professional attorney-at-law. I spit the cigarette out in a trash bin but left the sunglasses on, mostly because of the hangover, as I crossed the courtroom and collapsed in the chair next to the prosecutor, Cortland Smith. She shook her head.

"You smell like booze," she whispered.

"I feel like some booze. You got any? Hair of the dog and all."

She lifted a file and set it in front of me. "No, no booze. Sorry."

I shrugged and picked up the file. On the inside flap, prosecutors wrote the deals they were willing to offer. This one said: *No deal.*

"Seriously?" I said.

"He's got a long history, Dani."

"Give me a plea in abeyance. Come on, you know you want to. Come on, come on, come on."

"Are you begging me right now?"

"Is it working?"

"No, it looks kind of pathetic."

"Ouch. You're hurting my womanly feel-goods." I sighed and closed the file. "Fine. Trial it is." I looked at the judge, a portly woman named Harkin, and asked, "How is she today?"

"In a serious mood. Watch your ass."

I stood up and moved toward the lectern. Attorneys were supposed to form a line and take turns, but I was so late there was no one left. I smiled at the judge. She rolled her eyes and said, "Ms. Rollins, take your sunglasses off."

I slipped them off and tucked one end into the front of my shirt. "You look lovely this morning, Judge. Have you done something with your hair? Cut and color?"

"Who's your client?"

"Mark Rodriguez, please."

My client came up to the lectern and stood to the side. "Your Honor, my client is a nice young kid, nineteen years old, busted for allegedly possessing cocaine in a parking lot with a prostitute in the passenger seat. Kids these days, right? They have no sense of decency." I looked at Mark. "You take that stuff to a shady motel room like any decent citizen from previous generations, young man."

"Ms. Rollins, what do you propose?" she asked, annoyed.

"I believe the prosecution is graciously moving to dismiss the case and issue an apology to my client."

Cortland stood up. "Your Honor, we'd ask for a trial date."

"August seventh. And Ms. Rollins, please wear appropriate attire next time you're in my courtroom. And maybe don't be so hungover."

"Hungover?" I said, looking shocked. "Your Honor, I am flabbergasted that you would suggest such a thing. Horrified, really."

She exhaled. "Get out of my courtroom."

"Yes, ma'am."

We turned and left. Mark stopped in the hall and said, "So, what does that mean?"

"It means we're going to trial. You got a suit?"

"A suit? Nah. I ain't got a suit."

"You're gonna need one. You're gonna have to testify and tell the jury exactly what you told me: you didn't know it was cocaine, and you didn't know she was a prostitute."

"Okay, yeah. So you think we can win?"

"Sure."

No, there definitely was no chance we could win, but a few months of hope wouldn't hurt him. Besides, you never knew with a jury. We might get some crazy separatist nut who hated the government and the police and refused to convict.

"Look, just stay sober, buy a suit from a secondhand store—a nice one but not too nice—and come by my office in a month so we can go through your testimony. In the meantime, no nose candy or girls named Candy. None of it. Got it?"

He nodded. "Okay, Dani. Yeah. I got it. Come by in a month."

I watched him walk out of the courthouse and knew what I was saying to him wasn't getting through. He would keep using and possibly get busted again before the trial. I'd go check on him and talk to his mother, see if I could influence events in any way, but unfortunately, everyone had free will.

I headed out of the courthouse to the Jeep parked on the street. I took the parking ticket stuffed under the windshield wiper and put it under the wiper of the cop car parked in front of me before I got into my Jeep and pulled into traffic.

Out on the freeway, I blared Led Zeppelin as I headed to West Valley. Despite being in Utah, statistically one of the safest states in the country, Hoover County had more crime than counties twice its size. The police force out there grew every year, and with it, the prosecutor's office. That meant more criminal cases filed and more clients for us defense attorneys. Crime was always a growth industry.

I stopped at a rundown house with several pimped-out cars in front. One pink Cadillac had brushed chrome trim and a couple of Hispanic gentlemen smoking joints inside. They eyed me suspiciously, and I said, "Real men drive pink," as I walked by.

I got up to the porch where a kid no older than twelve said, "Who the fuck is you?"

"Now what kind of grammar is that? It's who the fuck *are* you?"

He stood up and tried to get in my face though he only came up to my chest.

"Easy, Snoop Diapers," I said. "I'm a friend of Franco's."

He slowly lifted his shirt, revealing the .22-caliber handgun tucked in his pants.

"You know, that's a good way to blow off your bits and pieces. Might I humbly suggest tucking the gun into the back of your pants?"

Franco opened the door. "Sit down, Hector. This here's my lawyer. Quit actin' like you hard."

"Shit," Hector said, "you lucky, bitch."

Franco slapped the back of his head. "Show respect to women, you little shit."

I walked past Franco and into the house. "Charming young lad."

"My cousin. He ain't so bad. Just protective." He glanced back at me as he led me to the living room and flopped onto the couch. "How you been, Dani?"

I sat down in the recliner across from him. A young girl was watching cartoons on the television in the front room. "Good. You?"

He said something in Spanish to the girl and she sighed, turned off the television, and left the room.

"I'm in some shit."

I held out my hands. "That's what I'm here for."

"No, this ain't like those other times. I really fucked up this time."

"What happened?"

He ran his hand over his head as he leaned forward, his gaze on the carpet. The tattoos of a naked woman with a skull for a face and the blade of a knife on his right arm were incongruous with the man I knew: the man who worked two jobs to feed his daughter and put a roof over her head, the man who attended night courses at Salt Lake Community College to get a degree in business to get his family out of the ghetto and into someplace decent. Sometimes, I guess, what's on the outside doesn't tell us what's on the inside.

"Some of the guys were doin' a deal down there in Richardson. They said they needed a ride. I told them I wasn't into that shit no more, and they said they just needed a ride. I didn't have to do anything else."

"Franco, tell me you didn't go down on a drug deal."

He shook his head. "They said they just needed a ride."

"Are you crazy? How many times did I tell you to cut that shit out? With your record, this isn't gonna be counselor meetings and fines anymore, man. You're looking at real time."

He blew out a puff of air, unable to look at me. "It's worse. We got pulled over. Cop said he smelled weed in the car and had us all get out. I knew they wasn't sellin' much, just what they had in their pockets. But they had guns. Three of 'em." He hesitated. "One of the guys was on parole. I couldn't let him go down like that, so I said the gun was mine."

"Shit," I said, flopping back in the recliner.

"Yeah, I know. But my homie said he'd come say it was his in court."

"You know that doesn't matter, right? You already confessed. They're gonna think you punked your friend into taking the blame."

"I know. I know," he mumbled. He swallowed. "There's more. The cop called down the task force. One of the detectives said with my record, they're gonna make it go federal, and they're gonna hit me as hard as they can. Twenty years. Is that true?"

Under Utah law, if a firearm was found anywhere near illegal drugs—it didn't matter the amount—it was assumed the weapon was being used to further drug deals. The US Attorney's Office frequently took over such cases and filed them in federal court.

"I haven't looked, but with your record, yeah. It could easily be that much."

"Shit." He paused. "He wants me to snitch. Says if I rat out everyone I run with, he'll let me slide. He's been callin' me all day, and I haven't answered. I wanted to talk to you first."

I leaned forward, putting my elbows on my knees. Snitching wasn't anything to take lightly. If he did it, he would have a target on his back the rest of his life, as would his family. I thought of the little girl in front of the television and what some high tweakers might do to her.

"The only time I ever recommend cooperating is if you're looking at time you can't do. Anything less, and you're gonna suffer."

"I'm already suffering, girla. I'm already suffering."

I thought for a moment. "Gimme the number for the detective. I'll talk to him."

He nodded. "Yeah. See if there's anything you can do."

"I'll see. But if I can't, you may need to do something drastic. You feel me?"

"Drastic?"

Technically, a lawyer couldn't tell a client to run. So I said as delicately as possible, "Run."

"What?"

"If I can't take care of this, run your ass off and don't look back. Go to Mexico. Hell, go farther south. Go to Brazil. But get outta here and don't come back. Even if I worked out a deal for you, it'd still be at least fifteen years. Run. In fact, don't wait for me to work anything out. Just run. Get your girl, get all your money, and run."

He nodded. "Yeah, all right. All right."

On my way out of Franco's, I saw the little man on the porch staring up at me. I crouched to eye level with him and said, "The small are the ones who need to carry a gun to feel big. Guns don't get you respect." I tapped my temple with my finger. "This is what gets you respect—being able to outsmart your opponents."

He rolled his eyes, and I left.

2

My office took up the corner of a floor in a building at least fifty years past its prime. The offices of criminal defense lawyers didn't matter. Clients wanted to know you could keep them out of jail, and the flash didn't matter one bit. In fact, the worst criminal defense lawyers in any city were found in the fanciest buildings, charging hourly rates that would make high-priced escorts blush. Better to hire the lawyers who shared office space with Pizza Hut or worked out of their shitty apartments—the lawyers willing to get their hands dirty, who would send an investigator out to see if the cop who arrested you was having an affair or if the prosecutor was going through a divorce that could be exploited to catch him off guard. It wasn't pretty, but it was necessary. The odds were stacked against defendants from the start, and they had to take any advantage they could get.

But I didn't feel like going back to the office, and I didn't feel like going home, so I headed to the bar.

The Lizard—yes, the actual name of the club—was in a section of the city crowded with sex-related businesses. Utah wasn't exactly the friendliest place for strip clubs or peep shows, but it couldn't just outlaw them either because of a little hindrance called the Constitution. So they put them as far from public view as possible, in a grimy section of the city known for factories and shady chop shops. My friend Michelle, who owned the Lizard, just happened to prefer the sleazier parts of town. Many of her clientele were judges, politicians, police chiefs, and doctors, so when they came out to play, they preferred to be on the wrong side of the tracks where nobody knew them.

I parked out front and went inside. Though it was around four in the afternoon, several cars were already there. The bouncer, a big guy wearing a sleeveless shirt, nodded to me and I nodded back.

The inside was almost too dark to see, and I had to let my eyes adjust before going farther. I saw the bartender restocking and I said, "Hey, where's Michelle?"

Someone slapped my back just then and I smelled the unmistakable scent of weed. "I missed you, Rollins," she said.

"Are you high already? It's like four in the afternoon."

"Drink with me," she said, slapping the bar top.

"Kinda early, ain't it? I was hoping for something to eat."

"We'll eat later." She turned to another bartender and said, "Tequila, Jim."

I lit a cigarette and sat on a bar stool. I didn't know how Michelle kept it together enough to own not one, but two bars. Maybe alcohol didn't require any business acumen or even sanity. It would be hard to fail when everyone wants the product.

"How you doin'?" Michelle asked.

"Same." I blew smoke out of my nose. "I think Stefan's really gonna marry that girl."

"Your ex is gonna marry a girl that's been in *Guns & Ammo*?"

"Looks like it."

The shots came. We tapped glasses, then swallowed the poison down. Michelle held up her fingers for two more.

"It's your fault, you know," she said.

"I know. Thanks for your support, friend."

"Hey, I'm proud of all my mistakes. Made me who I am."

"How can I be proud of it? My ex-husband is marrying someone else. It doesn't feel exactly like winning the lottery."

"There's only two ways to make it in life, Rollins. Jim Morrison, or John Rockefeller."

"What?"

"Life as art or life as project, woman. See, Rockefeller knew what he wanted from an early age. He built his life around it. He told himself that his life was going to be a certain way, and he planned the trajectory so it would go in that direction. Anything that didn't add to his vision of that life, his project, he wouldn't do. His family, his friends, his health, all of it came second to his project.

"Morrison went the opposite way. He painted a canvas with his time— a beautiful painting of emotion, imagination, and poetry. Experience coming together to weave this tapestry of pleasure and pain. That's it, sister. That's all you got. Life as art or project. So you gotta choose. In my opinion, the best choice is the painting. Make life your painting."

I stared at her. "Are you the same girl I saw projectile vomit red wine over a cop?"

"Hey, wisdom is found everywhere. Don't knock it. See, now, my life is a painting. I wake up in the morning with no idea what I'm going to do or where I'm going to go. I surf whatever waves there are. And that's it. I go where life takes me. My father lived his life like a clock. I mean, down to the *minutes*. Exactly eleven minutes to take a dump in the morning, fifteen minutes to shower and dress. When my mother and he had sex, it was scheduled: one time a week for fifteen minutes, always missionary . . . it was crazy."

"I'm not gonna ask how you know your parents only did it missionary, but I get what you're saying. But that doesn't apply to me anymore. I'm not twenty, Michelle. I've got a kid."

She put her hand on my arm. "That's exactly when you need to choose which one to be."

3

My day usually started with figuring out where the hell I was. This morning, I was in my own bed. True, I was still wearing my clothes from yesterday, but still an A plus for waking up someplace where I could shower and change.

I put on a gray suit with a white shirt and thought I looked like my father. I didn't remember much about my father in those early years—mostly how little he was around. I was eight when he finally left, and I don't remember being sad about it. My mother and I accepted it. At least I thought my mother had accepted it, until the day she abandoned me to the foster care system.

The thoughts were bringing me down and I didn't want to be down. The sunlight came through the windows, I heard birds somewhere, and the weather was pleasant and cool. I wanted today to be a good day. So I changed my suit into something that didn't make me look like a virgin schoolteacher—black blazer and jeans—and I checked my fridge for something to eat. Beer and a bottle of ketchup. I chugged half a beer and left the house.

Looking at today's calendar on my phone, I had a court appearance in the morning, a motion hearing in the afternoon, and two client consults in the evening. Not a bad day at all. I got into my car and looked over to my neighbor Beth's house. As always, she was standing on her porch, and she waved to me. I waved back. Before I could pull out, she came over and shoved a granola bar through the open window.

"I washed your dish," I said. "It's inside."

She brushed my hair out of my face with her fingers and tucked it behind my ear, making me look a little more presentable. "You're a beautiful girl," she said. "You need to show it to the world more."

I thanked her for the granola bar and pulled away. If it wasn't for Beth bringing me food, I might have just been drinking beer all day.

I listened to the Stones on the way to court in Draper City, the most affluent part of Salt Lake County.

The bailiff knew me, and on my way into court said, "You look like shit, Dani."

"Thank you, Hank. Always a pleasure to get insulted by a man who still lives with his mother."

"I told you that was temporary."

I went into the courtroom and saw the prosecutor at her table. Christina Montoya grinned at me and leaned back in her seat. "Quite a spectacle at the jury trial. I think that's the fastest verdict I've ever gotten."

I crouched down near her. The trial she mentioned had been a disaster—a DUI where my client got on the stand and said he had drunk sixteen beers that night but felt fine. I don't know what possessed him to say that; we'd gone over his testimony ten times. Christina did have a sweet quality that made people want to be honest. Maybe my client had just been caught off guard. The jury convicted him in less than a minute.

"Gloat much?" I asked.

"I'm not gloating. Well, maybe a little. You were trying so hard to win. It was adorable actually."

"If he'd stuck to our game plan, the shoe could very easily be on the other foot. I like to think I'd be lady enough not to gloat."

She shrugged. "When we hanging out again?"

"How about lunch?"

"It's a date. I can't get out of here till one." She opened her file. "As for our dear Mr. Passey, I'll reduce it to an infraction and give him a reduced fine in exchange for a guilty plea."

"Done."

An infraction was a crime that wasn't a crime. It wouldn't show on a criminal history report and no incarceration was possible. The judge could issue a fine, but had no means to enforce it other than dinging the defendant's credit. By any measure, it counted as a solid win. I turned to the audience and saw my client, an elderly man with white hair, sitting in the back. I motioned for him to follow me outside.

We stood to the side of the courtroom entrance. "Marty, you gotta take the deal I've worked out. They've got you on video hitting that girl."

"She was mouthing off to me. I already told you. And I've never done anything like that before."

I don't know why clients always said that—as though they deserved to have their problems disappear because they'd never been caught doing it before: *"I know I shot that dude but I ain't never killed anyone before." "I don't understand why they putting me on trial; I ain't never run over anyone before now." "I know I beat my wife but I've never been convicted of that before; they should just dismiss it." "I know I drove drunk but it's the first time I've been caught. They should just make the case disappear."*

"Marty, it's being reduced to an infraction. It won't be on your criminal history and the judge can only impose a fine. You can pay it or not pay it, and he can't really do anything to you."

"Would I have to say guilty?"

"Yes."

He shook his head. "No way then. I didn't do nothin' she didn't deserve."

This was probably the hardest part of my job: convincing the unreasonable to be reasonable. Three witnesses saw him strike the woman, there was a cell phone video, and the judge had five daughters and a pet peeve for males who laid a finger on females. Sometimes it felt like my job was nothing more than falling on swords.

"Trial then?"

He nodded. "Damn straight."

We went back in, and the judge grinned and said, "Ms. Rollins. Wearing your Sunday best again, I see."

I glanced down at my jeans and blazer and thought they looked fine. Then I noticed my shoes. I'd put on my white Chuck Taylors. Well, that was a risk of the profession.

"I tied them, Judge. Just for you."

"I appreciate that." He turned to his computer. "What are we doing with Mr. Passey?"

"Trial, please."

"Sixty days out okay for everyone?"

"It is," I said.

"That's fine, Your Honor," Christina said.

"Your Honor, may I just say that it's refreshing to be in a courtroom where fuckery has no place. I mean that in the nicest way."

I think I heard a gasp from the audience. Maybe it wasn't the court to drop an F-bomb in, but I had to let the judge know how much I appreciated him not yelling at me or degrading me or my client. Cool and collected. Even after I cussed, all he said was, "Please be here a half hour early so we can go through jury instructions on the day of trial."

I leaned toward Christina and said, "Leave the offer open. I'll try to get him to take it."

"No promises."

A Gambler's Jury

I checked my phone when I got outside and didn't see any calls from Stefan or our son, Jack. The two people I most wanted to hear from.

I didn't have the patience to talk to Marty right now. I would hit him up the day before trial, when a lot of clients grow afraid of conviction, and see if I could convince him to take the deal. I had a few hours before my next court appearance so I went to a local bookstore, something that soon would go the way of the dodo so had to be enjoyed now.

The store smelled of coffee, dust, and books. I got a cup of coffee and wandered around for a while.

A quick lunch with Christina followed at some sushi place where we talked about anything but work. I had met her outside of the courtroom when she gut-punched a defendant who grabbed her boob. It was an instant friendship from then on.

"You seem sad," she said.

I didn't know how to respond so I ordered us two beers. She didn't want any so I drank them both.

When I left, I headed to the Salt Lake City Justice Court and was trying to parallel park when a lawyer named Farley pulled into the spot from behind me.

"Are you serious?" I said. I rolled down my window and shouted, "Get your own damn spot, Farley."

"I was here first."

"The hell you were. I'm halfway in already."

"So am I, and the front end gets priority."

"What? That's not a thing."

"Yes it is. Now move your ass."

I backed up a few more inches and lightly tapped his car.

"What the hell are you doing, Danielle! You hit me."

I began revving the engine, my back bumper pushing against the front bumper of his car. The curse words spilling out of his mouth would have made a pimp blush. I made one hard push, and he finally

15

backed up and flipped me off as he drove around the block to find another spot.

The metal-detector bailiffs waved me through, past a crowd of onlookers waiting in line who scowled at me. "Hey," I said as I turned to them, "I suffered through three years of law school and got an anal fissure from the stress. I should get some recompense, don't you think?"

"No. Get back in line," someone said. I ignored them and went to the courtroom.

The case was a simple charge of exhibition driving. My guy and another had raced their souped-up cars on the street and got busted by a cop who was sitting outside a bagel shop. My client was in the back row, with his girlfriend. He had spiky black hair, a giant silver chain, and a tattoo of a naked stripper on his arm, which he felt the need to expose in all its glory to the judge and prosecutor today.

I was in and out in less than ten minutes. Quick plea, six-hundred-dollar fine, and good luck to the client.

4

My office always seemed colder and emptier in the afternoons, and I tried not to be there if at all possible. Client consults were the only reason I came in after two. Kelly sat at the front desk typing something up. I had found Kelly at a big firm, fresh out of college, when I went there for a deposition. Everyone there treated the staff, particularly the female staff, like crap. At the deposition, the partners forced her to sit quietly in the corner. One of them, a big guy in an expensive gray suit with massive male boobs, said something that pissed me off and I called him Adolph Titler, which caused her to laugh to no end. The partner fired her right there, and I immediately hired her.

She said, "One consult cancelled, the other one should be here in a sec."

I sat at my desk. My degrees hung on the wall along with various honors that meant nothing but somehow impressed clients. I leaned my head back and thought about my conversation with Michelle yesterday. I didn't see how it was fair that a girl like Peyton the Duck Serial Killer got a guy like my ex. Stefan was humble and sweet, and she was flashy and cruel and a hunter who posed next to beautiful animals she had just slaughtered, with a ridiculous grin on her face. But what could I do about it? Life seemed to be random chaos on top of random chaos, dragging you by the short hairs. Maybe the point was not to show life how much power it really had. Also, I'd cheated on Stefan. He had every right to leave me and marry whoever he wanted, and I had no right to complain.

The comm buzzed and Kelly said, "They're here."

"Send 'em back."

A moment later, a middle-aged couple walked in with a boy. The man was in a red jacket with a logo for FHY Pharmaceuticals over the breast and gray sweatpants, and the woman wore a nice sweater. The boy was probably around sixteen or seventeen. He was black and the parents were white.

The boy crossed and uncrossed his fingers as he held his hands up, and he smiled widely as he looked around the office. He had bits of food stuck to his chin and lips.

The woman held out her hand and I shook it.

"I'm Riley Thorne, nice to meet you," she said softly. "This is my husband, Robert, and our son, Teddy."

"Nice to meet you guys."

Teddy said, "I rode the elevator here."

His voice went from a low pitch to a high one, and the wide smile stayed on his face. I didn't know what type of disability he had, but it was severe enough that he couldn't keep his gaze on anything for too long. His eyes went from me, to the diplomas on the wall, to the window, to the desk, to the floor, back to me . . .

Riley Thorne pulled out an iPad and giant headphones, and put them on the boy. Teddy immediately laughed and began to play some game as the three of them sat down.

"His official diagnosis is severe intellectual disability, but we don't use those words around him," she said, sensing my curiosity. "We adopted him at three months and didn't find out until . . . I don't know, a year later maybe. We couldn't put him back into that awful foster care system, so he's been our boy now for seventeen years."

I just gave a dopey, understanding grin, unsure what else to do. I knew the foster care system well, and not once did anyone ever consider adopting me. It was the dream of every foster kid that some loving family would take you in as their own, and I wondered how different my life would've been had a nice couple like this adopted me.

"My secretary told me you guys had a family member charged with drug distribution, is that right?"

She nodded. "It's Teddy."

I looked at Teddy, who made a noise between a laugh and a hiccup as he tapped ceaselessly on the iPad.

"Teddy?" I said.

"Yes, it's a complete joke, Ms. Rollins."

"Call me Dani. Why's it a joke?"

"Teddy doesn't go out. He doesn't have any friends, not really. Just some kids from a class that we take him to four times a week. There's this neighbor boy who Teddy just worships—Kevin. Teddy's known him his whole life." She paused. "Kevin's just, I guess, everything Teddy isn't. He plays sports; he's on the high school baseball team; he dates girls . . ."

Robert Thorne chimed in, "He's got a scholarship to play for Arizona State." The pride in his voice was clear, as though he were talking about his own son. "He's a good kid. Like Teddy. They both are."

"Yes," Riley said sadly. "So you can imagine that Teddy really likes him. I don't know why, but he asked if Teddy wanted to come play games at their friend's house. We don't let Teddy out on his own, so I said that he couldn't go. Teddy really wanted to, though, so he sneaked out and went with Kevin. I don't know all the details, but the next thing I knew, the police were at our house saying Teddy was arrested for trying to sell cocaine. Teddy doesn't know what cocaine is. He has no conception of money or wealth. He couldn't sell something if he wanted to."

Victor Methos

I looked at Teddy again, whose mouth was open as he lost himself in the iPad. A handsome boy who wore a shirt with too many stains to count. He had large, soft, brown eyes that looked like a doe's eyes: innocent and open.

"Is this the first criminal charge Teddy's ever had?"

"Of course. He never even leaves the house except to play in the front yard and watch Kevin with his friends."

"And he's seventeen?"

"Yes, but he turns eighteen soon."

"Do you mind if I talk to him?"

She gently took the headphones off her son and said, "Teddy, this is Danielle. She would like to ask you some questions."

Teddy looked at me and breathed out of his nose before he said, "I rode the elevator here."

"I know. Was it fun?"

"Yeah, it goes really fast."

"Little too fast for me. What are you playing?"

"Um . . . it's birds and they fly through the air and hit these pigs."

"I've played it." I leaned forward. "Teddy, do you remember going out with your friend Kevin the other night?"

"Kevin . . . Kevin is my friend."

"Is he?"

"Kevin is my friend, yeah. He says we're pals." He looked down at the desk. "He says we're pals."

"That night you went out with Kevin, do you remember what happened?"

"No, because Kevin said we're pals, see. So I don't remember."

"I know Kevin's your pal, buddy, but he would want you to tell me what happened. I'm here to help you."

His brow furrowed a moment. "Yeah, Kevin's my pal. And he said he would take me to play games, see. And that we could play basketball

20

because he has a ball. I can't play basketball. My mama says I'd get hurt. I'd get hurt. So Kevin will take me to play."

"Where were you with Kevin on that night you went out with him?"

"At a house. And they had fruit punch there." He laughed. "They had fruit punch, and Kevin said I could have as much as I want, and they were playing games."

"Do you remember what happened after you had the fruit punch?"

"Yeah, we drove, we drove, and then the police came and then I went home. I went home. Kevin said that it would be okay, and he would take care of me. I went home."

Riley said, "The officer said they weren't taking him to jail because of his condition. He was a nice enough guy. He brought him back to us."

"Yeah, I rode in a police car, and they said I can't hear the siren, see. The siren is only for emergencies."

"That's right, buddy, it is." I thought for a second. "Did Kevin tell you to do anything that night?"

"Yeah, we're playing games, see. And we were going to play basketball but not football because Kevin says football eats ass."

"Teddy!" Riley gasped.

I couldn't help but laugh. I cleared my throat when his parents looked at me disapprovingly. "Tell me about the police, Teddy. When did the police get there?"

"Yeah, the police said I could ride in the car but I couldn't hear the siren, see. Because it's only for emergencies."

I nodded. I leaned back in my seat and watched the parents as Riley put the headphones on her son again.

"We were referred to you by someone in our church. Billy Nielson. He said you helped him out once."

I remembered Billy. He had been accused of sexual battery after misreading some signals and groping a girl he had been on a Tinder date with. In addition to the ass whooping the girl gave him—she was an MMA fighter—he was also arrested. I got him released with a fine and a few sessions of therapy.

My gut twisted into knots as I stared at Teddy. I had no concrete ideas why, just that something about this case was already sending off signals to stay away. "What county did this happen in?"

"Hoover."

"Hang on one sec."

I knew one of the screening prosecutors at the Hoover County District Attorney's Office, Lauren Hailey. I hadn't talked to her in months, and I couldn't remember why. I called her cell, and she answered within a couple of rings.

"Danielle Rollins," she said. "As I live and breathe."

"I don't know what that expression means, but I take it that you're happy to hear from me."

"You calling to set up a time to make out with my boyfriend again?"

That's right. That's why I hadn't talked to her in so long.

"I told you," I whispered, hoping the Thornes wouldn't hear. "He kissed me before I could push him away." We were awkwardly silent for a second. "Anyway, I didn't take you as the type to hold grudges."

"Oh, I got over it. You're not that important. And I dumped his ass."

"I agree with that. Guy was a scumbag. But hey, I need a quick favor and please don't hang up. I've got a young kid in my office named Teddy—"

"Theodore," his mother whispered.

"Theodore Thorne. He was busted a couple nights ago for distribution. I just wanted to see if that's in the pipeline yet."

"Hang on," she sighed. I heard her punching keys on the computer. Then she said, "Yeah, we got the detectives' reports today."

"And?"

"And we should be filing on it this week."

"Filing on it? Did the detectives mention Teddy's . . . condition . . . in their reports?"

"Yeah, they put that he has some possible mental issues. So what?"

"I got him here right now, Lauren, and it's pretty severe. No way he knew what he was doing."

"I don't know what to tell ya. People fake mental health issues all the time to get out of criminal charges. Work it out with the line prosecutor once it's filed."

"You won't do me a solid and hold on to the case for a while so I can look into it?"

"It's a lot of coke, and we have three witnesses saying Teddy was the one who did the deal."

I put my head back on my chair. Now it was making sense. "They pointed the finger at him, huh?"

"All four of them are charged with distribution, but yes, they said that it was Theodore's coke and his deal."

That was Utah law for you. The "constructive possession statute" said if someone knew drugs were in the vicinity, the drugs officially belonged to them. Four guys in a car with some weed in the console? If all four knew the weed was there, it didn't matter whose it actually was; even if none of them wanted to smoke it, all four would be charged. Teddy was just in the wrong place at the wrong time.

"Can you give me a few days to try to convince you not to file this?"

"Sorry, Dani, it's already approved by Sandy."

"That quick?"

"I told you, it was a lotta coke."

"How much?"

"Eight."

"Eight kilos? You're sure?"

"Positive."

I looked at Teddy, who was absorbed by the iPad again. "Well, I appreciate you telling me. I'll let them know."

23

I hung up the phone and turned to Riley and her husband. The husband stared out the window with a look that told me he didn't want to be here. Only Riley showed any real concern.

"He was busted with eight kilos. Street value, that's almost two hundred thousand dollars' worth of coke. I have a feeling the other boys pointed the finger at Teddy hoping they wouldn't get in trouble. Still, that's a lot of coke for just some ordinary teenagers."

"Of course they blamed him. That's why we need your help."

I stared at her a second. Teddy's case would be in juvenile court. Most judges didn't like sending kids to detention unless they had to, and certainly not for drug offenses. The likelihood was that even if Teddy pled straight guilty, he would get community service. It wouldn't even be on his record when he turned eighteen since we could get it expunged when he came of age.

Still, I wasn't sure I wanted it.

"To be honest, Riley, I'm not sure you need me. He won't go to jail because he's a juvenile, and you can ask them for a court-appointed attorney if you like."

"But we want you."

"I'm not sure you need me."

She hesitated a second. "Why don't you want this case?"

I couldn't answer that question honestly. How would I explain to a mother that I thought her child was innocent and I didn't need that kind of pressure in my life? True, he probably would get a slap on the wrist, but maybe not. Hoover County had the most aggressive prosecutors, police, and judges in the entire state—the type who thought breaking the law in order to enforce it was just good policy. They could try to land him in detention, and a kid like Teddy wasn't equipped to handle even a short stay.

"Can I think about it for a night?" I said.

"If this is about the money, we have a little nest egg. It's the least we can do for Teddy before . . . before he turns eighteen."

"It's not the money. Just let me think about it for a day and I'll get back to you tomorrow."

I shook hands with them as they left. Teddy kept his head down over the iPad, and when his mother removed the headphones, he said, "Are we gonna ride the elevator?"

"Yes, sweetie."

He whooped like he'd won the lottery and sprinted out of my office.

5

That night, I sat in my house and tried to watch a rerun of *Alf*. The show brought back good feelings from childhood, what few there were. I watched two episodes and then turned the TV off. I kept thinking about Teddy. I told myself that I didn't want the case, but I knew that something interesting was up. The case had run through the prosecutorial gamut too quickly. A detective actually finalizing and submitting a report in a couple of days was amazing, and then a screening prosecutor getting the go-ahead to file on a case a day or two after that was incredible, and the fact that this was a juvenile case . . . it just didn't make sense. Why go through all this trouble for a case that would end in community service, if that?

I had no delusions about the mentally disabled in the criminal justice system. They got no breaks. If the disability wasn't directly responsible—and how the hell could anyone prove it was?—for the crime committed, they were held to the same standard as everyone else. Teddy's disability would be a point of sympathy, a mitigating circumstance for the judge to consider, but it likely wouldn't negate the intent to commit the crime. He would be judged by the same standard as any other kid his age.

I didn't feel like being alone, so I got into my car and drove up the hill to the ritzy-shmitzy Federal Heights neighborhood. I turned my lights off as I rolled to a stop in front of Peyton the Pheasant Assassin's house. Stefan had moved in with her six months ago, about a year after our divorce. By the time the divorce was finalized, I was a mess and we both agreed that Jack would be best served living with his father. But I had no idea they'd be shacking up with a woman I despised.

Parking across the street at the curb, I saw a few lights on in the house but couldn't see anyone in the windows. Even though it was twenty different kinds of creepy to sit out here and stare at your ex-husband's new house, it brought me a level of calm that I couldn't get anywhere else.

Someone knocked on the window and I jumped.

"Holy shit!" I said, seeing my son's sweet face through the glass. I rolled it down. "I think you owe me new underwear."

"Gross, Mom."

"Don't hate the truth."

"What are you doing here?"

I put an unlit cigarette in my mouth, then took it out and got some gum instead. "Just being a stalker. What are you doing out?"

"I was over at a friend's house."

"What friend?"

"Just a friend. You don't know her."

"Her?"

"Don't be a dork." Jack put his forearms on the door and rested his chin on them. "How was work?"

"Crappy."

"Why?"

"Just a client who needs defending that I don't want to defend."

"How come you don't want to defend them?"

"You are a nosy little bugger, aren't you?"

He grinned. "How come? You always told me criminal defense lawyers either defend everybody or they defend nobody, because you're really fighting for the Constitution and not people."

"I said that?"

He nodded.

Shit.

"Hmm. I don't know. This one . . . I don't know. Kid's got a disability, and I don't think he's guilty."

"So? That should make your job easy, right?"

"I wish." I looked at the house. "Your dad home?"

"No. Come inside."

I didn't really think Peyton and Stefan would approve, but my curiosity overwhelmed me. I followed my son into Peyton's house. I'd been inside several times, but never without Peyton or Stefan right there with me. Now, I could actually look at things—assess my competition.

The photos on the mantel were worse than I thought. There were easily twenty of them. Stefan laughing or smiling in each one. A particular photo sent a nasty chill up my back: Peyton kissing him at sunset on some faraway beach I could never have afforded to take him to. The psycho used her money like a weapon.

I didn't know all the details, but from what Jack had told me, the two of them met when Stefan gave a talk at a fund-raiser about the importance of history to modern lives. Peyton didn't strike me as the type to give a crap about history, so I wondered if she just saw him as a trophy. A good-looking intellectual she could take to galas and charity balls to hang on her arm like a decoration.

"How's your dad doing?" I asked.

"You mean is he happy?"

He was perceptive, this one. Or maybe I was too obvious. People seemed to grow more obvious as they got older. "Is he?"

"I don't know. Maybe."

"Does he ever ask about me?"

"Not really. Hey, you want something to eat?" he said.

"No, but I'll take juice if you've got it."

"Orange okay?"

"Sure."

I moved from the mantel to the stairs leading to the basement. I'd never been downstairs.

"All of Peyton's stuff is down there," Jack said. "Guests aren't allowed."

Oh, now I was *definitely* going down there.

I took the stairs quickly and turned on the light. It was a man cave/woman cave of epic proportions. Bar, flat-screen television on the wall, pool table, video-game systems, and the heads of about twenty animals mounted along opposite walls. Deer, antelope, bear, mountain lion, moose, and a tiger. A mother-freaking tiger. Who had a tiger's head mounted on their wall?

I scanned the bar and grabbed a bottle of beer. As I sipped it, I spotted another collection of photos. These were Peyton in all her pseudo-manly glory. Peyton holding up the head of a dead buck, Peyton holding up a dead fish, Peyton next to the carcass of a shark, Peyton standing over the body of an elephant with one boot on its prodigious head . . . It was like looking at the internal thoughts of a serial killer. *"Yeah, she loved to kill animals,"* a neighbor would later say, *"but we had no idea she'd go on to make furniture out of people's bones. That just came out of left field."*

"Mom?"

"In the basement."

He came down the stairs and shoved a glass of orange juice into my free hand. I sat on the couch in front of the television and put my feet up on the coffee table made out of some fancy wood. Probably a sapling tree she chopped down and made its parents watch.

"Mom, can I ask you something?"

"You sure can, my half pint of sugar."

"How come you don't have a boyfriend? I mean, I know you date, men love you, but, like, how come you don't have a boyfriend?"

"Men love me? Where'd you get that from?"

"Please. Every one of my friends' dads that sees you falls in love. And I see some of the texts you get from people. But, like, how come you don't have a boyfriend?"

I exhaled through my nose and took another sip. "Sometimes, babe, you love someone so much that even when it's over, that love sticks to your ribs and won't let go. Not until the last moment, when hope finally goes out forever, or you find someone else to take their place. Until then, you're stuck."

I remembered the first time I met Stefan. A goofy nerd who fell off the back of a motorcycle and broke his arm. His girlfriend at the time, a girl not so much unlike Peyton, was too put out to take him to the hospital and told him to drive himself. I happened to be in the quad of the college where it happened and overheard her say that. Disgusted, I took him instead. He broke up with her the next day, and we were an item a week later, and married two years after that.

"Mom . . . Dad's not going back to you. He's not going to let himself go through that again."

"Your father and I were going through a rough patch and I was alone. I felt . . . No, that's an excuse. There are no excuses for what I did. I cheated on him and he was loyal to me. I deserve what I'm getting. Still doesn't make it hurt any less."

The door opened and I heard the deep bass laughter of Peyton the Tiger Sniper.

"Jacky?" Stefan yelled.

"Down here, Dad, with Mom."

The laughter stopped. There was a brief pause, and then two sets of footsteps came rushing down the stairs. Peyton stood there in a stunning black gown and gleaming watch, and Stefan wore a suit and tie.

His blond hair cropped short and his glasses some new, sleek model I'd never seen him wear.

"Hello, Danielle," Peyton said through what I thought were clenched teeth.

"Peytony girl, what's shaking?"

"Please," she said, tapping my feet off the coffee table, "make yourself at home."

"What are you doing here?" Stefan asked.

"Just wanted to see Jacky. I'll be going now."

"Nonsense," Peyton said. "Finish your drink."

Stefan looked at her and said, "Well I'm gonna get ready for bed. You too, Jack."

Jack wrapped his arms around my neck and kissed my cheek. "Love you, Mom."

"Love you, pumpkin pie."

He smiled as though he felt bad for me. I watched him go upstairs, but I didn't see the teenager in front of me. I saw the six-year-old boy who would run to me every morning and jump on my stomach. He'd tried so hard to impress me with things he knew back then, only a small portion of which were actually true, and then at night when he was in bed, he'd throw his arms around my neck and tell me he loved me. It felt as if those moments would never end, that he'd never grow up, but they were just a flash. A spark in a fire that glimmered for a second and was gone before I even knew what I had.

When the boys went upstairs, I was left alone in a basement with a woman who loved guns and killing. She smiled at me something wicked and then went to the bar to fix herself something.

"You're still in love with him," she said.

"With who?"

"Don't be an idiot."

She sat down next to me and crossed her legs. "You can never have him again, Danielle. I'm the better woman, and he'll always see that."

"Wealth doesn't make you better than anyone, Shake-and-Bake. It just amplifies what's already there. If you were an asshole before you had money, you'll be ten times the asshole after you get it. Hence the assholiness you see in the mirror now."

She chuckled. "It's all a big joke to you, isn't it? Well, here's a funny joke: I'm going to go upstairs, wait for Stefan in bed, and then I'm going to ride him until—"

"You better shut your mouth right now."

She laughed. "What's the matter? Can't handle the imagery?" She guzzled her drink and went to set the glass down on the bar. "Good night, Danielle. I'm sure you can find your way out."

I was left alone. I stood up, my guts in a tight knot, and scanned the basement. I ran over to the tiger's head, ripped it off the wall, and then sprinted out of the house with it like an NFL star running from a giant linebacker.

I was halfway to the car when I heard, "Mom?"

I turned around, trying to hide the massive tiger's head behind my back, and saw Jack looking down at me from his second-floor bedroom window. "Yeah, honey?"

"I want you to take that case."

"What case, baby?"

"The boy that you think is innocent."

"Oh. I haven't decided yet."

"Well, I think you should. It'd be good for you." He paused. "What are you gonna do with the head?"

"What? This?" I held it up. "I shall return it to the wild whence it came."

"'Night, Mom."

"Good night, honey."

"Mom?"

"Yeah."

"Don't be lonely."

"Who says I'm lonely?"

I walked to my car and tossed the head into the trunk. As I was getting into the driver's seat, I glanced toward the house and saw Stefan looking at me through the window upstairs. I waved to him, and he turned away.

Once in the car, I sat there a few minutes. I looked back at the house, at Jack's window, then took out my phone and put a reminder in my calendar: *Call Riley Thorne and tell her I accept the case.*

6

Whenever I accepted a new case, the first thing I did was bring the client in for a full vetting. I'd have them run through their version of events two or three times, sometimes more if I felt they were bullshitting me. It served several purposes, the two most important being that I could get a sense of how a jury would see them—once I'd spent time with a client my view of them would be tainted, so the beginning of the case was the best time to stand in the shoes of the jury—and that *they* could begin to see the holes in their nonsensical stories. The stories, through each iteration, would usually change.

I wouldn't do that with Teddy. I had a feeling I'd gotten what I could from him. So I just called his mother and told her I would accept the case.

"How much will you charge, Ms. Rollins?" she said.

"Normally I'd ask for a ten-thousand flat fee."

"I don't have that much. We have six thousand two hundred in our savings. You can have it all if you'll do it."

I sighed. On the one hand, it was never good to let a client determine the price of a case. They got a sense of entitlement, and there'd be things down the road that they would feel like they had a say in that they didn't or shouldn't. They had to know I was in charge, and the easiest way to show that was to not budge on price. Still, it'd been fairly slow the past month and this was only a juvenile case. I guessed that I would put in about twenty hours' work for that six grand.

"Okay, six it is. I'll start today. My secretary will email you a representation agreement. I'd like both you and your husband to sign it."

"Okay. Thank you so much for this."

"You're welcome."

I hung up and flipped on my computer. I checked my spreadsheet with all my open cases. I currently had seventy-one, sixty-five of which would be settled. Another five were still under investigation but settlement offers were in the works. One had just signed up and hadn't had a court date yet. That meant I could spend some hours on Teddy's case in the next couple of days.

I had Kelly draft an appearance as counsel of record, letting the court know I was Teddy's attorney, and send it to the prosecutor's office. Though the case hadn't been filed yet, they would send me the discovery—the evidence—as soon as it was ready. Then I called my investigator and told him I had something new for him. It sounded like he was busy, but he still said he would drop everything and come by.

Within twenty minutes, Will Dylan stood at my door. He was lean with slicked-back brunette hair and always reminded me of a good-looking Wall Street banker who actually had a sense of humor but without the drug addiction.

"What've you got for me, my pasty-white friend?" he said.

"That shit's racist right there, Will."

"Hey, I'm a quarter Irish American. I know what it's like to be oppressed, so I can say things like that."

"The only time you've ever been oppressed is when they asked your mom to leave a buffet because she ate all the pie."

"That was unjust treatment. It said 'all you can eat.' And I'm still hurt you wouldn't sue them." He sat across from me. "What do you got?"

"Drug distribution by a juvenile. Here's the kicker: the client is mentally challenged. I think his neighbor used him to try to get this drug deal done and things went bad."

"He's retarded and they're still going forward?"

"Seems so. Not sure 'retarded' is PC anymore, by the way."

He shrugged and picked up the case file on my desk and tossed it back when he saw it held no reports. "I'll interview the codefendants. That's probably a good place to start. Send me the police reports as soon as you got 'em."

"I will. Also, check out the criminal histories of all the codefendants."

"What is this, amateur hour? I've done a few of these, you know."

"I know. Sorry. I just want this case over and done with as quickly as possible."

"Why? Is the client an asshole?"

"No, not at all. Just don't want to spend too much time."

He exhaled. "I'll get it done quick. I'm still moving to Fiji."

"That's become a real thing, huh?"

"That's right, baby. I'm leaving the rat race, opening a little bar like my dad owned in Iowa, and spending my days on white sand." He rose. "Well, I'll get to it. So you're still not wanting to move to Fiji with me, huh?"

"Afraid not. Not yet, anyway."

"Well, the offer's always open. I could use a best friend over there. I gotta run. Catch ya later."

He owned a security firm with thirty employees and, as far as I could tell, was a millionaire, and it still baffled me that he was running down criminal histories and interviewing drug dealers as part of his day. The move to Fiji would be a good one for him.

I leaned back in my chair. The entire exchange could've been handled through email, but Will was old-school. When I had a case, he liked to come into my office and sit down and go over it. I didn't begrudge him that. Besides, on some days Will was the only noncriminal I dealt with. I needed that link to the outside world. Dealing only with drug dealers and rapists could mess with my mind.

I decided to ignore a motion I had to write and take a nap. I lay down on my couch and instantly wished I'd sprung for something more expensive than IKEA.

When I woke up, a couple of hours had gone by. I stretched and looked out my windows onto Main Street. A new sandwich place had opened down by a bank, and I headed out to try it. I lit a cigarette at the intersection and smoked while I walked. The air was gray and hazy today, and it was colder than it should've been. Two young men smiled at me, and one of them said something that made the other laugh. I turned around and walked backward as I winked at them and, as usual, they didn't know how to react. Men liked the fantasy of strong women, but when faced with a strong woman, they turned into children.

The sandwich shop was crowded and I had to wait in line nearly twenty minutes to place my order, but they made it for me right then. I took the sandwich and sat down at a corner table. I had a good view of the street and could see people walking past: people in business suits ignoring people in jeans, who ignored people in tattered clothes begging for food.

I took one bite of my sandwich and it was terrible. I tossed it and went next door to a pizza place and got two slices. I took them outside to a homeless guy sitting against a tree. Behind him, parked at the curb, was a Maserati, and the contrast of those two things made me uncomfortable.

"Mind if I sit?" I asked.

"Free country. You can park your ass wherever you want."

I sat down next to him and placed the plate with the pizza in his lap and took one slice for myself. We began to eat and we watched people stride by, ignoring both of us now, as though I had stepped inside an invisibility chamber.

"You stay at the Road Home?" I said.

He shook his head. "They only got ninety beds, and there's a lotta families here. I don't wanna take some kid's bed. I just sleep at the park. It's warm enough. Just passing through, anyway."

"Where you headed?"

He shrugged. "California, I guess. I been back and forth between the coasts three times. California's my favorite."

"Mine, too. I lived in LA before moving here."

"What made you come out here?"

"I thought in Mormon country I could have as many husbands as I wanted. Turns out that shit's been illegal for a century."

He chuckled, and bits of food fell from his mouth. "Shit, I had a wife once. Don't think I can handle more than one spouse at a time."

"Amen to that, brother."

I finished my pizza in a few bites and then rose and said, "Take care of yourself."

"You, too."

When I walked into the office, Kelly was watching something on her computer and eating a chicken sandwich from a fast-food joint. Without looking at me, she handed me a stack of papers: the discovery for Theodore Thorne. They had officially filed charges in the Hoover County Juvenile Court, charging him with a first-degree felony for distribution of a controlled substance.

"Kinda thick for a drug case," I said.

"Lotta witness statements. There's some recordings, too. I'll get them in the next week."

I sat down at my desk and began to read.

7

The police reports were detailed, but like all police reports, they were filled with so many grammatical and spelling mistakes and confusing descriptions that it made you want to tear your hair out. I wondered if it'd be that hard to set up an English class at the POST academy to train officers on the difference between "meat" and "meet"—unless two suspects actually did "meat" at a house on State Street and "meat" was some new sexual act that I hadn't learned about yet.

The reports started with the official charging document. I read the probable-cause statement.

> During a surveillance operation on a known drug house at 1435 N. 100 E. in Richardson, Utah, an individual by the name of Theodore Montgomery Thorne contacted our confidential informant and asked if he was in the market for a large shipment of cocaine. Arrested Person Thorne did this of his own accord with no initiation from our CI. AP Thorne set the time of 7:00 p.m. on April 2 to bring the narcotics. AP Thorne showed up at the CI's residence here in Richardson, Utah, at approximately 7:20 p.m. with three

other individuals later identified as Kevin William Simmons,
Fredrick Taylor Willmore, and Clint Russel Andrews.

The APs came to the residence's porch with what appeared to be
a large package in a gym bag. Through audio and video surveil-
lance, we recorded the AP Kevin Simmons and Theodore Thorne
speaking with the CI. AP Thorne stated that they had the drugs
and wanted the money. He then proceeded to hand the package
to the CI. At this point, we felt we had enough to initiate an
arrest and proceeded to take the APs into custody. AP Kevin
Simmons resisted arrest and attempted to flee on foot. He was
gently guided to the ground by Detective Gonzalez and placed in
handcuffs. I arrested AP Thorne and double locked and checked
the handcuffs. I asked AP Thorne what he was doing at the
house and he stated, "Giving him the bag." Based on where he
was looking, I deduced AP Thorne was speaking about the CI.

Subsequent to arrest, a search of the gym bag in AP Thorne
and Simmons's possession revealed eight kilograms of a white,
powdery substance that later field-tested positive as cocaine.

We proceeded to the Hoover County Sheriff's Office, where
AP Thorne again admitted to selling cocaine. AP Simmons,
AP Andrews, and AP Willmore all admitted that the drugs
belonged to AP Thorne and that he had initiated the contact
with the CI and that they were there simply driving him at
his request, as AP Thorne had stated he was too frightened to
go himself. All three stated independently that they did not
realize they were there to sell narcotics.

Shit. Really boys?

I wondered how long they had been planning to bring Teddy with them to take the fall in case the cops got involved. Since all three had the same story, they had to have discussed it beforehand. These boys sat down and methodically came up with a plan to hose a boy who didn't have any friends and who believed they were being nice to him.

I read the witness statements twice. Simmons, Andrews, and Willmore all had nearly identical statements: Teddy needed a ride to drop off some drugs and was scared to go by himself. I read the confidential informant's statement, hoping he would say he didn't remember Teddy ever speaking with him, but he didn't remember much of anything. He just said someone called him and told him they would be dropping off a package—a convenient case of sudden amnesia.

No rational human being would believe that Teddy masterminded this whole thing. But cops weren't rational; they wrote reports and dropped a big pile of witness statements, recordings, and narratives onto a prosecutor's desk and let them decide who to bring charges against. The real question was: Why was Hoover County bothering with Teddy?

Didn't matter. I would work out a great deal on this case and that would be the end of the story.

I checked my email and saw that Riley had called and paid the six grand. Today was turning out to be a good day.

I had a consultation with a current client in the afternoon. He had burgled a cell phone store, and they'd caught him on camera shoving over a hundred phones into his backpack. I'd gotten a deal for probation and restitution for him, but he was unhappy. He kept saying that some friend of his who had done the same thing last year had gotten his case dismissed.

"Maybe I should hire his lawyer," he said.

"Maybe you should."

I had little patience right now and didn't feel like coddling him. Besides, I'd earned the three grand he'd paid me four times over and would not be issuing any refunds.

He huffed and puffed a little more and then left the office. Again, for what seemed like the millionth time, I sat in my office and wondered what the hell had inspired me to become a lawyer. I decided I needed a break.

The Lizard was just gearing up for the night, and I figured Michelle would be there. I pounded on the side door as I smoked, and she opened it up. She punched me in the gut harder than I would've liked. "Come in, want you to try something."

Ever since I'd known her, she either punched, pushed, shoved, or kicked people she really cared about. In fact, we'd met in high school detention after she hit a boy she liked so hard that he fractured a rib.

I sat at the bar as she mixed and whirled and blended. In less than a minute, some glowing green concoction sat in front of me on the bar.

"What fresh hell is this?" I said.

"New drink I'm trying out. Get a lot of enviro-nazis in here and I thought I'd make 'em something special. I call it 'Earth.'"

"That's it? Just *Earth*?"

"Just Earth. Tell me what you think."

I lifted the glass and smelled the contents. I took a sip and nearly gagged. "Shit, it tastes like it has dirt in it."

"It does have dirt in it. What'd you think?"

"You made this with dirt?"

"Not any dirt. I didn't go outside and pick it up. Bought the good stuff. Soil from a flower shop. Just a hint of dirt to give it that earthy taste. What do you think?"

"I think it tastes like dirt, Michelle."

"Well, what the hell do you know? You've got no taste."

She took the witches' brew away and set a beer down in front of me. I took a long drink and she said, "Rough day?"

"Not really. Good day, actually. Made six grand on a case I'm not going to have to do much work on."

"That is a good day. So why the long face?"

"Do I have a long face?"

"You do."

I took another drink. "Just get sick of the bullshit sometimes. This wouldn't be a bad gig if it weren't for the clients."

"Hey, if you're unhappy, you should take what money you got and invest it in a club or escort agency. Sex industry is always booming."

"I've got a son. What kind of message would that send him?"

She shrugged. "That men are pigs."

"True, and a good lesson to learn, but let's not go down the pimp road just yet."

"Suit yourself. But you know I'm here for you. You can always run the bar with me."

"I know. And I'm here for you. And as your lawyer I cannot let you serve dirt to your customers."

"Yeah, I kinda figured."

My phone buzzed. I checked the ID, and it was from my after-hours line. I rarely answered that, but I felt in a good mood, and signing up another client would be a nice cherry on this sundae.

"This is Danielle Rollins," I said.

"Ms. Rollins, sorry to bother you. This is Riley Thorne."

"Oh, hey. What can I do for you?"

"Teddy's been arrested."

"What do you mean, 'arrested'? For what?"

"Two police officers came to our house and took him to jail. They had a warrant. It was for this case."

"What? They said that? Jail?"

"Yes, they said they were taking him to the Hoover County Jail and that we could bail him out after he gets booked in."

"It's gotta be some mistake. They almost never issue warrants for juveniles. And when they do, they take them to detention, not jail. Let me make a couple of calls."

I hung up and dialed my bail bondsman, Chip. Every time I thought of him, I pictured his parents sitting around at his birth trying to decide what dignified, appealing name to give him, and then going with "Chip."

"Chip," he said.

"Hey, man, it's Dani."

"What up, yo? Haven't heard from you in a bit. What you been up to?"

"You know me, nothing good."

"I heard that," he said.

I watched as Michelle mixed some new monstrosity in the blender. Instead of green, this one seemed to be turning out purple.

"Hey, can you check on a warrant for me?" I said.

"Sure thing. For who?"

"Theodore Thorne. He's seventeen, and his mom just called me and said some cops picked him up and took him to jail. She says they said jail but I'm wondering if they meant detention."

"All right, hang on."

I heard him walking around and then the groan of a chair as he sat down.

"Yeah, man, that's weird. We got a warrant here for fifty grand."

"Fifty? On a drug distribution for a seventeen-year-old? You sure you got the right Theodore Thorne?"

"Yeah, man, lists Danielle Rollins as his attorney. It's filed in the district court, not the juvenile court."

I shook my head. Clerks, bless 'em, were human and made mistakes. They were overworked and dealt with a segment of the public that had to take the frustration of the process out on someone, and the clerks were usually the closest ones available. I'm sure some douchebag yelled at the poor clerk and, flustered, she accidently punched it in as an adult case. Easy fix. I could get down to the jail and fix it myself.

"I appreciate that, Chip. I'll take care of it."

"Cool, man. Hey, if he needs a bondsman, you know where to send him."

"You don't even need to say it. You've been good to me, brother."

I hung up and told Michelle I had to go.

"Come back after," she said. "I think this batch is gonna be good."

I left and started the drive down to the Hoover County Jail about half an hour away, certain I would get my client out immediately and be hailed a hero by all.

8

Richardson was . . . unique. The city, it was rumored, was founded when the original pioneers who settled Utah decided that the criminal element—and probably the mentally ill—shouldn't proceed to the Salt Lake Valley with them but instead found their own city. They were forced to splinter off, and Richardson was born. That's not knowledge you can get from history books: you only learn that stuff once you live in Utah. I wondered if every city had knowledge like that—things no one wanted to see made public.

I parked outside the county jail and hurried in. The clerk at the counter looked about as grumpy as an old man could get, and before I said a word, he groaned as if I were asking him to change my tires.

"Hey, there," I said, smiling. Old people loved smiling. Or hated it. I don't know; I didn't get old people.

"Visiting hours are over."

"I'm counsel," I said, pulling out my Utah State Bar card. I showed it to him, and he wrote down my Bar number on a sheet of paper.

"Who's your client?"

"Theodore Thorne. I think there's been some sort of mix-up. He's only seventeen. He shouldn't be in here."

He typed in a few things and said, "Birthday on the sixteenth?"

"That's him."

"No mistake. He's being charged as an adult."

My heart jumped into my throat. "What the fuck are you talking about?"

"Hey! Watch your language. I will not tolerate language like that."

"Sorry. Just caught me by surprise. He's not charged as an adult— it's just a drug distribution case."

He swiveled the computer screen around so I could see it. "Look for yourself."

And there it was. Theodore M. Thorne, charged with first-degree felony narcotics distribution, out of the Hoover County District Court.

"It's a mistake. They must've filed it incorrectly. I've already talked to the DA's office about this case."

"I go off what the computer says. You wanna see him?"

"Listen, I'm telling you, that's a mistake. Can we get someone on the line? The kid's mentally disabled and shouldn't be in here."

"I go," he said very slowly, "off what the computer says. Now you wanna see him or not?"

I stared into his beady little eyes, eyes that had hardened to the plight of anyone who walked through those doors. He seemed to be enjoying my shock, as if the more he hurt or offended the person standing in front of him, the more strength it gave him—a trait I'd seen too many times in lifelong bureaucrats.

"Yes, I'd like to see him."

I went through the metal detector and was searched by a guard before being led back to a little room with steel benches. The slam of the door filled the concrete space. I had a recurring nightmare that I was trapped in a room like this when the jail staff forgot about me, and I had to fend for myself until they found me. I didn't remember how the dream ended.

The door opened a minute later and Teddy was led in. The guard said, "Call me when you're done."

Teddy wore a white-and-gray jumpsuit, and his right eye was swollen. His cheek was red, and he had a cut lip.

"I didn't want the cake, see," he said, his fingers crossing and uncrossing compulsively as he looked toward me but not directly at me. "I told them I didn't want the cake."

"Teddy, what happened to your face?"

"I told them that I didn't want the cake, but they gave me the cake anyway."

He paced in front of me, his fingers rubbing each other. Agitation poured out of him and filled the room as his voice got louder.

"I told them I didn't want cake I wanted pudding but they put cake on my tray and I said I didn't want it and the lady said—"

"Teddy," I interrupted, "did someone hurt you?"

"They were not nice," he said, stopping and staring at the wall. "They were not nice and I said they were rude and they said I had to have the cake because—"

"Teddy," I said, this time standing up to get in front of his eyes.

He jumped back, his hands covering his face as he pushed himself against the wall. He was trembling as he stared at the floor, his eyes wide.

"I'm sorry, buddy," I said softly. "I'm sorry."

I sat back down and watched him. He couldn't stop trembling.

"You shouldn't be in here. I'll get you out as soon as I can. Hopefully tomorrow or the next day. I just need to straighten it out with the courts. There's been some sort of mistake on your case, and they're charging you as an adult."

He glanced at me and then back to the wall. His middle finger started furiously rubbing against the top of his index finger.

"Just hang tight, okay, buddy? I'll get you out of here as soon as I can."

I rose and knocked on the door. The guard came.

"Hey," I said, "he's getting worked on in there. Can you guys transfer him to another cell block or administrative segregation? He needs to be by himself or closely monitored."

"Don't got the room," he said, brushing by me to grab Teddy.

"Hey," I said, gently putting my hand on the guard's shoulder.

"Get your damn hand off me."

I lifted my hand, surrendering. Those with egos the size of their penises had to be handled gently. "Easy, big fella. I'm just trying to help him. He's mentally disabled and he's clearly getting hurt. He needs to be in a more mellow cell block."

"Retard probably ran into somethin'."

I stared at the guard as he dragged Teddy away. As they were leaving, Teddy looked back at me once and then turned a corner with the guard and was gone.

———————

Outside, evening had turned to night. The sky was clear and the stars sparkled above me like gems. I stared up at them a long time. Jack and I used to lie in our backyard and stare at the stars. He would ask me the names of the constellations. I had no idea so I made them up. Later, when he found out I had been making them up, he said he liked my names better. I wondered if anyone had ever lain with Teddy and looked at the stars.

I exhaled and took out my phone.

"This is Chip."

"Hey, I need you to bail Theodore Thorne out. Tonight. Like right now."

"Okay. Family ponied up the ten percent, huh?"

"No, I'm paying it."

"What? You're paying five G for a client? They paying you later, though, right?"

"Chip, don't worry about the money. Just get him out."

I slipped the phone back into my pocket and looked at the jail. A monolith of steel and brick, a testament to humans' ability to hurt each other and our ability to throw mercy out the window. I couldn't look at this jail or any jail very long, and I never liked visiting clients in them. A cold rush always filled my guts, and I had an overwhelming urge to run away. I don't know if it was claustrophobia or what, but jails were hell on earth for me.

Once, in foster care, the father of the family had locked me in the basement without any lights or food. I think I was in there for two days, but really couldn't tell. I sat against the wall and cried at first, but then I stopped crying. I decided I wouldn't give the bastard the satisfaction. I wondered if sitting in a cell was similar.

A mother and child walked up the steps. The mother looked at me. "Do you know where we go to visit inmates?"

"Through those doors right there. Visiting hours ended at five, though."

"Oh." She looked down at her daughter. "We'll come back tomorrow, sweetheart."

The daughter's face lapsed into a sadness that pierced me as she turned around and headed back to their car. She held a little sheet of paper with the words "Love you, Daddy" written on it.

I got into my car and drove back to Salt Lake, relieved, at least, that Chip would have Teddy out within the hour.

9

I had a restless night. I drank a few glasses of whiskey and tried to watch Netflix but couldn't concentrate. I ended up just lying in bed with my eyes glued to the screen, the sound off while blue images flickered in front of me for a couple of hours.

When I woke, I took a quick shower and threw on the first suit I saw and a pair of actual pain-in-the-ass heels. Then I took them off and put on Chuck Taylors, because screw men if they needed me to torture myself to look their version of good. The sun burned my eyeballs, and I put on sunglasses before I even left the house.

I had one quick hearing in the morning, then I went straight to the office, said hi to Kelly, sat down at my desk, and began making calls. My first was to the Hoover County District Attorney's Office. I asked to be transferred to the assigned prosecutor on the Theodore Thorne case, and she said the two words I least wanted to hear: Jasper Diamond. They called him "Double D" for Double Diamond because his middle name was Diamond, too. Jasper Diamond Diamond. Maybe his parents figured he would forget that he was a Diamond, or something.

I'd had two previous cases with him and both were disasters. One was a simple theft case where he wouldn't give me a deal, and we had to go to trial. He'd withheld a nice little fact: the police officer who had cited my client was currently under investigation for rape. He arrested women for minor traffic offenses and misdemeanors, and then told them they could go to jail or have sex with him. My client, an attractive female, had no doubt been one of his targets, but there were too many people around for him to make his move, so he just wrote her the citation and left.

My client really had been stealing something, but that was beside the point. Prosecutors had a duty to disclose all the relevant information to the defense. I didn't find out about it until the day of the trial, when an anonymous tipster called my office. Someone on the Hoover County police force still had a conscience. I was sure that would be weeded out in time.

During the trial, I filed motions for sanctions. Instead of fighting it out with me, Diamond dismissed the case.

The second case was a DUI where he kept trying to introduce evidence the judge had already ruled was inadmissible: the fact that my client belonged to the Black Panthers in the 1970s, which would clearly prejudice the jury against him. I objected so many times my throat was sore. Finally, he just told the jury in his closing. I moved for a mistrial and it was granted. The case was then given to another prosecutor.

"This is Diamond," he said. Not Jasper. Diamond.

"Double D, this is Dani Rollins." A second of silence. No doubt he was happy to hear from me. "Good to hear from you, too. Anyway, you're the assigned prosecutor on one of my cases and I thought I'd give you a ring. There's been a misfiling."

"Thorne, right?"

"That's right. Kid's seventeen and he's in district court."

"That's not a mistake. We're certifying it."

Now I was the one who was silent for a moment. "You can't certify it. It doesn't fall under the statute as one of the qualifying offenses."

"Take it up with the judge. I filed certification on it with the information. See you at the hearing, Counselor."

He hung up on me.

To certify a juvenile case meant they were seeking the judge's permission to try the defendant as an adult. But only certain offenses qualified: aggravated arson, burglary, robbery, murder, attempted murder, sexual assault, or discharge of a firearm. Drug distribution wasn't anywhere near that list. And there was a set procedure: the case had to be filed in juvenile court, and the juvenile court judge had to find that there was probable cause and that trying the defendant in the district court didn't offend the interests of the child. It was bullshit because of course it always offended the interests of a child, but I could see why they'd want some kid who murdered his neighbor for fun to be tried as an adult.

Just in case I had missed something, I looked up the statute: section 78A-6-702 . . . nope, drug distribution wasn't listed there. What the hell were they doing?

My cell phone buzzed: it was Will.

"What up?" I said.

"Hey, lady, I tried interviewing your boys in that Thorne case."

"Already? Look at you, all efficient."

"Well, I'm retiring a young man of thirty-two, remember? Wanna get this over and done with."

"What'd you find out?"

"Nada. They wouldn't talk to me."

"Since when has that stopped you?"

"Uh-uh, not gonna happen. I am not getting some ethics violation now that'd keep me from my paradise island. They lawyered up and don't wanna talk. End of story."

I leaned back in my seat. "Hoover just did something weird."

"What?"

"They certified the Thorne case. But there was no hearing in juvenile court. They filed the certification and got it right into the district court."

"They can't do that."

"You're preaching to the choir. I'll get it kicked at the first hearing. But why would they even try this? It's clearly against statute."

"Hm. Maybe they don't like the statute."

My heart skipped a beat and my guts turned to ice. "Gotta go," I said. I dialed Double D again, and he answered, this time sounding more put out than before.

"Hello?"

"You *want* to lose," I said. "Are you trying to take the Serious Youth Offender Act up on appeal?"

"What I am and am not doing is no concern of yours, Counselor."

"Don't give me that bullshit. You guys have always hated that you don't have the power to charge juveniles as adults whenever you like. This is someone's life, Jasper. This kid's mentally disabled, and you guys are trying to use him as a guinea pig? Send your lobbyists to the capital like every other corrupt corporation and bureaucrat."

He sighed. "I already told you, take it up with the judge."

"Who's the judge on the case?"

"Roscombe."

Shit.

Mia Roscombe. And no, not female. I don't know why his parents decided to name him Mia but they had, and now he made the lives of every defense attorney in Utah miserable. I wondered if his parents and Double D's had gotten together to come up with names that would screw up their children.

Most judges would have declined the filing and told the DA to take it to juvenile court. Roscombe hated the Serious Youth Offender Act more than Hoover County did. He wanted to be the one deciding the fates of youth offenders, not some "soft-hearted juvenile court judge"—his actual words.

"Find another case, Jasper. This kid doesn't deserve it. Use one of the codefendants."

"Your guy confessed, and everyone else said he was the one who set it all up."

"There's no way with his mental—"

"That's for the psychiatrists to decide when you have him evaluated. Not for us. Can I get off the phone now? I've got things to do. I can't drink all day and hang out with male strippers like you do."

"I resent that. Only half my day is spent drunk with strippers."

"Good-bye, Dani."

I hung up the phone and shook my head. Then I called Riley.

"Hello?"

"Hey, it's Dani Rollins."

"Oh, Ms. Rollins, I was going to call you. We got a call from your bail bondsman, and they let Teddy out last night."

"Yeah, I know," I said. "I paid him five grand to do that. We can talk about that later. Anyway, got some news. It looks like the DA has filed this correctly. They want to try Teddy as an adult."

"Is that bad?"

"Very bad. If they lose on the issue of jurisdiction, they want to appeal it and overturn the law. If they win, Teddy could be facing a five-to-life sentence. This particular judge has told me before it's his policy to always send defendants to prison for drug distribution cases, so at a minimum Teddy would do five years."

There was silence for a moment. "I don't think he could survive that."

"I don't either. So I'm going to do everything I can to get him out of this."

"Whatever you think is best."

A lot of parents would have been screaming about the injustice of the system. Riley seemed less concerned than I thought she should be. But what the hell did I know? I certainly wasn't June Cleaver. My son would soon be the stepson of my polar opposite and learning how to harpoon whales or whatever Peyton the Animal Cannibal had planned.

"Anyway, I'll keep in touch. And make sure he's at his court date."

"We will. Thank you."

After hanging up, I lifted Teddy's file and stared at it a minute. I had a motion to write on another case, but I didn't feel like doing that right now. I opened the file to Kevin's address and then thought, screw it, and left the office.

10

Will wouldn't interview Kevin, but who said I couldn't give it a shot? I hadn't officially been notified that he had a lawyer and could always play dumb later. But I didn't want to do anything as obvious as knocking on his door and asking to speak with him. So I did the creepy stalker thing and went to his school.

Skyline High School was surrounded by green shrubbery and plenty of pine trees. The air was cleaner here, above the muck of downtown Salt Lake. The school was a flat building that had been designed in a lost decade.

I parked and watched the kids coming out. I had seen Kevin's driver license photo in my file and knew who I was looking for. Although if a thousand kids came out at the same time, I'd be hard-pressed to spot him. I called Will.

"What up?" he said.

"You busy?"

"Always."

"I need to know what kind of car Kevin Simmons drives."

"Why? What are you doing?"

"Better you don't know."

"I hate those. All right, give me a minute."

I hung up and watched a group of girls heading to their cars. They didn't look like the girls I remembered from high school. These looked like children—children who dressed like hookers. I felt myself sounding like an old lady and stopped the thoughts immediately. Every generation had their own style, and no generation was better or worse than any other. Then I saw a girl in a miniskirt and what could only be described as stripper heels and decided to revise my theory. Something was wrong with the current generation.

I got a text from Will: *White BMW*, followed by a license plate number. I drove around the lot until I saw a white Beemer that matched the plate. I parked across from it and turned on iTunes. In just a few minutes, I was nearly falling asleep. Fatigue crept up on me like that. The older I got, the harder it was to judge how tired I really was.

After half an hour, I got out of the car and lit a cigarette. The sun was shining and there were few clouds in the sky, but the cool air sent a chill up my back. I walked over to the football field. The cheerleaders or whoever sat on the ground gossiping while the boys showed off. Most of the cheerleaders I knew from high school who had hooked up with the popular athletes were now either divorced with several kids or, worse, stuck in a marriage that made them miserable. Marriage to someone you disliked was the American coffin that people willingly got into.

When I turned back toward the lot, several stragglers were still piling out of the school. I watched the Beemer. Someone was headed for it.

Kevin wore a beanie and white T-shirt. He had a girl with him, blonde and pretty and tan with vacant eyes. I approached and said, "Excuse me. Kevin?"

He looked at me but didn't say anything.

"Need a few words with you, my man."

"Who are you?"

"You're gonna wanna talk in private."

He unlocked the car and told the girl, "Hang on."

Once she was in the car with the door shut, I sat on his hood and sucked at my cigarette. He looked nervous, but it was a nervousness that had backup: Will had included in his report that Kevin's father was a big shot at a local detergent company and was loaded.

"That's cold-blooded of you, man. Teddy didn't deserve that."

He folded his arms. "You a cop?"

"Why? What do you have to hide?"

"I already talked to the cops, and I've got a lawyer. He says I don't need to talk to any more cops."

"Seems weird," I said, ignoring everything he was saying, "that Teddy would be the one to know the CI, a known drug dealer. Teddy doesn't have any friends. Well, you. At least he thought so."

He shook his head and looked away. "Talk to Teddy."

"I did. He doesn't understand."

"He understands more than people think."

"No shit? Could've fooled me. What about you? Do you understand more than you let on? Did your lawyer explain to you that you're gonna have to testify against Teddy and that, if at any point, they find out you're lying, you'll be charged with felony perjury on top of your drug charges?"

"I'm not lying," he said angrily.

I paused. His anger was genuine.

"Tell me what happened," I said.

"I already told the cops like—"

"I wanna hear it from you."

He looked at his girl and then turned his back on her and sat on the hood next to me. "We were just going to a buddy's house, and he wanted to come play games."

"How'd you end up in Richardson?"

"Teddy brought this, like, gym bag with him. He said he needed to drop it off. It wasn't far from where we were going so I said yes—I help him out sometimes. He only told us what it was about when we got there. He was scared to go up, so I went with him."

"Why'd you go along with him if you knew what he was doing?"

"I tried to talk him out of it. I don't know if he understood what I was saying. It was, like . . . he got this idea in his head, and then he wouldn't let it go. So we drove him down there, and he kept saying he was too scared to go to the door. The other guys wanted to leave as soon as he stepped outside, but I wouldn't let them. He told us it was drugs, but, like, I didn't really believe him, you know? I was gonna call his parents but he said not to. So I went with him to the door thinking the bag had, like, toys or something in it. Then Teddy and this guy traded bags and the cops were on us."

"You just went along with a drug deal? No questions asked?"

"I didn't believe him, and he wouldn't let me look in the bag. We were headed up near Richardson anyway, so I thought I'd go with him and make sure he was okay, whatever he was doing. Like, we didn't think he'd actually have coke on him. I mean, how could you think Teddy could do something like that?"

I stared hard at the kid, thinking that his lying soul would be revealed to me from the effort, but . . . Shit. I think I actually believed the little turd.

"Kevin, it doesn't seem to me like he could put something like that together."

"I know. It was really weird. Like he had it in his head that he had to do this and nothing would make him stop." He looked back at his girl. "I gotta go."

I hopped off his car and watched as they pulled away. Kevin seemed sincere enough to me, but if he was the type of sociopath to use a mentally disabled kid as a scapegoat, he could certainly be the type that could lie convincingly.

I tossed my cigarette on the pavement and stepped on it. I'd have to visit Teddy and get a take on him. As I headed to my car, a couple of young boys smiled at me.

"Got some condoms in my car," one of them said with a grin.

"I'd break you," I said, brushing past them.

I texted Kelly to send me Teddy's address.

11

When I got to the Thornes', the first thing I noticed was that the lawn sparkled in the sunlight, freshly mowed and watered, with flowers on either side of the porch. Not a single blade of grass was out of place. I parked in the driveway behind a Lincoln and got out. The car was probably twenty or twenty-five years old, but looked like it had just rolled off the assembly line. Not a speck of dust to be seen.

I knocked on the door and waited. The welcome mat said: "Bless This Mess."

Riley opened the door and seemed surprised.

"Hey," I said. "In the neighborhood. Thought I'd stop by."

"Did something happen?"

"Just thought I'd talk to Teddy for a little bit, if he's here."

"Yes, he's up in his room. Come in."

The home wasn't much different from the lawn and the car: I could still see the wave pattern on the carpet from a recent vacuuming. Plastic on the furniture. Photographs on the mantel turned just so.

Riley led me upstairs to the first room on the right. Teddy sat on the bed looking through a photo album. He wore shoes with the laces tied and superhero stickers on them.

"Teddy, Danielle is here to see you. Isn't that nice?"

"How are you, Teddy?"

"I'm looking for pictures, see. I'm looking for pictures."

"Yeah? What kind of pictures?"

I sat on the bed next to Teddy and looked down at the photos. One was of Riley; her husband, Robert; Teddy; and two other little boys at a campsite.

"Do you have two brothers?"

"No those are my cousins, see. My cousins. But they don't see me anymore. They said that because I have black skin I wasn't really their cousin, but my mama said I'm their cousin in every way that counts, see. That's what she said."

I looked at Riley, who stared at us a moment. "I'll give you two some time," she said, and left the room.

"Teddy, I wanted to ask you about Kevin."

"Kevin is my friend."

I sat silently for a moment and watched him flip a page in the album. "Yes, he is. But I wanted to ask you about the night the nice policemen brought you home. Do you remember that night?"

"Yeah, I wanted to hear the horn and see the lights, see, and they wouldn't do it. They said they wouldn't do it."

"Do you remember the house you were at? A man lived there. Do you remember him?"

He flipped another page.

"Teddy, did Kevin ask you to go see this man with him? The man that gave you the money?"

"I wanted to play games. Just to play games, see. And then the policeman drove me home. But he said I couldn't see the lights."

I exhaled and leaned back on the bed. He kept flipping through the album, and I looked around his room. On the nightstand was a copy of *The Adventures of Huckleberry Finn*. I picked it up. Several of the pages were dog-eared, and I opened it randomly to one of them and found a passage highlighted:

> *Well, it made me sick to see it; and I was sorry for them poor pitiful rascals, it seemed like I couldn't ever feel any hardness against them any more in the world. It was a dreadful thing to see. Human beings can be awful cruel to one another.*

"Do you read this book, Teddy?"

"Yeah, Jim and Huck are friends, see. They're good friends and Huck won't write a letter telling them where Jim is. 'Cause they're friends."

I nodded slowly and put the book back. "Did Kevin tell you to hold the bag you gave the man that night?"

"Kevin's my friend."

"I know, buddy, but did he give you the bag? It's okay—I saw Kevin today, and he said you could tell me."

"Kevin said I could play games."

"Did you know what was in Kevin's bag?"

He looked away and began kind of rocking back and forth slowly. He kept his eyes on the photo album, and it seemed the conversation was over.

"I think it's time for his nap," Riley said, reappearing at the door.

I rose. "I'll see you soon, Teddy."

"I'll see you soon, Danielle. Bye."

I don't know why, but the phrase cut me. It was so sincere. It had a tinge of hope to it, like he enjoyed my company and was genuinely looking forward to seeing me again. In most of the world, no one said anything so truthfully.

We got downstairs, and on the way out I said, "Does he read *Huck Finn*?"

"Oh, yes, it's his favorite book. I don't think he understands it, but he really enjoys it. I used to read it to him when he was a child." She cleared her throat. "That was a lifetime ago."

"What do you mean?"

"Nothing. Just that . . . when your child's a baby, you have so many hopes for them. You want them to have better than you did. And then one day someone tells you that it will never happen—that instead, your child will always need you. He will never be able to live on his own or do anything by himself. And then you realize that it would've been better not to have him. For both of you."

"What about his birth parents? Ever tried to find them?"

She shook her head. "They abandoned him at the entrance of a hospital. No one knows who they are."

We stopped at the door and I stared at her. "Did Teddy know the other two boys that were there with Kevin?"

"No, Kevin is his only friend outside of school."

"What do you know about Kevin?"

"They're wealthy . . . I don't know. They don't really have that much to do with us. We bought this house twenty years ago before this area went up in price and a lot of the neighbors look down on us because we don't have much. We don't know anyone around here really. But I will say that I once saw Kevin and his friends in his backyard when his parents weren't home. They were smoking marijuana."

I nodded. "Do you think Teddy could've had contact with anyone else that put him up to this?"

"No. He never leaves the house. The only person that could've possibly done this is Kevin."

12

The day dragged on like an anchor through mud on the ocean floor. Every second had to be endured rather than enjoyed. I wrote motions; I answered client calls. One new client signed up: a Catholic priest accused of sleeping with a prostitute. Apparently he and the hooker were on the way out of the motel when she asked for two grand or she would call the cops. The priest refused—mostly because he didn't have two grand—but the argument alerted the hotel staff, who called the cops. They were both cited for sex solicitation. It was an old hooker trick. They'd get cops, preachers or priests, school principals, politicians . . . whoever held positions where they shouldn't be sticking their members in ladies of the night, and then blackmail them. Another trick was to solicit a john and then pull out a fake badge, and tell him if he didn't want to be busted it would cost fifty, sixty, or a hundred bucks.

The priest paid me fifteen hundred bucks and said it was all he had. Who knew if that was true? He had just betrayed every vow he'd ever taken for five minutes of pleasure.

I didn't get out of the office until darkness had fallen over the city. Every city was different at night. It was as if two separate sets of people lived there, and one only responded to the sun and the other only to the moon. I had always been a night person . . . until I had Jack. And then the days were my time, because they were his time.

He was smart from a young age, and well ahead of the other kids in his classes. I wondered just now how it would've been to raise a child like Teddy. Constantly depending on you, unable to do anything by himself. Watching your child fall behind as the other kids of the same age advanced . . . I suddenly felt saddened for the Thornes.

My cell phone rang as I walked to my car. It was Michelle.

"What up, you crazy honky?" I said. "I was just about to head down to the Lizard for a drink."

"Forget that. Got you set up on a date."

"What kind of date?"

"Best kind: blind date. It's with my sister's friend."

I leaned against my car and stared up at the stars. It was a clear night, and I could see the twinkles of color from an airplane high overhead. "Michelle, I don't feel like a date just now. I want a drink."

"Go drink with him, dork. I need this favor. My sister's goin' out with her beau and she feels bad leaving her friend alone."

"Why don't you go out with him?"

"I gotta be at the Lizard tonight. The mayor's coming by."

I sighed. "Fine. But fair warning: I'm getting trashed."

"Understood. Pick him up at the Lizard."

I drove down to the bar and parked at the curb. I texted Michelle I'd arrived, and she and a man stepped out. He was skinny and white, with fine hair that came down to his shoulders and glasses that seemed too big for his face. He wore some rap group's T-shirt. I didn't like to judge people right off the bat, but he looked like an idiot. I could see it from a mile away: this was not a guy whose conversation would come sliding out, all lubricated and ready. It would have to be dragged out like nails pulled from wood. Also, he looked familiar.

Michelle opened the passenger-side door of my car, and he got inside and grinned before glancing away. She put her head in the window after shutting the door and said, "This is Chris. Chris, Danielle. Have fun, you two." She left, and I sat staring at him.

"She's something, isn't she?" I said. "Like a Neanderthal with too many hormones."

"Yeah, she's great."

I pulled away from the curb. We didn't speak a word all the way to the next light. Then he said, "That was a minute and fifty-one seconds."

"What was?"

"We were silent for that long. That's a long time."

"It certainly is. Too long." I stopped at the red light. "So how do you know Michelle and her family?"

"Oh, her sister's an old friend. I've known her and Michelle since we were kids."

"Chris . . . wait, you're not Chris Peterson, are you?"

"Yeah."

"I'm Danielle Rollins. Do you not remember me?"

"Oh . . . um . . . Sorry. No."

"You sat in front of me in Mr. Tate's geometry class."

"Oh really? Wow. Small world, huh?"

"Yeah. Small world."

Now I knew why he looked familiar. Chris had been a part of a group of boys who thought they could harass girls to no end—they pulled down girls' shirts, groped their asses in the halls, and were rumored to have gang-raped a girl they got drunk at a party. They were supposed to be the cool kids—played sports, drank, had nice cars, blah-blah-blah. All the crap that dimwitted fathers of high school sons forced their children to think was cool. Chris had once asked me to a dance, something I had never been to, and I was so excited I couldn't concentrate all day. At the time, I was living in a foster home with a single lady named Mrs. Tanner, who had to be in her seventies. I told her I had been asked on a date and she was so excited she went out right then and bought me a dress. Secondhand, for five bucks, but still, it was the thought that counted.

I went to the library that night, my favorite place to be, and studied all I could find about modern dancing. I was there until closing time and then checked out a book on dating and one on the art of conversation with men.

The next day, I smiled at Chris in the classroom, and some of his friends giggled. He turned to me and said, "Hey, about the dance—I'll only go with you if you give me a blow job. Like, right now, in the bathroom." He tried to grope me under my shirt and I had to push him off.

I slapped his face and left school for the day, making sure no one saw me crying.

I glanced over to him and took in what twenty years had done. He didn't look like the spritely athletic boy anymore. Time had a way of destroying those who were concerned only about their looks: the more someone cared about their outward appearance, the worse they looked with age. Some sort of universal principle granted dignity in old age to people who saw appearances as ultimately unimportant.

I turned the car around and headed for the police station.

"Oh," he said, holding the grab bar above his window. "Where we going?"

I smiled at him. "Trust me. You'll have fun."

13

I pulled to a stop in front of the satellite police station—a small community center that only housed a handful of cops and was primarily used to test suspected DUIs—and parked.

"Um, are we going to the police station?" he asked.

"It's a surprise. Come on."

We went inside. I saw Ryan leaning against a desk with a Styrofoam cup in his hand. He wore his jersey over his obese frame like a linebacker wearing a tight football uniform.

"Rollins," he said. "What the hell you doin' here? I didn't hear any ambulances for you to chase."

"I don't chase ambulances. Well, not anymore. Hey, this is Chris. Chris, my buddy Ryan."

They said hello and Ryan tossed his cup in the trash and grabbed his jacket.

"You heading out?" I said.

"Yeah, I got patrol tonight."

"Mind if we tag along?"

"Sure."

Chris looked from Ryan to me. "Um, tag along?"

"Yeah," I said. "It's called a ride along. I do it all the time. Don't worry, you'll have fun."

I got into the passenger seat of the patrol car outside, and let Chris sit in the back. Ryan got in and immediately turned on some hard-rock, '80s hair-farmer metal station, and pulled out.

"So you guys on a date?" Ryan said.

"Sure are."

"You know how to show a gentleman a good time, Rollins. Shit. What, was the 7-Eleven out of nachos or something so you had to find something else to do?"

"Hey, we had fun last time, didn't we?"

"You mean when you almost got me suspended? Yeah, that was fun."

"Oh, don't be such a Debbie Downer. You had a blast."

We drove for only a few minutes before he got a call about a drunk driver. We found the car about a mile from the bar that the report had come in from, and Ryan pulled the driver over for not using her signal while turning.

"Stay in the car this time," Ryan said.

He got out and went to the driver's window. He asked her to step out of the car, and she had to lean against it to keep from falling over. She had the swaying motion of someone who couldn't hold her liquor, and she looked barely over age.

"So . . . um, do you do this a lot?" Chris asked.

"Oh, yeah. Best form of free entertainment there is. You never been on a ride along?"

"No. Um, listen, do you wanna maybe just go to dinner or something?"

"Yeah, we can grab something. Trust me, food is not something cops go without for very long."

The woman was in handcuffs in about five minutes. Ryan opened the back door and stuck her in next to Chris. Chris looked like he wanted to get out and run.

"Shit," the girl said. "Hey, can't you just let me go this one time? I can't have my license suspended again."

She didn't sound good. Her speech was slow and slurred, her eyes glazed, and she stank of powerful, cheap alcohol.

"Now, what's a nice girl like you doing driving around drunk?" I asked, turning around to face her.

Chris said, "Danielle, maybe we should—"

"Fuck, I don't feel so hot."

"Danielle," Chris said, "I think I'd like to—"

The first motion was a dry heave: a shot fired declaring the war about to come. Nothing came out, but it may as well have. Chris was clawing at the door until he figured out that it couldn't be opened from the inside.

"Danielle, I'd like to get out, please."

"What? Why? We gotta take the little miss back to the station for testing."

"I'd like to go now. Right now. Please."

I sighed. "Fine. Let me get you out."

Another dry heave, and then the vomit burst out of her mouth and over the backseat, spattering droplets onto Chris's face.

"Danielle," Chris yelled, vomit rolling down his cheeks. "Danielle, please get me out!"

I stepped outside the car and lit a cigarette before opening the door. Chris jumped out like a caged animal. He backed away from me and said, "I just remembered I have somewhere to be. Thanks for the night out."

"What? That's it? Let us drive you back, at least."

"No, no. I'm fine. I can call an Uber. Thanks again."

I grinned as I watched him walk away and take out his phone. He went into a convenience store and waited inside.

"Hey," I heard. "Hey, you. What's your name?"

I leaned into the car. The stench of booze and puke burned my nostrils. "Young miss, do you need a barf bag?"

"No, no, listen to me. I can't have my license suspended again. Can you guys just let me go?"

I took out one of my cards and put it on her lap. "Tell the cops I'm your lawyer and that I told you not to talk. You gotta take the breath test because they'll suspend your license longer if you don't, but don't say anything to them and I'll take care of this. I charge thirty-five hundo, though."

"Fine. No problem. Just as long as you can save my license."

I went over to Ryan, who was inventorying her car—a nice way of saying he was searching it without a warrant before it got impounded.

"You slip her a card?"

"Yup," I said. "I appreciate you letting me come on these."

"Hey, you got my son off on one to fifteen for that bullshit check-fraud charge—don't think I'll ever forget that."

He got out of the car and leaned against it. Though it didn't seem like much effort, he had a sheen of sweat and he was breathing heavily. He reached into his jacket pocket and pulled out a package of mini-donuts.

"Wow," I said. "I can't believe that stereotype is true. That shit'll kill ya."

He shrugged as he shoved the first powdered donut into his mouth, getting sugar on his lips and chin. "Gotta die of somethin'." He pointed to the convenience store. "Who's the bro?"

"Blind date."

He shook his head. "This wouldn't be my idea of a good date."

"Mine either." I leaned against the car and tilted my head back, staring at the stars. "How's the wife?"

"I tell you somethin', you promise it stays between us?"

"Scout's honor."

"I think we might be divorcing."

"Now? After twenty years?"

"It's just getting to the point where neither one of us can stand to see the other one anymore. I hear her come home, and I just get anxiety in my stomach, you know? It's the same for her. We barely talk."

"Well, take it from someone who's been down that road: divorce won't make you happier. It just makes you lonelier."

"That's easy for you to say. You love the shit out of your ex. You're the one who screwed it up."

"Yeah, maybe."

He chewed for a moment. "You wanna go bust up a frat party or something? Those are always fun."

I shook my head. "Not really feeling up to it tonight. You mind dropping me off at the station?"

"Yeah, sure." He tossed the empty donut wrapper into the passenger seat of the car and shoved the last two in his mouth. "I gotta process your client anyway," he said through a mouthful of donut.

14

After being dropped off at my car, I drove around for a while. I passed the main homeless shelter for Salt Lake, and I watched the crowds gathered around outside. The beds would already have been assigned, so everyone not yet inside would be sleeping on the pavement, if they had sleeping bags, or in the park if they didn't.

I drove by that twice a day, every day, and I'd grown immune to it and all the utter suffering, the predation on the weak, the rape and murder and exploitation that happened right in front of me. It was a brutal, bloody jungle contained within a half-block radius, and I saw it now as nothing more than scenery. I used to drop off food and clothes every month when I first got my office. Then it gradually became every other month as I got busier with work, then once every few months, then once a year, and now I couldn't remember the last time I had donated anything. Maybe there was some evolutionary mechanism within people to numb ourselves to suffering so we could still function.

The thought of going home or to the office filled me with dread, so I drove up to the University of Utah, where crowds of people filled the sidewalks after a football game, and made my way slowly over to Federal Heights. I texted Stefan.

Is Peyton home?

Why?

Because I'm outside your house.

No reply. I parked for a minute and then decided my initial plan of getting trashed was the best option. I was about to pull away when the front door of the house opened and Stefan stepped out. He wore a red shirt, jeans, and a scarf, though it wasn't cold. I got out of the car, leaned against the hood, and lit a cigarette. He stood next to me and looked over the neighborhood. He grabbed the cigarette out of my hand and took a puff before handing it back.

"I thought you quit," I said.

"I did." He paused for a moment. "You know you can't keep showing up. I'm going to be a married man soon, and Peyton isn't going to like it."

"I don't think I care much what Peyton the Deer Molester thinks."

"Deer molester?" He grinned.

"Come on. You've seen the basement. Tell me she doesn't have a hard-on for those poor animals. What else would explain her fascination with killing them other than she's attracted to them? It's like how the most homophobic person in a crowd is scared they're really gay."

He chuckled. "You're such an ass. It's not like that at all. She's just tough and likes tough things."

"Yeah, nothing tougher than shooting Bambi from a hundred yards away dressed in camo. She might as well be playing a video game on her couch. Now, if she hunted with her bare hands like our furry ancestors—that shit I could respect. I don't think she'd want to get her heels dirty, though."

I watched him. The way the moonlight struck his face, he looked like a ghost. A thread of fear slithered through me: one day, he would be a ghost to me.

"You can't love that chick."

"Of course I love her."

"How? You almost have a PhD in history, for shit's sake. How the hell do you love a Neanderthal like her? Are you doing it just to torture me?"

He took my cigarette and had another puff. "Believe it or not, what happens in my life doesn't revolve around you, Dani."

"Sure it does. I'm like that with men. I stick around like the clap."

He chuckled again, and I could tell he hadn't wanted to. He turned to me, and the sight of him sent a jolt of nervous energy through me, much like the first time I saw him in the hallways at college. "What about you?" he said.

"What about me?"

"Any special man in your life? What happened to the doctor?"

"Is that a hint of jealousy?"

"No," he said, mocking me. "I just care about who you're bringing around our son."

I blew out some smoke. "Doctor didn't work out."

"Why? Wait, let me guess: he wanted to be in a relationship, and the second he talked about it, you lost interest."

"See, that's why we belong together. No one knows me like you do."

He laughed. "You're just a cliché. It's not hard to tell what happened." He looked up to the sky a second before saying, "Danielle, you need to move on. You have a lot to offer someone, and you need to find that person. You're not the type who can be happy alone."

"What if this is it, Stefan? What if I had my shot at the perfect life with you, and now I'm condemned to walk the earth by myself, like that show *Kung Fu*?"

"Then that's heartbreaking. But I think life is what we make of it."

I exhaled and then took another drag off the cigarette. "I wonder if that whole mother-dropping-me-off-at-a-girls-home thing has anything to do with my distrust of people."

He looked at me with a serious expression and said, "I know you joke about it, but . . . have you ever thought of reaching out to her?"

"Who, my mother? What the hell would I possibly want to do that for?"

"It might bring you some closure."

"There's no such thing as closure." I paused. "You know what she told me to get me into the car that day? She said she was taking me to Disneyland."

"I know," he said softly.

"I've never been to Disneyland, and I can never go. I don't think I could handle it. I was so . . . excited. I thought it was the best day of my life. When we pulled up to the girls' home, I knew what it was. I don't know how, but I knew. I just kept crying and telling her that I would do better. That I would listen more, and I'd be a better daughter. She was crying, too. She gave me a kiss and then put me into the hands of two men who worked at the home. I remember running to the window after they'd dragged me inside and pressing my face against it as I watched her drive away, how cold the glass was against my skin, the noise . . . it was so noisy there."

Stefan placed his hand over mine. "You're not that girl anymore."

"Yeah."

He took my face in his hands and looked into my eyes. "You're not that girl anymore."

My heart sank, and I lifted my face to kiss him. He turned away, and I thought I sensed the pull in him, the tearing in his soul. My coming here had hurt him, and I felt awful for it.

"I'm sorry," I said.

"I better go. Peyton'll be home soon."

He walked away toward the house, but I saw the tears on his cheeks glistening in the moonlight. I watched him walk inside the home of another woman, another woman who would grow older with him, who would be there for him during his dark moments, who would share Christmases and Fourth of Julys and calamities and upheavals and joy so powerful it would make the soul hurt. And I felt like that kid again, with her face pressed against the cold glass, watching someone I love leave me.

15

Teddy's first court date came quickly. Nothing really happened at the initial appearance, but judges loved their formalities and forced everyone to appear. I arrived early and stepped out of my car into the heat.

Richardson looked as dirty as ever. It seemed like the oil refineries that spewed out black air from their cylindrical monstrosities had painted the sky today. The air always tasted of exhaust. The courthouse was set up as a cylinder, too, almost like a factory chimney, and I headed up to Roscombe's courtroom on the third floor.

The moments before a courtroom door opened were always awkward. Everyone sat around staring at everyone else, trying to guess what they were there for. The lawyers were the only ones laughing and joking.

I was glad the doors were already open. I looked in. Roscombe was screaming at some poor lady standing at the lectern and crying. I stepped inside, past the audience, and sat down at the defense table. Roscombe saw me.

He was slim but had this weird droopy skin on his chin. His white hair was combed over to hide a pink scalp, and I had never—not once—seen anything but a scowl on his face.

He stopped spewing words as his eyes fixed on me. We knew each other.

Roscombe had locked up a single mother of three for stealing diapers from a Walmart. He'd told her at sentencing she could pay the fine of three hundred dollars or serve thirty days. She could no more pay three hundred dollars than a million, so she was jailed. Her kids were taken into foster care. I was told about the case by the public defender, who'd had her plead guilty without even the slightest fight. I took the case for free and immediately filed a motion to withdraw the guilty plea due to "gross incompetence and general son-of-a-bitch-ness by the bench." I made sure to underline the "son-of-a-bitch-ness." Then, knowing what was coming, I immediately sent a copy of the motion to my friend at the *Richardson Herald*, who published it in its entirety. The online comments called me "a hero fighting a dictator."

Judges did not fear lawyers; they did not fear politicians; they did not fear city councils or the general citizenry. The only thing they feared was bad press, because bad press would force those lawyers, politicians, city councils, and citizenry to really take a look and see if a judge needed to be removed. It was damn near impossible to remove a judge in the state of Utah, but enough bad press might just do the trick.

Roscombe released the woman when he saw the news stories, but not before finding me in contempt and making me spend a night in jail.

He seemed to snap out of whatever trance I had put him in, and he stared at the woman at the lectern as though he'd forgotten why she was there. Finally he said, "That's all. Get out of my courtroom."

The woman ran out with tears still streaming down her face, humiliated. I rose and smiled at him. "I see you still have your charm with the ladies, Your Honor."

He leaned back in his massive leather chair. "I didn't think you'd show up in my court again, Counselor."

"I let bygones be bygones, Your Honor. And I'm really here to learn from your great legal and humanitarian base of wisdom."

He made a clicking sound through his teeth. "I'm afraid we have a full calendar. You're just going to have to wait to learn from me, Ms. Rollins."

It was customary for attorneys to go first rather than those people representing themselves, since we had to get to other courts. "Your Honor, I just have a quick initial appearance. Shouldn't take but two minutes."

"Yes, but then you'd have to butt in line before all these good people. We can't have that, now can we? Have a seat, Counselor."

I sighed and sat down. I scanned the audience and saw Teddy and his mom sitting in the corner. Teddy had his headphones on again and was smiling at the iPad. His mother stared straight ahead, and if she noticed me, she didn't acknowledge it.

The calendar ground away. Other attorneys' cases were called, and when I tried to sneak in after them, Roscombe said, "Now now, Counselor, the end of the calendar is the proper time to learn from my great base of legal and humanitarian knowledge."

"Right," I said, sitting back down. Perhaps I'd spoken a little too quickly with that comment.

I had to have Kelly ask the courts and prosecutors to put off my afternoon court appearances, as there was no way I'd make them in time. By noon, I was sweating, aggravated, and again questioning why I had become a lawyer. I looked back at Teddy and his mom. Teddy was asleep on the benches and Riley was leaning her head against the wall as if she was getting there. Only a handful of people were left in the courtroom.

The prosecutor was a slim man with glasses. He leaned back and said, "That's what you get."

"Nice," I replied. "You're a true credit to your profession."

"Hey asshole, I'm doing God's work. You're the one doing the devil's."

"The devil has *Game of Thrones* and bacon donuts. Choir music and angry sermons don't compare."

He shook his head and turned away. That'd teach him to talk to strange lawyers loitering in courtrooms.

By one thirty, I wanted to slash my wrists. I lay down on the floor behind the defense table, Teddy's file covering my eyes from the harsh lighting. I slept a little, and then I listened to the defendants answering to Joseph Stalin on the bench. I made a game of it, trying to guess what each defendant looked like based on their voice. I was wrong every time.

"Ms. Rollins, are you awake?"

I jumped to my feet. The only people still in the audience were Teddy and Riley. I wiped the drool away from my lips and stood at the lectern.

"Theodore Thorne, Judge."

"Mr. Thorne, please step forward."

Riley woke Teddy and helped him up to the lectern. He stood next to me and said, "Hi Danielle."

"Hey."

"Mr. Thorne, you are charged with one count of distribution of a controlled substance, a first-degree felony, punishable by a commitment of five years to life at the Utah State Prison. Here is a copy of the information against you. Do you understand the charges?"

Teddy turned a vacant stare to me. This wasn't the time to go into his competency, since if he said "no," all that would happen is the judge would read it again. So I just nodded.

"Yes," he said, "my mama told me. And she said we could go to McDonald's after and get an ice cream."

I thought maybe a pang of sympathy would cross Roscombe's face, but the man was like stone. He nodded as if Teddy had said the most logical thing in the world. "Looks like he's made bail. I'll set this for a scheduling conference in two weeks."

"Your Honor, actually, I'll be filing a motion to dismiss and would ask for a hearing."

"I don't entertain motions until after a preliminary hearing, Counselor."

"He shouldn't be forced to go through a preliminary hearing. The State completely lacks jurisdiction in this matter and—"

"I know what the jurisdictional issues are. I approved the certification that he be tried as an adult."

"Then you understand, Your Honor, that this is just a ploy by the State to attempt to get around the legislature trying to, just a little bit, restrict their seemingly endless power to ruin the lives of average citizens. The district attorney's office wants me to appeal this, and the supreme court is where this is gonna play out, so why don't you just let me file my little motion, deny it, and let's get this up to the big boys?"

"The big boys?" He chuckled. "You just don't know when to keep your mouth shut, do you?"

"That's never been my strong suit, no. But in the words of Forrest Gump, I know what love is."

He sighed. "Mr. Thorne's preliminary hearing is set for two weeks from today. After which, if I find enough evidence to bind the case over, you can file whatever motion you like. Now, are you done?"

I looked at Teddy, who had this wide-eyed expression on his face like he was at the circus, and I knew he had no idea about what was going on. In his hands I saw a small doll: a monkey.

"Fine, two weeks," I said. "Good to see you again . . . Mia."

I turned and left before he could jail me again, and Riley and Teddy followed. We rode the elevator down in silence until I said, "What's the monkey, buddy?"

"My daddy got it for me at Lagoon. You had to throw the ball and he threw the ball and won this for me."

Riley smiled softly. "He was ten. He's kept it ever since."

We stopped on the courthouse steps. "The prelim is a mini-trial," I told Riley. "They're gonna put on witnesses and we're gonna cross-examine them. I'm sure Mia there is going to find enough evidence to move forward, and then we'll file our motion to dismiss this case. If it's not granted, I'm going to file what's called an interlocutory appeal, meaning an appeal while the case is still pending, and eventually I'm sure the Utah Supreme Court will smack down Hoover County. What they're doing is blatantly illegal. That's just how they roll, I guess."

She nodded. "Thank you." She looked at Teddy. "Let's go, Teddy."

"Danielle," he said, putting both hands on my shoulders. "I have great news."

"What is it?"

"It's my birthday on Friday. And . . . and I'm gonna have a party. Will you come?"

I paused. I had never, not once, mingled with a client. I kept it strictly business, and that had served me well. But something in his face told me I couldn't refuse.

"Sure, buddy. I'll be there."

He turned to his mom. "Danielle's coming!"

She just looked away and led him down the stairs. I thought I should ask them what time and where, but she didn't seem to be in a talking mood so I let it go. I went back to my car and sat there in the boiling heat for a moment.

This wasn't some random attack on a statute that Hoover County didn't like; this seemed more orchestrated, and I had a feeling Roscombe knew more than he was letting on. I would have to be careful going forward. I couldn't trust Hoover County or Roscombe any more than a pretty girl could trust an unguarded drink at a frat party.

I started the car and pulled away. I would need to talk to the other boys in the case before meeting with the big cheese: the confidential informant.

16

Clint Andrews and Fredrick Willmore. I had to confer with these two gentlemen to find out if Kevin was telling the truth. Will refused to break the professional rules of conduct and speak with people already represented by attorneys because he was retiring soon. I couldn't blame him. The prosecutor would file disciplinary proceedings against him and try to take his private investigator license. They'd lose, but it could mean months of proceedings, and he was on the verge of getting the hell outta here.

Clint Andrews went to a private school named Laterford. It was locked down tight, unlike public schools. The entrances all required scan cards to get in. I thought for a few minutes and then got out of my car.

Inside, I waved to the secretary in the front office, who said over the intercom, "Yes?"

"Hi, I'm Patty Andrews. Um, Clint Andrews's mom. I just needed to talk to him really quick."

"You're his mom?"

"Yup. Sure am."

She eyed me but didn't say anything. It looked like I had struck gold and she didn't actually know who his mother was.

"I don't need him released," I said. "I just need to talk to him for five minutes and he's not answering his phone. We can do it right here in front of you if you're worried I'm a serial killer or something."

Apparently my joke didn't go over well because she sat there eyeing me like she was debating calling the cops, but then just said, "Wait a moment."

I turned around and stared out over the parking lot. I had the urge to light a cigarette but thought the warden might have an issue with it.

I turned back and saw a young man speaking to the secretary: Clint. I turned away so he wouldn't see my face and just waited. Eventually the doors opened and he stepped outside onto the sidewalk.

"Clint!" I said, giving him a hug.

"Who are—"

I put my arm around his shoulders and turned away from the secretary so she couldn't see our faces.

"I'm a lawyer on the Teddy Thorne case. I didn't want to alarm your secretary so just play along."

"I, um, like, got a lawyer."

He spoke with an upward inflection at the end of everything he said, as though the entire world was a question mark to him. Ol' Clint may have been a couple of arrows short of a quiver, probably from constant pot smoking—something I could smell on his clothes and hair from a mile away.

"You remember the night you got arrested?" I said, ignoring his statement.

"Um, yeah."

"Tell me what happened."

He shrugged. "We went down to Richardson. Kevin said they had to do something."

"Who's *they?*"

"Him and Teddy."

"What'd he say they had to do?"

"I don't know."

"You don't know? You just accepted that you guys were gonna stop in a shady neighborhood with a gym bag for no reason?"

"I didn't ask. He said we had to go do something and I said okay." He looked back toward the secretary. "Um, can I go now? I'm missing gym."

"In the police reports, you said Teddy was the one who suggested you guys go down to Richardson and visit somebody. You remember telling the cops that?"

He shook his head. "No. I mean, yeah. They were like . . . I don't know. They were saying, like, is this what happened. And my dad was there and he just kind of nodded and so I said yeah."

"Teddy never said anything about going to Richardson to deliver a bag?"

"Yeah. I think. He just, like, kept talkin' about games or some shit. Playing video games."

I folded my arms and leaned back against the wall. Hoover cops, man. They got a theory in their heads about how this played out, and then they coached the witnesses into saying what they wanted them to say.

"Thanks, Clint. Have fun in gym."

"All right."

I watched him go back inside and then hurried to my car before the warden deduced that I wasn't his mom.

Unlike Clint, Freddy Willmore didn't go to a fancy private school. He went to Central High, a high school devoted to one of the most poverty-stricken districts in the state.

I parked as close to the building as I could and got out. Central didn't have the pristine lawns and nice cars like the parking lots of Laterford and Skyline. It had crumbling brick walls and a couple of broken windows. The front doors looked like they could fall off their hinges at any second, and the interior smelled like an old gym locker.

I went to the administrative office. The secretary here was on the phone and rolled her eyes when she saw me. The walls were covered in chipping paint and black stains.

"What do you need?"

"Hi, can I speak to Freddy Willmore, please?"

"One second and I'll page him."

No questions about who I was or what I needed to see him about. I suddenly felt bad for the kids who attended here, knowing that the school cared about nothing but churning them out as quickly as possible. I wondered how big the advantage was for the kids twenty miles away at Laterford.

A few minutes later, a slim cat with short hair and a red T-shirt came in. The secretary pointed to me. I offered my hand and Freddy shook.

"Freddy, I'm an attorney on the Teddy Thorne case. I just have a couple of questions for you."

"I'm already represented. You should probably get in contact with my attorney."

"I know you are . . . but Teddy's had a hard enough life without this shit being hung on his neck, hasn't he? Can you just give him a break and help me out?"

Apparently, Freddy instantly knew what I was speaking about because I saw the sympathy in his eyes—an emotion I had looked for and didn't see in Judge Roscombe.

"He wasn't the one who suggested you guys go to Richardson that night, was he?"

Freddy glanced at the secretary and then shook his head. "I didn't hear him say it."

"Did the cops feed you that?"

"They said that Kevin and Clint had already told them it was Teddy. When I tried to tell them I didn't hear who said it, they said that they had what they needed. So I just kind of agreed with them."

"So who did suggest it? Kevin?"

"I don't know. I was playing a game, and then Kevin said we're going to Richardson. I didn't hear who first said it."

"Freddy, they've charged Teddy as an adult, in front of a judge who sends all adults convicted of distributing narcotics to prison. Do you know what would happen to Teddy in prison?"

He looked away in disgust. "I know. I feel horrible about it. But I swear, I don't know why we went down there or whose idea it was."

Unlike Stonerboy back at Laterford, Freddy was articulate and intelligent. It seemed odd that he would so willingly go along with stringing up Teddy for something Teddy might not have done. Then again, cops can be extremely intimidating, especially for people with no exposure to the system. I had no doubt Freddy was terrified of what would happen if he didn't agree with the story Kevin and Clint had already put forward.

"So what happened when you got to the house?" I asked.

"Kevin hopped out and took Teddy with him. They went to the door, and a few seconds later all these cops swarmed us. That's all I know."

"You didn't know he had coke in the bag?"

"No. I never would've gone with him if I'd known that. I've got a scholarship to the University of Florida. If I get a drug conviction, it's gone."

"So you let Teddy take the blame, hoping you'd slide, huh?"

He swallowed. "I . . ."

"Yeah, well, thanks for talking to me anyway. You did wrong, but you can make it right. I'm going to send my investigator out to interview you and he's going to record it. Is that cool?"

He shrugged. "I don't know. I guess."

I nodded. Despite what he'd done, I felt bad for the kid. I could see holes in his shoes and his shirt looked a few years past its prime. He probably came from poverty, and poverty had given him the drive to work hard and find a way out. He was just trying to preserve that. I would be careful with him and make sure I didn't get him into any more trouble than I needed to.

"Hey," he said, "tell Teddy I'm sorry."

"I will," I said, handing Freddy my card. "Call me if you want to talk about anything else. I'll send out that investigator today or tomorrow."

I was leaving when I stopped and said, "Hey, out of curiosity, how'd you get a lawyer already?"

"Kevin's dad hired one for me."

"Huh. Who is it?"

"I don't know. Some family lawyer for them."

"How do you know Kevin and Clint? You guys all go to different schools."

"We grew up together. We lived in the same neighborhood when we were kids. My dad left us when I was, like, ten, and we had to move. But they're still my best friends."

I nodded. "Thanks again, Freddy. You're doing the right thing."

I left the school with a light, airy feeling in my guts: I'd get Freddy on record explaining the cops had fed him that story, and Hoover County would cut us a deal. They wouldn't risk that coming out to a jury because then all three of the boys' stories would be put in doubt.

I felt so good that I decided I would celebrate with a midday drink.

17

After my drink, I went to my next hearing, which was only an arraignment, and I literally did nothing but stand there and verify my client's address. Young kid, twenty-one, the girl from my blind date, who had puked on Chris.

As we were walking out of court, she said, "You think you can save my license?"

"Probably. There are deals we can work out that don't suspend it. Just make sure to stay out of trouble until then."

"I will. I'm just glad they didn't find the pot and gun under my seat."

"Let's just keep that between us and never bring it up again, shall we?"

"Oh, okay. That's probably a good idea."

The rest of my day wasn't much different. One court appearance after another, followed by paperwork. Will and I had had lunch at the Purple Iguana, and he talked for an hour about all the things he was going to do his first week in Fiji. Finally he said, "Listen to me going on and on without asking about you. How's the Thorne case?"

"Good. Found out cops fed at least one of the kids the story. I need you to go out and interview Freddy Willmore. He's going to verify that he doesn't know who suggested driving to Richardson and that the cops pressured him into saying it."

"Isn't he represented?"

"Just get him on record waiving his right to have his attorney present."

"That's still skirting the line, lady."

"Will, just do it."

I noticed a few women at a table next to us checking Will out. It always happened when we were in public and he seemed completely oblivious to the attention.

He held up his hands in surrender. "All right, all right. For you, anything." He took a bite of food and then wiped his lips with a napkin. "So that's pretty cool, huh? You think you can get it outright dismissed?"

"Who knows? If it was Salt Lake I'd say yes, but Hoover fights everything to the death, even when they're wrong. It may still have to go to trial."

"Hey, so, I talked to Chip. I was sending him something and he mentioned that you paid Teddy's bail. That true?"

"It is."

"So the parents are paying you back, right?"

"I don't know. I don't think they have any money."

"So . . . you got six grand for the case, and you paid five of it to get him out? And at least another three to me for my work. That's not exactly good business, Dani."

I shrugged. "I couldn't leave him in there."

"Why not?"

I shook my head but didn't answer.

"Look," he said, "I grew up poor. My dad owned a bar but when he left me and my mom, we had nothing. Government cheese and bread for breakfast, lunch, and dinner. I swore I'd never go back to that, and I haven't. I've lived the American dream, and you know how I did that? I realized that everybody suffers. That you help one person, and the next one needs it, too, and the one after that, and the one after that. You gotta look out for yourself first, and then help others when you can."

"I don't know . . . I just couldn't leave him in there."

"Well, I'm doing this one gratis. I'm not taking money from you," he said.

"I won't say no. Thanks, Will."

"Anything for you, m'lady."

We paid and left the restaurant, and I decided I would go home. I didn't have it in me to sit at the office and answer one more client call, hear one more rant about how unfair the system was or how the cops had planted evidence or how the CIA had bugged phones or aliens were beaming down messages into people's brains.

Driving past the homeless shelter, I didn't see as many people as I normally would. A few were huddled on the corners and a few were in the street in small groups, but the large masses had dissipated today. I remembered that I'd told myself I would drop off some clothes for them since I hadn't done it in so long. I ran to the thrift store up the block and bought out a bin of sweaters and sweatpants for twenty-two dollars and drove back and dropped them off at the shelter.

At home, television didn't sound appealing, and neither did music, so I sat in the dwindling light and watched a tree outside my living room window. It swayed in a breeze and the sunshine hit it just right, causing it to sparkle as it trembled. My eyes were beginning to close when my phone buzzed. It was a text from Jack.

You wanna see a movie with us?

Us?

Me and dad

I typed out: *Pretty tired, honey. Maybe another time*, then deleted it and just said *Yes*. I stretched my neck and arms and then got back into my Jeep and drove up to Federal Heights.

I had no idea what prompted them to invite me, but I wasn't going to say no. They probably had a daddy-son date planned and Jack insisted I come.

When the door opened and my two boys stepped out, my heart stopped. It was one of the most beautiful things I'd ever seen: the two people I loved most in the world, laughing as they came to me.

"Gentlemen," I said as they hopped into the Jeep.

"Hey, Mom," Jack said, giving me a quick kiss on the cheek.

I looked at his father and said, "No hello smooch?"

"I'm here. That's a big step for now."

"I'll take what I can get."

We drove down to the movie theater. Jack told us about a girl he liked, and I pretended to vomit, which made him cackle.

"What kind of parenting is going on at that house? He's thirteen. Crack the whip a little."

"Oh, please," Stefan said. "I had my first girlfriend at fourteen."

"That's too young. You need to lock him down. I'm sure Peyton's got an atomic bunker or something, right? Lock him up until he's thirty and then release him into the world. It worked for Lizzie Borden."

Stefan smiled. "I still remember my first girlfriend. Patricia Omakasu. She was Japanese and sixteen, with eyes like emeralds and the body of a yoga instructor."

"Are you trying to make me crash?"

"We made out once in my car, looking out over the city."

"Oh, hold on." I rolled down the window and pretended to vomit again. Jack laughed and it was the sweetest sound I had ever heard. "So this is what I'm missing, huh? The entire family thing. I always thought it was the part of life that had to be endured, and now that it's too late I finally see it was the most beautiful part. The cosmos put one over on me, didn't it?"

"It's not too late," Stefan said. "I mean, for you. You'll find someone and settle down and we'll just live our separate lives. That's how divorces work, Dani."

"Yeah, but I sure as shit wish they didn't."

We parked at the theater and went inside. I bought them both popcorn and drinks and tickets to the movie Jack wanted to see—something about hot teenage vampires. The dialogue in the first five minutes made me nauseated, so I just stared at Jack and Stefan as long as I could without them noticing. At one point, Stefan did notice and grinned at me. I leaned back in my seat and suffered through a teen romance between a vampire, a werewolf, and something else—a witch or something.

I fell asleep and woke up to Jack taking my hand.

"Thanks for coming, Mom. I know you didn't like it."

"Nonsense. I thought the part where the girl has to choose between two unbearably good-looking monsters was interesting."

He took my arm and led me out. I noticed Stefan staring at us, and a smile crept to his lips. Maybe it was just watching Jack with his mother, or maybe it was that he enjoyed the movie and spending time with his son . . . but there was always the chance that he missed the shit out of this as much as I did.

I dropped them back home, and Jack hopped out first. Stefan sat for a second and said, "You need to move on. I don't want you to be alone."

"Kinda hard to do when you're in love with someone."

"If that were true, you wouldn't have cheated on me." He leaned in and pecked me on the cheek. "Thank you for coming with us. He really wanted it." He hesitated. "He really wants something else, too. And no matter how much Peyton and I try to talk him out of it, he won't budge." He exhaled. "Jack wants you at the wedding. He says if you're not there, he won't go either."

"Why?"

"He says it's a big moment of his life and he wants you at all the big moments of his life."

I looked at the house. "He is wise beyond his years."

"If you don't want to come, there's no pressure. He'll get over it and eventually understand why you couldn't be there."

"No, I'll be there. I mean, I'll have to get completely shitfaced."

"Fine, but you have to behave."

I exhaled loudly and leaned back in the seat. "You sure about this? I mean, you're gonna go through with it?"

"I love her. I'm sorry, I know that hurts you to hear, but I do." He opened the door and got out. "Good night, Dani."

I watched him walk inside the house. When he got to the door, Peyton opened it. She kissed him and then noticed me and grabbed his ass. I rubbed my eyebrow with my middle finger before driving away. A lead weight inside made me feel like I'd dropped through to the center of the earth, complete with fire and burning and gnashing of teeth. The rage got so bad that I had to pull over and get control of myself before I could put the Jeep in drive again.

Move on. Yeah, I was sure that would be easy.

18

The upcoming wedding hung over me. I dreaded the idea of running into Stefan at romantic dinners with his wife, seeing them skiing up in the mountains together, or the absolute oh-shit moment: seeing Peyton pregnant with his seed. I couldn't handle even imagining it.

The next few days melted into each other. In a haze, I'd work a full day, then go get thoroughly trashed at the Lizard and pass out somewhere—Michelle's house, my own, or even in the VIP room of the Lizard. I kept dreaming I was standing at a port as some massive black ship docked in the night, carrying something wicked to be unleashed on me.

While I was in court on Friday, I got a text from Kelly reminding me that it was Teddy Thorne's eighteenth birthday. Since the parents had never contacted me about attending a party, I figured I wasn't really invited. I'd pick up a small gift for him, and maybe I'd drop it by his house to make up for not being there.

On this particular midnight dreary while I pondered weak and weary, I thought about Edgar Allen Poe. He died alone and in the gutter, full of regrets of lost love that could've been his. Was that my destiny, too? That, and worse? At least Poe left behind all his books for generations to enjoy. I would have nothing but a string of criminals I'd helped free or got reduced sentences for.

I drove by the homeless shelter and saw a few groups of men huddled around. The night was warm so it wasn't too packed. In the middle of the road, between the shelter and the free medical clinic across the street, a few guys were pushing someone around. Looked like a young black kid. One of the men was up in the guy's face, while the others searched his pockets. It was a common occurrence at the shelter when someone new was brought in. The guy they were hustling looked like . . . Teddy? It couldn't be him.

I pulled to the side of the road and got out, but not before grabbing my mace from the glove compartment.

By the light of the streetlamps, I could see three of the men and the back of the mark who was getting robbed. "Hey, guys, lay off. I already called the cops."

I got a few steps closer and the men turned. The last thing the homeless wanted was a pat down by the police. Inevitably, the officers would confiscate the drugs that made their situation tolerable for a few hours.

I froze in my tracks.

The mark actually was Teddy Thorne.

"Teddy?"

The three men hurried away. One of them dropped Teddy's *Huckleberry Finn* and took off. I picked it up and went to Teddy. He was rubbing his fingers together and walking in a circle.

"Teddy, what are you doing here?"

"And I told them that they had to give it back, see. That they had to give it back because my mama gave me that."

"Teddy," I said, moving in front of him. "What're you doing here? Why aren't you home?"

"I said they had to give it back but they wouldn't give it back. And I said that the book—"

As gently as I could, I placed my hands on his shoulders to get him to stop going in circles. He couldn't look me in the eyes and instead kept his gaze on the ground. His fingers were rubbing together so hard that even in the dim light I could see the skin rubbing off. I covered his hands with mine to get him to stop and just held them there a moment. Slowly, his eyes rose to mine, then dropped back down, but he stopped walking in circles.

"Why aren't you home?"

He didn't move or say anything.

"How did you get down here?"

"I told them . . ." he began halfheartedly, and trailed off.

He must've gotten lost. My office wasn't far, and I wondered if his mom had run up to see me and left him in the car or something. "Come on," I said, "I'll take you home."

———

Teddy sat in the passenger seat and rocked back and forth. When I gave him his copy of *Huck Finn*, he squealed like a five-year-old. It sat on his lap now, his fingers tracing the outline of the words on the cover.

"I'm sorry I missed your party, buddy."

"Danielle you said you're coming. You said you're coming to my party."

"I did. I'm really sorry about that. How was it? Did you get some good presents?"

"I saw . . . I saw a butlerfly today."

"Really? A butlerfly?" I didn't have the heart to correct him. His way sounded so much more dignified.

"I saw it at my house. At my house. And I chased it but it didn't stop. I was going to put it in a jar and take care of it, see. I wanted to take care of it."

"Butlerflies don't like living in jars, buddy. They have to be free. If they're not free, they'll die."

"Yeah, but I would take care of it and we would be friends. They need friends, too." He paused. "My mama said I can't have a party. I can't have a party because I'm going somewhere."

"Where?"

"I'm going somewhere, see. So I couldn't have a party."

We got to his house, and I helped him out of the Jeep. As we headed up the steps of the front porch, I could see a light on in the front room. I knocked. I knocked again and rang the doorbell. Then I knocked, rang, knocked, rang. Still, no one answered.

"Are your parents home?"

"They like to . . . they like to go to the movies without me, and Mrs. Hatcher comes over to watch me. We watch *Jeopardy* together."

"Is Mrs. Hatcher a neighbor? Does she live around here?"

"Mrs. Hatcher likes *Jeopardy*. Because Alex Trebek is handsome."

I grinned. "Do you know where Mrs. Hatcher lives?"

"She lives over here."

He led me down the street, gripping his *Huck Finn* tightly. We came to a little white house with rocks in place of a lawn. "Mrs. Hatcher lives right here but she doesn't like visitors."

"I'm sure she'll make an exception."

I went up to the door, but Teddy stayed where he was on the sidewalk. I knocked, and an old lady with glasses answered. She was short and pudgy and looked at me like she was trying to remember who I was.

"Hi, um, you don't know me, my name's Dani Rollins. I'm the Thornes' attorney. I found Teddy wandering around but I can't find his parents. You know where they are?"

She looked sad, and I noticed that she wouldn't look at Teddy.

"Yes, they're probably home."

"Oh, no, I was just knocking and ringing there for like a full minute."

"I don't think they'll be answering," she said somberly.

I immediately pictured this crazy old lady going Menendez brothers on poor Teddy's parents—blood and buckshot and the scent of Vicks VapoRub everywhere.

"Um . . . any particular reason why they wouldn't be answering?"

"I'm afraid you'll have to ask them."

She moved to shut her door and I stopped it. "Sorry, one sec—Teddy said you watch him sometimes?"

She closed her eyes and exhaled loudly through her nose. "You'll have to leave."

"Can you at least tell me what's going on? I found Teddy at a homeless shelter by himself."

She glanced at Teddy and somehow it seemed to pain her. "I couldn't take him. I can barely take care of myself. They asked, but I couldn't do it."

"Couldn't take . . . Holy shit. Are you telling me his parents dropped him off at that shelter on purpose?"

"You'll have to go. Now please, move your hands from my door before I call the police."

I was frozen in place for a second and then I backed away. The old lady shut the door. I turned back to Teddy. He was humming to himself and appeared to be counting the stars in the sky. I couldn't believe Mrs. Hatcher was right. Something else had to be going on.

I led Teddy back to his house. The light that had been on was now off. There was a small patio on the side of the house with an awning over it and an open window just above.

"Teddy, wait here."

I ran up and climbed onto the metal beams supporting the awning before wriggling up onto the awning itself. I started to fall backward, but I grabbed the window frame like a drowning man and held on. I climbed inside to a hallway on the second floor. Standing in the dark, I listened until I heard quiet talking coming from down the hall. I found

Teddy's parents sitting on their bed. The father was watching television with the volume down, wearing a polo shirt with a giant food stain on the chest. Riley sat with her arms folded, staring off into space.

"Excuse me."

They both gasped. Fury raced across Robert Thorne's face as he jumped out of bed. I held up my hands and said, "Whoa, big fella. I'm just bringing your son home."

"How the hell did you get in here!"

"I was knocking for like an hour. Did you guys not hear?"

"You need to leave. Right now!"

"My pleasure. Teddy's outside. I'll go bring him in."

The two of them glanced at each other.

"No way. It's true, isn't it? You fuckers dropped him off at the shelter."

"He's eighteen now," Robert said. "What he does is up to him. I gave him everything for eighteen years! Eighteen years of my life. I'm not giving him what few years I got left."

I stared into the man's eyes and saw nothing but anger. "You gotta be kidding me. He's your son."

Riley got out of bed and put her hand on his shoulder. This seemed to calm him down enough that he turned away from me and sat back on the bed, staring at the floor. Riley gently wrapped her arm around mine and led me out of the bedroom.

"You have no idea what it's like to raise a son like him. We've exhausted ourselves. Financially, physically, spiritually, mentally . . . there's just nothing left. Robert has had two heart attacks. I had a nervous breakdown three years ago and was institutionalized for over a week. We've given our all to that boy. I swore that I would raise him because he was my responsibility, but now that's done."

"What the hell are you talking about, 'done'? He can't take care of himself. Do you know what the other men were doing to him when I found him? They were robbing him. Which is what will happen to him now for the rest of his life. He won't have anything. Not even his body, because a lot of those guys are fresh out of prison and if there are no women available—"

"I don't want to hear it," she said, raising her hand and closing her eyes.

"Well, you're gonna hear it, lady."

"Ms. Rollins, it's easy to judge people until you're put in their position."

"You're damn right it's easy to judge, because most people, like you, are assholes. How could you do that to your kid?"

"We've thought about it for years, we've prayed, we've consulted lawyers, we've looked for homes that would take him . . . everything."

"There've gotta be some nonprofits set up that would take him."

"Not when he's emancipated, and not in Utah. If he finds his way to a bigger state, maybe they would be able to help him."

"Ummm . . . hello? How about you *take him* to another state?"

"Ms. Rollins," she said sternly. "I'm speaking to you as a courtesy. What I should do is call the police for you breaking into our home."

"And how about I tell the cops you threw your son out onto the street?"

"What we did is not illegal. We've consulted with lawyers."

Unfortunately, what she said was true. In Utah, once children turned eighteen, the parents were not required to take care of them—even if they did have mental disabilities.

"I don't believe this. You dropped him off at the shelter like a sack of garbage. What kind of person are you?"

Tears filled her eyes. "I'm the type of person who's been a prisoner for eighteen years. I don't have that much of my life left, but I'm not spending it as a prisoner anymore. Now please get out of my house. You've been paid your full fee, and we don't wish to have any more contact with you."

I left the house in a stupor. How could human beings do that to another human being, much less their child? When they'd dropped him off, they had to have seen what kind of men Teddy would be with: eyes like sharks', blank, looking for any little fish to tear apart. His parents didn't care. How long had they been waiting for his eighteenth birthday to do this? How many breakfasts and holidays did they go through with Teddy, knowing full well they were going to dump him on the streets?

Back on the sidewalk, Teddy clutched his book tightly and hummed to himself.

"Can I go home now?"

I looked down. Now I was the one who couldn't look him in the eyes. "No, buddy. You're going to be staying with me tonight."

"A sleepover?"

"That's right, a sleepover."

19

We got to my house, and Teddy went in and stood in the living room. He looked like a child checking out a zoo he'd never been to—fascination, wonder, and disgust all at once. I got some blankets and pillows and put them down on the couch and said, "All right, bud, we'll have you sleep here tonight."

"No, I can't. It's a couch."

"Yeah, but it's big. Plenty of room."

"Couches are for sitting, see. They're for sitting and not sleeping."

"Yeah, but . . ." I could see there was no persuading him. Couches were indeed for sitting and not sleeping. I led him back to my bedroom.

"Well, the bed is yours, then."

"Okay."

I'd started to leave when he said, "I need to brush my teeth."

"What?"

"I need . . . I need to brush my teeth and watch a show."

"What show?"

"We watch *SpongeBob SquarePants*. I need to brush my teeth and watch *SpongeBob SquarePants*."

"Buddy, I don't have *SpongeBob SquarePants,* and you can go for one night without brushing your teeth. It's cool, I promise."

I turned to leave again and he shouted, "I need to brush my teeth and watch *SpongeBob SquarePants!*"

He was trembling. His hands shook so violently I thought *Huck Finn* might drop. His lower lip curled and straightened in a slow rhythm.

"Okay," I said calmly, "we'll figure something out."

Teddy and I roamed the aisles of Smith's, the local grocery store, until we found the toothbrushes. He took five minutes to choose one, and then said he needed the toothpaste with Iron Man on it. I bought both for him and the cashier said, "I like your toothbrush."

"Thanks," he said. "We're having a sleepover."

"Oh," she said, looking at me, "that sounds fun." She smiled and said, "I worked with special needs children a while ago."

"Oh yeah? Hey, do you know of any shelters that take, um, special needs adults who don't have anywhere else to go? Like somewhere safe?"

She looked at me like I had just announced I was an animal rapist. Quickly putting the brush and toothpaste in a bag, as though she didn't want to touch something I was going to touch, she said, "They're just like you and me. No different. They don't deserve that."

"I just meant . . . never mind. Thanks."

"Bye," Teddy said, waving to her.

"Bye," she said with a smile, before trying to shoot poison at me from her eyeballs.

We got home, and I set him up in the bathroom. The first thing he did was drop his pants and sit on the toilet. I turned around and said, "Whoa, bud, you gotta warn me when you do that."

I went to shut the bathroom door and he said, "Danielle?"

"Yeah?"

"Can you leave the door open? I get scared."

"Sure."

After he went to the bathroom and brushed his teeth he said, "Where's my jammies?"

One more trip to Smith's and we picked up red Santa Claus pajamas. The same woman checked us out, and she glared at me the entire time. Once outside the store I said, "Teddy, is there anything else you need? Anything at all? Because I'm not coming back here."

"Ummm . . ." He thought for a few moments, slowly shifting his weight from foot to foot. "We have Fruity Pebbles every morning, see. Fruity Pebbles and orange juice."

"Fruity Pebbles and orange juice . . . okay. Anything else?"

"Um, SpongeBob—"

"Yeah, I know about Mr. SquarePants. Anything else you can think of while we're here?"

He shook his head. We went back inside and purchased Fruity Pebbles and orange juice, and the cashier stared at me again. I said, "You're kinda cute when you're hateful."

She rolled her eyes, and I thought she was going to throw the cereal at my head.

Back home again, Teddy got into his pajamas and we purchased the first season of *SpongeBob SquarePants* from Amazon. As he watched, I stood in the doorway and watched him. He was a child in the body of an adult, and I wondered how many other people I'd met who I could say the same thing about. At least half the judges I knew.

I went and lay down on my couch and closed my eyes.

20

In the morning, I heard someone in the living room. I opened my eyes and saw Teddy standing over me. I gasped and nearly jumped off the couch, which made him laugh to no end.

"Buddy, you can't sneak up on me like that."

"It's time for *My Little Ponies* and Fruity Pebbles."

"*My Little Ponies*? What happened to *SpongeBob*?"

"It's not bedtime, silly."

I lay there a second and then swung my feet out. I bought the first season of *My Little Ponies* and Teddy ate in front of the television: a massive bowl of Fruity Pebbles with a tall glass of orange juice. I had court in an hour. I called Will.

————————

Twenty minutes later, I was showered and in a suit when Will walked in. He wore jeans and a beige jacket, and I thought he looked like a model for Gap.

"You're kidding, right?" he said. "This was just an elaborate ploy to get me over here."

"Afraid not. He's in the bedroom watching *My Little Ponies.*"

He quietly sneaked down the hall and looked into the bedroom. When he came back out he said, "You really want me alone with him? I don't know anything about kids."

"He's harmless, and he's eighteen now. I don't have anyone else to ask. Michelle's a psychopath and would probably get Teddy some hookers. It's just for a little bit. I'll hit this court appearance and be right back. I already called the office and told Kelly to start looking for a group home for him."

He folded his arms. "Dani . . ."

"What? How is this my fault?"

"You can't just take him in. You don't know—" He glanced back to the bedroom and then whispered, "You don't know the first thing about taking care of someone with special needs."

"What was I supposed to do? Let him get raped at the homeless shelter?"

He shook his head.

"Look," I said. "You're awesome for doing this and I love you for it." He cracked a smile, and I kissed him on the cheek. "Thanks again."

Today's appearance was in one of the roughest courts in the state: Magna Justice Court. It sat in the middle of a barren desert, and the moment I got out of my car, dust blew into my mouth. I spit it out, grabbed the file for Hernando Ramirez, and ran inside the courthouse. The building used to be offices for a Frito-Lay plant next door, which had been torn down.

The inside of the building smelled of sewer with a hint of dead rat. The doorknobs were greased with fingerprints, boogers, saliva, and whatever other bodily fluids people saw fit to toss on them. The windows were never clean, and the bathrooms were unusable. In fact, the entire place reminded me more of a bathroom at a public park than a court of law. Still, somehow, it was fitting, considering Judge Borth was one of the craziest bastards this side of the Mississippi.

I found my client pacing around in the hall.

"Hernando, how you been?"

"Good, D. You gonna get me outta this today, or what?"

"I'll see," I said, opening his file to see if there were any updates. "You testing clean on those UAs?"

"Yeah. Two months now."

"That's good. Sit tight. I'll be right back."

I pushed my way inside the crowded courtroom and saw the prosecutor sitting in a side room with someone representing herself, a pro se. I waited outside the door until they were done and watched the crowd gathering inside. It seemed like the place was made for fifty people and a hundred fifty had crowded in. I leaned my head back and stared at the ceiling, pretending I was sitting on a beach somewhere, listening to the waves, Stefan lying next to me with Jack playing somewhere near us. Will close by, hanging out. Paradise.

The door opened and the pro se stepped out and vomited.

She had bloodshot eyes and stank of booze. She nearly fell and I grabbed her, and bits of vomit splattered my suit. The bailiffs rushed over and snatched her away. The stench, mixed with the already unpleasant air of the court, made me want to gag. Instead, I stepped inside the side room and shut the door. I grabbed a few tissues from a box on the table and wiped at the vomit on my suit.

"You catch some shrapnel?" the prosecutor said.

I remembered him only as Bob, and the last time I was here we had gotten into a shouting match. His wide smile indicated he didn't remember, so I said, "What can you do? Occupational hazard."

"Ain't that the truth. Who you here on?"

"Mr. Ramirez."

"I've got four Ramirezes on the calendar today."

"Hernando."

He flipped through his stack of files and pulled one out. "Oh, yeah. The public pisser. Didn't he piss on a cop car?"

"That would be him."

"Little shit. He's lucky they didn't mace him."

"Little shit though he may be, he's got a minimal history. What do you think about amending it to an infraction and having him pay a fine and be done with it? He's been sober now for two months and we've got the UAs to prove it."

He nodded and closed the file. "Here's what I say to that: go fuck yourself."

"What?"

"You think I don't remember you, Rollins? You embarrassed me last time in front of my judge. For you, you just stroll in here once every few months. But me, I gotta be in front of this psychopathic prick every day. He gave me shit about that motion I lost for months."

"It wasn't my fault your cop was a liar."

"He wasn't a liar, you just made him seem that way. And you pulled me down into it, too. So no, no deals. You can set it for trial and take your chances."

"You gotta be shitting me! You wanna waste both our time on a trial for someone who pissed on a car?"

"Yes. And you better win, or I'm gonna ask for as much jail as I can get."

"Here, throw this away for me, would you?" I put my vomit-laden tissue into his file.

I left the room and saw Hernando standing by the door. He raised his eyebrows, asking me what the verdict was. I shook my head and I heard him say, "Shit" from across the room. Nothing to do now but wait for the judge.

Borth, I had heard, had suffered a psychotic break in his fifties, after he was already a judge. The rumors said it was dementia brought about by severe alcoholism and untreated mental illness. Sometimes I'd come to this court and he'd smile and ask me how my family was, and sometimes I'd come here and he'd scream so much his face became a chubby, sweaty mess of red flesh as he wore out his vocal cords. No way to know ahead of time whether you were getting Jedi Borth or Darth Borth.

The bailiff finally announced, "All rise, Magna City Justice Court is now in session. The Honorable Judge Clarence Borth presiding."

I rose and watched as Borth strolled in, wearing a jogging suit—something a retired old man would wear in Florida. The light-green velour didn't look all that different from the vomit I had wiped off of myself only a few minutes ago.

He mumbled to himself as he took his robe off a coat hanger behind the bench and put it on. Then he sat down and leaned back, drawing a deep breath. "Any private attorneys ready to go?"

I stood at the lectern and said, "Danielle Rollins for Mr. Hernando Ramirez, please, Your Honor."

Bob sat down at the prosecution table and stared at Borth. Neither of us knew exactly who was going to get yelled at today. Bob glanced at me and then flipped me off by pressing his palm against the table with only the middle finger up. I'd done what I had to do to win the motion he was so pissed about, but I didn't think I deserved this kind of treatment. So I stuck my tongue out at him, and he shook his head.

"Ms. Rollins," the judge said calmly, "how are we doing today?"

"We're doing just fine, Your Honor. How's everything with you?"

"Oh, you know, just enjoying my grandkids. That's the reason to wake up in the morning for me, now. I have eight of them." He reached into his pocket and came out with a wallet full of photos. "Come look."

I glanced at Bob, who rose slowly. We approached the bench as the judge pointed to each photo and named the child. "This is Suzy, and Eric, and Catherine, and . . ."

He didn't have eight grandchildren. He had ten grandchildren, and he listed each one. Then he put his wallet away and looked at me and then looked at Bob and said, "What are you two standing here for?"

I looked at Bob and said, "You were considering dismissing this case, Your Honor."

"I was?"

"No," Bob said, "that's not what you were doing. You were showing us photos of your lovely grandchildren."

"Oh, yes. Did I tell you I had ten grandchildren, Ms. Rollins?"

"Each more lovely than the next, Judge. Now how about ruling on that motion to dismiss?"

"There is no motion to dismiss!" Bob said too loudly.

The judge closed his eyes for a second and when he opened them, you could tell something was different. The shouting had snapped something. "Mr. Macalusso, we do not shout in my courtroom. Least of all . . ." His voice was now rising in volume. "Least of all to me! Do I make myself clear?"

"Yes, Judge."

"What do you think this is?" Borth said, his voice going up again. "A whorehouse? Do I look like a whore for you to yell at, Mr. Macalusso?"

"No, Jud—"

"Ms. Rollins, do I look like a whore to you?"

"No, Your Honor, but if you were, I must say you would make an absolutely lovely one."

"Damn straight."

He turned back to Bob. There was no stopping him now. The floodgates of sanity had crumbled.

"Damn it, Bob, I don't deserve to be treated like this!" Borth said, slapping his palm down on the bench. "I went to Harvard, for heaven's sake. Do you know I worked full time and was still top of my class? Did you know that?"

He was full-on shouting now. He didn't seem to realize that a court-room full of people were hanging on his every word.

Borth shouted for five minutes. I leaned my elbow on his bench and watched. Bob had turned bright red. He stared at the items on the bench—pens, pads of paper, the gavel—letting Borth's abuse go in one ear and out the other. Eventually, the flush in his cheeks faded and he just looked tired.

"Now," Borth finally said, "I'm going to make my ruling on that motion to dismiss. Ms. Rollins, I found your argument persuasive. I'm dismissing the case against your client."

"Your wisdom astounds me sometimes, Judge. Thank you."

"Your Honor," Bob said, the flush in his cheeks returning, "there is no motion to dismiss. She hasn't filed anything."

"Next matter, please," Borth bellowed.

We left the bench and Bob whispered under his breath, "I'm appealing that. No way I'm letting it stand."

"Fine. But Borth is the one you have to file the appeal with. I'm guessing he won't be too happy with you questioning his omniscience."

"Up yours, Rollins."

I couldn't help but slap Bob's shoulder and grin. "You need to get more enjoyment out of life, Bob. Quit taking this shit so seriously."

"This is a court of law, and you treat it like it's a circus."

"No, a circus has to make sense. This"—I motioned around the room with my hand—"is random chaos. Entropy is the only rule here. You roll with it, or you break, and you're gonna break if you keep taking everything so personally."

I grabbed Hernando just as Borth began lecturing a man in a truck-ing cap about the proper way to change lanes. I didn't feel I had escaped until I actually inhaled the sour, dusty, smog-infused air and knew I was out of Borth's clutches for certain.

I contemplated heading back to the office, then I remembered the cluster I had waiting for me back home.

"What did you do?" Hernando asked.

"Just got lucky. No more booze. I'm serious. Especially in Magna. It went our way this time, but Borth could've easily taken his wrath out on you."

"No more, man. I swear."

We shook hands and I headed to my car, wondering if Will hated me yet.

21

When I got home, I heard laughter. I rounded the corner and saw Will at the dinner table, or what passed for my dinner table, playing cards with Teddy. He would throw down a card and Teddy would squeal and clap his hands.

"Danielle!" Teddy said. "He knows how to do magic."

"Does he? And where did we learn magic?"

"I wanted to be a magician when I was a kid. No joke. I went to a magic school and everything. My mom was the one that was really pushing me to pursue it."

"What happened?"

"I mean, you know she died when I was . . . I think twelve. And I had to go back and live with my dad who didn't want me and didn't give a shit about anything I was interested in. He got remarried and that was that. He wouldn't pay for the lessons anymore." He shuffled the deck with one hand. "Still kinda regret it. I think I would've made one helluva magician."

I turned to Teddy. "You have fun with him?"

"He does magic," he said with a laugh.

I smiled at Will, and he rose and said, "It was very nice meeting you, Teddy."

"No, do more magic. One more. Please!"

"I think Danielle can handle more magic tricks. I have to get back to work." He looked at me. "Some of us actually have to work."

"Ouch. Careful with that poison tongue, you devil you."

I walked him out. At the front door I said, "I really appreciate this."

"It was actually fun. He's a great kid. Did you find somewhere for him?"

"Haven't heard from Kelly yet. I'm sure we'll have somewhere for him by tonight."

He shook his head. "Hard to believe his parents would do that. You take good care of him, Dani."

He walked to his car, and I watched the entire time. At the car door, he turned and looked at me and a grin came across his face. I wondered, briefly, what life would've been like being married to a man like him instead of Stefan. Will was spontaneous and fun. One time, he picked me up at five in the morning on a motorcycle he had rented and took us skydiving. Another time we were at a waterfall and he jumped in, dressed fully in a suit, because it looked too good to resist. Stefan was the opposite. He was intellectual and had to have everything planned to the last detail. In hindsight, that didn't seem like any way to live.

When he was gone, I turned and saw Teddy mumbling to himself as he tried to do magic tricks, getting frustrated and groaning. I took out my phone and texted Kelly.

Any news yet on homes that would take him?

Nothing yet.

Did you find any other relatives who might?

None. Will said Riley has one sister, who didn't want anything to do with Teddy.

Well, that meant I had another day to kill with him, at least. I googled the day's events in Salt Lake and found that the Salt Lake Bees, a minor league team, were playing at four.

"You ever been to a baseball game, buddy?"

"I can't do magic, Dani. I can't do it." He had grown emotional, to the point that I thought he might cry.

I approached the table and sat down next to him. "It's okay, you just gotta keep practicing."

"No, no, I can't do it."

"Here, let me show you." I picked up the cards and said, "Tell me when to stop." I flipped through the entire deck. "No, Teddy, you have to tell me when to stop."

"Stop."

"Well, wait until I'm flipping through the deck."

I flipped through and he shouted "Stop!" like he was trying to halt an oncoming car. I showed him the card, a two of diamonds.

"Now watch. I give you this card, but I peeked at it when I stopped. See? Watch, here's the move." I showed it to him again, a quick glance downward. His brow furrowed and I showed it to him again.

"But that's not magic," he finally said.

I put the cards down. "Let's grab something to eat. Are you hungry?"

"Yes, I'd like my French toast."

"What French toast?"

"We have French toast for lunch with maple syrup."

"For lunch? All right, who am I to judge? French toast it is."

The first thing I noticed about taking Teddy out were the stares. It seemed as though every person needed to catch a look. Most of them weren't malicious—just people curious about him. A few even gave him warm smiles as we walked into Feeders Bakery.

We ordered French toast for him and a coffee and donut for me. Teddy and I sat down at an open table by the window. Then again, most tables were open since Feeders specialized in breakfast and closed at one.

He immediately took out the sugar packets and the small containers of jelly and began to stack them into little houses. The houses were perfectly symmetrical, one identical to the next. When he ran out of packets, he borrowed some from the table next to us.

"You like building things?"

"Yeah, I used to play with Legos, see. With my Uncle Roger. He would buy me Legos and we would play with them, see."

"Oh, yeah? Is Roger your dad's brother?"

"No, Uncle Roger. He lived next to us. But he went to heaven."

He said it with a certainty that I was sure no saint had ever possessed. He absolutely knew that when death came, it was only to transport people to paradise. I felt sorry for him and envied him at the same time. I had no belief in anything other than random chance. Life had begun on this little backwater planet by accident, and its inhabitants struggled to make sense of it all. I wished I could believe the way Teddy believed. It would give meaning to all this muck.

A man came out of the back and spoke to the cashier. He looked over and smiled, and then he saw Teddy and his smile went away. His name tag said: "Billy—Owner." I'd never seen the owner of a business put "Owner" on a name tag.

Billy was a middle-aged man with slicked-back thinning hair and a paunch. He shook his head, and said something about "retards." We were close enough that I heard the word clearly and knew I wasn't mistaken.

"I'm sorry," I said, "did you say something?"

He looked at me. "Nothing."

"No, you said something, don't back down now. What was it?"

"Nothing," he said again, "Just . . . you know, I'm sick of all these special privileges, that's all. I mean, I'm sure you can relate. I think the government should just stay out of personal business."

"I'm not sure what that has to do with you insulting my friend here."

"Wasn't an insult. It's just, like, take the gays . . ."

"*The* gays?"

"Yeah. They whine and bitch so much they finally get what they want, and they use the power of the government to force me to bake for them. You believe that? So, you know, just with retards, and I don't mean any offense by this, but it's the same thing. I had to put in a two-thousand-dollar ramp to stay in compliance with the ADA bullshit. Two grand. You believe that?"

"You had to build a ramp for people who can't walk . . . wow. You poor thing. How tough your life must be. You had to actually spend some money to help the disabled; how *do* you go on?"

"See," he said, shaking his head again, "this is what I'm talkin' about. I can't even talk to you people."

"'You people?—what, rational adults? You want something to complain about? Try switching places with this kid. You wouldn't last a day, asshole."

"Hey, I don't appreciate that kinda language in my place."

"Yeah, well, we were just leaving anyway. Let's go Teddy."

"I don't have my French toast."

"We'll go somewhere else and get your toast."

"No, I need my toast."

I rose and took Teddy by the arm, trying to lift him. "Let's go, I'll get it somewhere else."

"No."

"Teddy, come on." I pulled on his arm.

He screamed. Then he began hitting his head with both fists, and I had to grab his arms and hold him down. He was screaming so loudly his face turned red and the veins in his neck popped out. I had to lean on top of him to keep him from pummeling himself. He began to cry.

"It's okay," I kept saying in his ear. "It's okay, it's okay, buddy. It's okay. I'm sorry I grabbed you. I'm sorry. I'm sorry."

His screams slowly died away, and he breathed heavily as he wept. I looked around the restaurant. Everyone was staring at us, and the owner had a smirk on his face. He pointed to the door. I let go of Teddy and went over to Billy.

"I'm not leaving without his French toast."

"You ain't getting squat from me, so you both can just leave right now."

"Look, dude, you saw what happened. We already paid for it. Just give him his French toast and you'll never see us again."

He pointed his fat finger in my face. "Screw. You. Now get out before I call the cops."

Some people just couldn't be reasoned with. This guy would fit right in with some of the judges in this state.

"I'll piss in your baking oven."

He chuckled. "What?"

"You can call the cops, but it'll take them ten minutes to get here, at least. And I'm a defense attorney—I couldn't care less about cops. I'll get fined for this. But after I piss in your oven, my first call is to KSL so they can immediately post the story online. It'll spread to all the other news sites by the end of the day. Doesn't matter how much you clean afterward; you'll always be the place where some crazy chick pissed in your oven. How many of these customers do you think will be digging into their éclairs after they read that?"

"Get the hell outta here," he said with a wave of his hand.

I went behind the glass bakery case and pulled down my pants but not my panties. The oven was in full view of the customers. "If you touch me, I'm gonna mace you and still piss in your oven. You just have to sit there and watch me do this."

His face went slack. He stared at me like I had come from some distant planet and was just flapping my tentacles. I reached my thumbs into my panties to pull them down. Some of the customers stood up to get a better look. One had his cell phone out and was recording.

Billy held up his hand. "Wait." He turned to the cashier. "Get him his toast."

I pulled up my pants and held my head high as I walked back to my table. The few customers in the place scurried away from us, and I sat down and looked at Teddy, who had gone back to making houses.

"You okay, Teddy?"

"I used to have Legos."

"I'm sorry I grabbed you; that was wrong of me."

His brow furrowed a little. "I liked Legos."

22

We sat at Franklin Covey Field later that afternoon. The Bees were playing a team from Philadelphia. I got Teddy a hot dog and a soda and the same for myself. The food was fine and the warm sun soothed my skin. I put my sunglasses on as I watched them warm up, and Teddy clapped whenever one of the players hit the ball. He smiled widely, revealing teeth that were clean but needed braces. No matter how many napkins I gave him, he always had food stuck on his face and shirt.

"You ever played baseball?" I asked.

"Yeah. Yeah, Kevin let me play."

"Really? Kevin let you play with him?"

"Yeah, I would hit the ball and they would laugh because they said I was funny."

My heart sank. I looked away and out over the players. I felt a hand on my shoulder, and Will appeared behind me.

"You made it," I said. "I didn't think you'd come."

"Since when don't I like baseball? Especially with my new buddy Teddy."

Teddy squealed with delight. "More magic, please!"

"We don't have any cards, buddy," I said.

He went quiet for a few moments, staring out over the field. Then a player hit a ball out to left field, and he squealed again and clapped.

"So how's your day been?" Will asked.

"Great," I said. "Living the dream." I took out a cigarette and put it between my lips. Since there were children nearby, I didn't light it. I glanced at Teddy, who was busy watching a boxelder bug scurry across the cement under his feet. "He told me he's played baseball before. His neighbor Kevin would play it with him. Teddy said they would laugh because he was funny. I don't think that's what they were laughing at."

"Kids can be so damn cruel."

"Shit—do you live in this world, man? Adults are much crueler." I paused and took the cigarette out of my mouth. "I lived with this family for a while in a small town where everyone knew everyone. I was like eleven, I think. There was this kid in my neighborhood—I think his name was Sandy or Randy, Andy, something like that. He was disabled. Me and my friends, we would invite him to ride bikes or run around—this was, like, fifth grade. He couldn't pronounce certain words, so everyone was always telling him to say this or say that. Everyone laughed. I did it, too. Then, just like that, we got bored, and no one invited him out anymore. He'd sit on his porch and watch us, and we would ride by like he didn't exist." I watched the field a second. "Hatred isn't the worst thing you can feel toward a person. It's indifference."

I put the cigarette back in my mouth. Will was staring at me now with his big eyes.

"What happened to him?" he asked.

"His family moved, and no one ever saw him again. I remember the next day at school, no one said anything. It was like he hadn't existed. I thought how weird it was. This was a kid who had grown up next to us, but no one knew he was gone." I exhaled. "Maybe you're right; maybe kids are worse."

He put his hand on my knee and gave it a squeeze. "Well, I guess I'm not the expert. Gale never wanted to have kids, one of the reasons we divorced actually, and now I think it's probably too late."

"Why didn't she want kids?"

"I don't know. She just was too into herself. When you're selfish, it's hard to give yourself over to someone else, even if it is your child. I guess that was the issue with my dad. What about you? Any more kiddos?"

I shook my head. "I got Jack. My world revolves around him. Wouldn't be fair to bring a baby into that." I flicked some piece of lint or something off my pants. "I still can't believe Stefan is marrying that chick, man," I said.

He shrugged. "What can you do? Life moves on without us sometimes. Sometimes it's worse when two people who should be apart stay together, believe me. You shoulda heard some of the fights me and Gale got into before the divorce."

"How's she doing?"

"I don't know. Once her alimony was done she took off and that was all she wrote."

I looked back over the field. The announcer was bellowing something over the speakers and the players disappeared. Teddy was on his feet, not understanding that they would be back. And then he leaned down and got his soda and took a few large gulps as the announcer kept going on and on about some product they were pushing, some sort of Tupperware.

Within a few minutes, the players were formally announced, and people started cheering. Teddy was jumping up and down. It put a smile on my face, and Will was smiling, too.

During the game, Teddy nearly had to be restrained. He kept jumping up with excitement whenever the crowd went wild, and he would boo when they booed. The joy that spilled out of him was contagious and, even though I couldn't care less about the Bees, I found myself cheering and yelling profanities at the opposing team's players. That always got me a soft elbow in my ribs from Will.

"Where's Jack?" he asked over the noise of the crowd during the third inning.

"I texted him and he said he was out with friends. That seems to be his MO these days. More friends and less family."

"Don't beat yourself up about it. You did it, and Jack's kids will do it to him. Then somewhere in your thirties you realize how ephemeral friends are, and you go back to your family. Unless you hate your family, I guess. Or they're dead."

"You're such a ray of sunshine."

He grinned. We held each other's gaze a second and then cheers erupted again as the batter struck out. Will stood up and yelled, and I turned away from the field and glanced down at my shoes. They were scuffed and stained. When Stefan had been living with me, he shined my shoes. I would tell him I didn't care, but at night, when I was asleep or out or had drunk myself into oblivion, he would shine them so they would look nice for court in the morning.

"Danielle!" Teddy squealed. "He caught the ball. Look! He caught the ball!"

Someone had caught the ball and everyone was going wild.

I began to cheer for whatever had happened on the field, but only because Teddy was cheering.

When the game ended, we left the stadium and strolled through the neighborhood. The stadium didn't have parking of its own, and we had to pay extortionate rates in the neighboring lots or find street parking. Teddy ran ahead of us with a stick in his hand. He poked at fire hydrants and trees and kept himself occupied.

"Oh, so get this. I went to interview that kid, Freddy. He has the same lawyer Kevin does and I wasn't allowed to speak with him."

"He told me he would talk to you."

"Well he must've changed his mind. And I wouldn't count on him telling anybody else that the cops fed him that story. That lawyer's probably got him scared shitless that if he says anything he'll be the only one going down."

"Shit. Well, it's set for a preliminary hearing. I'm hoping to get it dismissed then, or afterward when I file a motion challenging jurisdiction."

"Seems weird that they're fighting so hard, doesn't it? I mean, for a kid like Teddy."

"They want to change the law, and this case just fell into their laps. It was just the wrong place and the wrong time."

"So justice is just a matter of luck."

"I wish it was a matter of luck. It doesn't even seem to be that."

He hesitated. "You know, I'm proud of you."

"For what?"

"For doing this. For taking care of him. You could've left him at the homeless shelter and your life would've been a lot easier."

We stopped. His car was parked at the curb in front of a building painted yellow and red. We both watched Teddy playing with a grasshopper. He picked it up as gently as possible and moved it away from the street. If it hopped back, he'd pick it up and move it to safety again.

"I've made a decision," I said. "After Stefan's wedding, I'm moving."

"Moving where?"

"Back to LA."

"When did you make that decision?"

"Right now. While we were walking." I put a cigarette in my mouth and this time lit it. "I can't handle it. He knows I love the shit out of him. And if I can't be with him, so be it. That's my fault. But I can't live in the same city with him and his wife, running into them everywhere, hearing from other people what they're up to. I gotta go and start over."

I don't know if it was just the way the afternoon light from the setting sun was hitting Will or what, but I thought he seemed sad. He folded his arms and looked down at the ground and nodded.

"If you think that's best," he said.

"What the hell do I know about what's best? But it seems like something that should happen."

"Wait, what about Jack?"

"I'm not going through a custody fight. I'll ask him who he wants to live with."

"Ouch. That's going to hurt one of you pretty damn bad."

I nodded as I puffed on my cigarette and then held it low as I watched Teddy. He was spinning in a circle and clapping as the grasshopper moved away from the road and went toward the building.

"Look, I gotta run," Will said. "But seriously, thanks for inviting me. I had fun."

I watched him get into his car and drive away. The smoke tasted bad right now, and I tossed the cigarette into the gutter and went over to Teddy.

"Come on, buddy. Let's get something to eat."

23

After a dinner of pancakes at Teddy's insistence, I put him in my bed again, and we went through the entire *SpongeBob* debacle. When he was finally asleep, I asked my neighbor Beth to keep an eye on him for a few minutes and then drove up to his parents' house. The lights were on. It was worth a shot—maybe they missed the kid and realized their mistake.

I went up to the door and knocked. Teddy's father answered.

"Don't come here again." He slammed the door in my face.

Okay, so maybe their hearts hadn't softened quite yet. I took out my phone and dialed Riley's number. It went to voice mail.

"Hey," I said, "it's Dani Rollins. Teddy's staying at my place for now. He really misses you guys. I thought maybe . . . I don't know. Maybe you've realized you made a mistake or something. Give me a call or stop by anytime." I paused. "No one said parenting was easy. If it was, everyone would be good at it, but no one is. You just do the best you can. This isn't the best you can do, Riley."

I hung up the phone and looked up to the second floor of the house. Riley stood at the window staring down at me. She didn't move or gesture and neither did I. Instead, we stared at each other awkwardly until I left and decided I needed a drink.

———————

The Lizard was more packed than usual. I had to hand it to Michelle—she had a way with marketing. She seemed to instinctively know who her demographic was, and she went after them with a sniper rifle.

This time I saw her before she saw me, and I hopped off my stool and sat at a table so she couldn't hit me. She wrapped her arms around my neck and shook me like a doll, splashing my beer everywhere.

"Wanna get high?" she asked. It wasn't really a question, though, because her answer was always "hell yes."

"I'm good."

"You haven't smoked pot since college. Why is that?"

"Not my thing."

"Suit yourself. So what's going on with you?"

"Got someone staying at my house, and I'll have to get back to him soon."

She sat down next to me and took out a silk pouch. The weed was fragrant, almost like perfume. She laid it on a small table and began taking out the stems. "Your kid?"

"No, a client actually. Kind of a kid."

"Since when do you take clients home?"

"Since never." I took a sip of my beer. "Hey, I may need you to do a favor for me."

"What's that?"

"CI I got on a case. They released his name to me under a protective order yesterday, so don't share it with anyone else: Salvador Zamora. Drug distributor in Richardson. He's the main witness against my client. I've tried calling him a bunch of times and he won't talk."

"And you think I just happen to know all the drug dealers in Utah because of my shady character." She licked a paper and began rolling the joint.

"Don't you?"

She lit up and took a long puff. "Hell yes I do. What you need this guy for?"

"The kid who's staying at my house, Teddy Thorne. They're saying he tried to sell coke to Zamora. Teddy's mentally disabled, though. I think he's the fall guy."

"The fall guy?" she said, chuckling and choking on the smoke at the same time. "You from an eighties detective sitcom or something?"

"Look. He's being blamed for something he didn't do. Can you help or not?"

"Take it easy, lady. You're gonna give yourself a heart attack with that shit. My dad died of a heart attack at thirty-seven. Believe that? Think you're a healthy young buck and then just keel over from the stress. Don't let that be you."

"Thank you for the PSA, Surgeon General. Now can you find this distributor for me?"

She nodded. "I got some hookups in Richardson. I'll ask around and see what I can find out."

"Thanks." I set my beer down. The urge to drink had left me.

"Where you goin'?" Michelle asked as I rose.

"Just tired. I'll see ya."

24

Preparation for Teddy's preliminary hearing consisted of going over the police reports and witness statements and creating a general outline of the topics I wanted to cover. Some defense attorneys planned out every question, but I didn't. Juries and judges sometimes picked up on cues that had nothing to do with what the witness was saying. Some witnesses just looked like they were liars, and others looked like they would rather die than tell a falsehood. Outward appearances, of course, had nothing to do with whether witnesses were actually telling the truth or not, but juries and judges liked to believe they could read people. And if I had my head down over my questions, I would completely miss what the jury or judge was taking in. So I stuck with an outline.

At the preliminary hearing, the judge was just looking to see if there was probable cause to move to trial. In every other district in the state, the prelim was handled by a different judge to ensure fairness. In Hoover County, it was handled by the same judge, allegedly to save money, but really as a middle finger to fairness.

The big question mark was Zamora. I had no idea what he was going to say. He could get up there and say Teddy sold him coke, the same way he had in the police reports, or he could get up there and say he had no idea who Teddy was and that Kevin had set everything up.

As I sat at my desk and reread the file for the third time, Michelle called my cell phone.

"Hey," I said.

"Got a line for you on Zamora."

"You are the magic woman. What'd you find out?"

"Coke distributor for the Kings. You know them?"

"I've defended a couple of them. Nothing in depth."

"Mexican street gang. They're the ones who shot that cop as retaliation for the cop shooting that Mexican kid."

"I remember that. Zamora runs with those guys?"

"Apparently he's one of the top dogs."

"No shit?"

"Yeah. The guy I talked to said he's been in and out of the can so many times all the guards at the prison got a pool on when he'll be back. Long history."

A guy like that might say anything to keep out of prison, if for no other reason than because of how boring the experience had become.

"Did you find out anything about a connection to Teddy?"

"Nah. No one's heard of your guy. Ask me, though, Zamora's not the type of guy some high school punk could just approach with a bag of coke. You gotta have connections to get to him. Your dude got connections?"

"Not one."

"Hm. Well, that's all I got. You need anything else?"

"No. That's really helpful. I owe you."

"Remember that when I ask for something. And be careful, Dani. These are some bad dudes."

I set the phone down and leaned back in my seat. Zamora was a bigwig in a violent street gang, and somehow Teddy knew him well enough to sell him several kilos of coke? No way. It didn't add up. But then again, Kevin didn't seem like the type of kid who would know Zamora either. Assuming Roscombe set the case for trial after the hearing, I'd appeal, but while the appeal proceeded, I'd use the months between now and the trial date to try to find out how *any* of these kids knew Zamora.

I was about to continue through the file when my phone buzzed with a call from the office line. I remembered why I had promised myself recently that I would turn my phone off while I prepped cases. It never happened, because no defense attorney could afford to miss a phone call from a potential client, but it was a nice thought.

Even though I wanted to keep working on Teddy's case, I couldn't pass up money to pay the bills.

I sighed and answered. "This is Dani."

25

The day of the preliminary hearing, I got Will to watch Teddy while I prepped, and he agreed to drop him off before the hearing started. I could've brought him along to the office, but I'd have to leave him alone while I prepared, and I had no idea whether Teddy could be alone during the day. Whenever I texted his parents to get some advice, they never texted back. I had called Riley so many times that I had her phone number memorized.

Kelly had researched every nonprofit in the state of Utah and found that there were few places that Teddy could fit into. There were shelters, and there were homes, and there were halfway houses, but nowhere that Teddy would be watched by someone qualified to supervise him. Every agency kept saying, "We'd love to help, but our funding got cut and . . ."

The "and" didn't matter. Not to Teddy. If I put him out on the street, he'd have nowhere to go, and I wasn't sure he could figure out how to get food. There was a real possibility he could die, a possibility that I'm sure wasn't lost on his parents when they decided to abandon him. The law—dating from 1901, when it was deemed that forcing parents to care for adult children would interfere with the harvest—protected

Robert and Riley. Some of our laws were so outdated I thought it might be better to delete them all and start over.

I showed up to the prelim early, and Double D sat at the prosecution table. He wore a ridiculous pin on his lapel: two revolvers crossed over an American flag. I nodded to him and he nodded back. I sat down at the defense table and checked the printed court calendar in front of me; Teddy was one of three cases. The public defender had the other two.

A few people, mostly families, trickled into the courtroom. No one was there for Teddy. I checked the clock on my phone. He and Will should've arrived fifteen minutes ago.

"All rise," the bailiff said halfheartedly.

Roscombe came out and sat down without looking at anyone. He booted up his computer and then leaned forward. "Who's ready?"

"I am, Judge," said one of the public defenders. He was sitting in the jury box with an inmate, who didn't seem to want to sign a plea form. The PD was telling him he didn't have a choice. Finally, the inmate relented and signed it, his shackles clinking against the wood of the jury box. In Hoover County, public defenders were contracted, and the contracts went to the lowest bidder. It wasn't the public defenders' fault, really: the county had set up the system to ensure their public defenders were overworked and underpaid, making certain they wouldn't actually fight cases, appeal constitutional issues, and generally call them on their bullshit. Dictators don't like naysayers.

The PD took to the lectern and did his thing. I kept checking the door for Will. Finally, I texted him and asked where he was. He said they were here but having trouble at the metal detectors.

In the lobby, the two bailiffs stood in front of Teddy, who was leaning against the wall, covering his ears with his hands and rocking back and forth.

"What happened?" I said.

Will looked up from trying to comfort him. "The bailiffs told him he had to take off his shoes because they kept making the metal detectors go off. He wouldn't do it, and they tried to grab him."

I turned to the bailiffs. "Is that really necessary? Can't you just wand his shoes?"

"I told him to take them off."

"He doesn't want to take his shoes off. Is it really that big a deal?"

"He don't take his shoes off, he ain't comin' in."

Gomer Pyle had made up his mind, and there was no changing it. I turned to Teddy and stood in front of him so he could see my eyes, and I smiled. Slowly, he removed his hands from his ears.

"You all right, buddy?"

"He said . . . he said to take my shoes off Danielle but I don't want to take my shoes off. I don't want to take my shoes off."

"I know. But you know what? This linoleum right here feels better without your shoes on. Check this out."

I slipped off my shoes, ran a few paces, and then slid on my stockings for maybe two feet on the smooth linoleum.

"See?"

He watched as I slid on the floor again and slowly he began to smile. He took off his shoes, flinging them to the side, and tried to run to me. I said, "Go through there," and pointed to the metal detectors. He went through without beeping and slid on the linoleum. I raced him around the stairs as he squealed like a kid. We slid into a bench, and he toppled over and thought it was the funniest thing in the world. Will held our shoes and watched us with a grin.

I picked Teddy up from the floor and said, "We gotta go upstairs for just a minute, but do you want to come back down after and slide again?"

"Yeah!"

"Okay. Get your shoes back on, and let's hurry and do this so we can slide some more."

We put on our shoes and headed to the elevators. The sliding had lifted his spirits so much he was skipping to the elevators. We got on, the three of us, and headed up to the courtroom.

Teddy sat down at the defense table. The PD finished pleading both of his clients and Roscombe sighed when he saw me. "No chance this is resolving today, Ms. Rollins?"

"No chance."

"Very well. We are here on the matter of State of Utah versus Theodore Thorne, case number 1645984925. Is the State ready to proceed?"

Double D stood up and said, "We are, Your Honor."

"Very well, first witness."

"State calls Kevin Simmons to the stand."

A bailiff stepped outside and, a moment later, came in with Kevin. Teddy clapped and said, "Hi, Kevin!" and I had to grab his hands to get him to stop.

Kevin took the stand and wouldn't look in our direction. I noticed someone else in the courtroom, too—a man in a pinstriped gray suit with hair the same color as the suit. He stood in the back of the courtroom with his arms folded and watched me. He had to be Kevin's lawyer.

Double D stood up and strolled to the lectern like he didn't have any other place to be in the world. He had one page of questions in front of him, and he was quiet a long time, reading each question beforehand to himself. Finally he said, "State and spell your name for the record, please."

"Kevin Simmons. Um, K-E-V-I-N and then S-I-M-M-O-N-S."

"Mr. Simmons, do you recall the events of April second of this year?"

"Yes."

"Please run us through what you remember."

Kevin glanced once at Teddy and looked down. He cleared his throat. "We were hanging out at my house in Salt Lake. Just like, I don't know, goofing around, playing video games and stuff."

"When you say we, who do you mean?"

"My buddies Clint Andrews and Freddy Willmore. We were I think playing a game when Teddy came by. He said that—"

"Let me stop you there. Who is Teddy?"

"Teddy Thorne."

"Is he in the courtroom today?"

"Yeah."

"Can you identify him, please?"

Kevin hesitated and then lifted his arm and pointed to Teddy. "That's him at the table. With the gray shirt."

"How do you know Teddy?"

"He's my neighbor. He's lived next door, like, forever."

"So you and your friends are hanging out and Teddy comes over. What happens then?"

"He seemed, like, really agitated. Something was bothering him. I could always tell because he paces. Just, like, paces back and forth. So I asked him what was up, and he said that he had a bag that he needed to take somewhere and could we take him."

"Did you see a bag with him?"

"No, he went and got it later. He said the place was in Richardson, and we were going up to Roy City to meet some other buddies so we said we'd take him. I just thought . . . I don't know. I don't know what he was doing."

"So you agreed to take him?"

"Yeah, it wasn't far from where we were going, so we said we would. Then he ran over to his house and came back out with a bag."

Double D went to the prosecution table and reached underneath. He came out with a dark-blue duffle bag, and then returned to the lectern. "Is this the bag?"

"That looks like it, yeah."

"Your Honor, we'd move to introduce exhibit one into evidence."

"Any objection?"

I rose. "None."

Diamond said, "May I approach?"

"Yes."

He handed the bag to the judge's clerk and then went back to the prosecution table and reached underneath again. He came up with several bricks of what looked like cocaine. He stacked them neatly on the table, taking his time to let it sink in how much coke was in the bag.

"So what happened when you drove him down, Mr. Simmons?"

"We got in my car and I drove. Teddy sat in the passenger seat. It takes like half an hour to get to Richardson, so we listened to music and talked."

"Did Teddy say anything?"

"Not really. Just that he had to deliver this bag."

"So what happened then?"

Kevin took a deep breath. "We drove down and got off on the Twenty-Fifth Street exit. That's when he finally told me what was in the bag."

"What did he say?"

"He said that he had cocaine in the bag."

"Those were his exact words?"

Kevin nodded. "He said he had cocaine and that he had to drop it off. I tried to talk him out of it. I told him that it was illegal, but he kept insisting that we do it. He has this tic, I guess, where he just keeps repeating something over and over. He started doing that and wouldn't stop until I told him that we would drop it off."

"What happened then?"

"I mean, I didn't believe he had coke," Kevin said, glancing at the judge. "I just thought he was kidding. But I thought he *did* have something to drop off. So he leads us to this house in Richardson. He sits there for a second and then says that he's too scared to go by himself, so I get out of the car and go with him. I mean, I haven't seen the coke, so I thought that maybe he was making it up. I don't know. So I go up on the porch with him and some Mexican dude answers. Teddy says, 'Hi,' and the Mexican dude takes the bag. Then it was just a blur after that, just cop cars and people throwing me on the ground, arresting me. It was unreal. I've never been in trouble before so, I mean, it was crazy."

"Did anyone, to your knowledge, put Teddy Thorne up to this?"

"No. I don't think so. I mean, I haven't heard anything else. As far as I know, Teddy was just down there to drop the bag off."

"Now, you've known Teddy a long time, you said."

"Yeah."

"He's slow, isn't he?"

"Yeah, he's retarded. I mean, not to the point that he can't do anything, but yeah."

"So how do you expect this court to believe that a slow man set up and executed a deal for this much cocaine?"

"I don't know. I'm just telling you what I saw."

"Thank you, Mr. Simmons. No further questions."

I sat quietly a moment and eyed Kevin, a pen to my lips. I put the pen down and rose. I passed the lectern and stood in front of the witness, something I knew Roscombe hated. I put my hands in my pockets and paced a little bit.

"Teddy led you to this house?"

"Yeah, that's what I said."

"You know he's never been to Richardson," I said, just taking a wild guess and seeing what Kevin would say.

"I didn't know that. Seemed like he knew the place, to me."

"How did he lead you there?"

"Just told us where to go."

I stopped directly in front of him. "Like was he telling you to turn right and left, or did he give you an address?"

"Right and left. He was directing us where to go. I don't think he's good with addresses."

"How many times did he tell you to turn?"

"What?"

"How many times did he give you directions?"

"I don't know."

"Ten? Twenty? Thirty . . . ?"

"Twenty, maybe. He just kept saying turn here or go up this road."

"What was he wearing?"

"What was he wearing?"

"Yes, Mr. Simmons. What was my client wearing on this night?"

Kevin swallowed. "I don't remember."

"You spent the entire night with him, did a drug deal with him, and then got arrested with him, and don't remember what he was wearing?"

He hesitated. "Jeans. Jeans and, like, a T-shirt."

"What kind of a T-shirt?"

"I think it was blue."

I took a step closer to him. "What kind of shoes did he have?"

"I don't know."

"Was he wearing a watch?"

"I don't know."

"What music did you listen to on the way to Richardson?"

"I don't remember."

"What topics did the four of you talk about?"

"I don't know. Just stuff."

"Just *stuff*? Seems like you would remember every detail about that night, doesn't it?"

"I don't remember."

"You don't remember much, do you? I mean, other than the fact that my client was responsible for everything?"

"He was."

"Where'd he say he got the coke?"

"He didn't say."

"Did you ask him?"

"No."

I glanced at Roscombe, who wasn't even paying attention. Preliminary hearings were perfunctory: defense attorneys rarely won, and judges seldom paid much attention. They would just rubber-stamp the case for the prosecution. It didn't matter, as I didn't really expect to win here. I was using it more to get the witnesses down into a story, and then I would get the recordings and the transcript from this hearing, and if they said anything different at trial I would shove it down their throats.

"Your handicapped friend has a bag full of cocaine, and you expect us to believe you never asked him where he got it from?"

"I didn't think of it."

"You didn't think of it? But you thought to talk him out of doing it?"

"Yeah, I did."

I paced a few times and then turned to him again. "How'd you do it?"

"Do what?"

"How'd you try to talk him out of it?"

"I said it was illegal and that we shouldn't do it. That we'd get in trouble."

"And you thought he'd understand that?"

"Yeah, he understands a lot."

"You just called him retarded, didn't you?"

"Yeah, but there's different levels of retarded."

I folded my arms. "Really? Do you have some psychology degree I don't know about, Mr. Simmons?"

"No."

"So you couldn't really say what *level* of 'retarded' Teddy is?"

"I guess not."

I went closer to him, close enough to put my hand on the banister in front of him and look into his eyes. I wanted to see how he would act under pressure. "That gym bag's kinda big, isn't it? Something you'd use in sports."

"I guess."

"Teddy play any sports?"

He shook his head. "No, I don't think so."

"What sports do you play?"

"Baseball and wrestling."

I folded my arms. "You did the coke deal, didn't you?"

"No."

"You took Teddy along to catch the blame in case you got busted."

"No, that's not what happened."

"It's easy to blame someone who's 'retarded.' He can't fight back. Not really."

"No," he said, shaking his head. "I wouldn't do that."

"Sure you would. It's easier than manning up and doing your time. Blame the retard, and this all goes away. How long did you act like his friend for?"

"It wasn't like that," he said, his voice rising.

"Was it hard to look at him every day? See him smiling at you, thinking you're his friend when you knew you were gonna screw him worse than anyone's screwed him in his life?"

"No!" he shouted. "It wasn't like that. He was my friend. He is my friend. I wouldn't do that to him."

His face was red and his hands trembled. He looked at Teddy, who sat there passively a moment and then said, "Hi Kevin!"

Roscombe immediately jumped in and said, "Mr. Thorne, do not address the witnesses in my courtroom."

I stepped a few paces back so Roscombe would have to look at me instead of Teddy and said, "No further questions."

I sat down and stared at Kevin.

Damn it to douchebag hell.

I think I believed the little shit.

26

One of the detectives testified next, repeating what Kevin said, and then Double D rested. Star witnesses, particularly CIs, were never called at prelim, but Zamora's written statement was submitted as evidence. The judge didn't even call for argument. He just said, "I find there's enough to bind this case over for trial."

"Judge," I said, on my feet, "if I may? No procedure was followed in the bringing of this case. This is a matter that should've been filed in juvenile court and is not listed under the Serious Youth Offender Act as a predicate offense to charge a juvenile as an adult. And even if it were, the juvenile court judge is the one who makes the determination as to whether the juvenile should be tried as an adult. Here, the prosecution has ignored several statutes upheld by the supreme court and filed directly in the district court in contravention to the law. I would demand this case not be bound over, due to lack of jurisdiction. Frankly, it's an offense to the citizenry of this state that the case has even gotten this far."

Double D stood up and said, "Your Honor, you yourself signed the certification to make this an adult case. If Ms. Rollins has a problem with your ruling, the proper remedy is an appeal to the court of appeals, and they can decide whether the court's actions are proper."

"Holy shit," I said, staring at him with my mouth open. "Did you two plan this or something?" It was quick, but Double D looked away from me, avoiding eye contact.

"Ms. Rollins!" Roscombe bellowed. "You will respect this courtroom and refrain from profanity, or I will lock you up so fast it will make your head spin."

"Your Honor, did the State come to you before this case was filed and ask if you would do this, or did you certify this on your own?"

Roscombe glanced at Double D, and Double D looked down at the floor and back up. It was minor. It was quick, but it happened. It wasn't a coincidence Roscombe had been assigned to this case; they had planned this out beforehand. I thought Roscombe certified this case because he wanted to get rid of the SYOA, but this had been a collusion between him and the prosecutors. They had influenced a judge to do what they wanted. There were so many judicial and ethical rules being broken right now I couldn't even think straight.

"Your Honor, I move for an immediate recusal of yourself from this case."

"Such request must be made in writing, Ms. Rollins."

I grabbed the pen off the defense table and wrote on a yellow legal pad my name, phone number, and Bar number, and then, *Excuse yourself, Judge* across the top, and on the side, *Motion for Recusal.* I gave it to the bailiff who walked it over to the judge.

Roscombe said, "Cute," before taking the page and tossing it in the trash. "But it doesn't follow proper form."

"I can't even begin to name all the laws you two are breaking right now, and you're telling me about proper form?"

"I would watch your tone in my court, Counselor." Roscombe turned to his clerk and said, "Kill the recording." When she had, he continued: "The State is going forward on a legitimate issue. They believe the statute to be incorrect and so do I. If you lose, appeal it, and we'll see what they say."

"And in the meantime an innocent boy's life is ruined." I shook my head. "I always knew you were an asshole, but I had no idea the supernova of assholedom you had stored away in that head of yours."

Roscombe looked like he might soil himself. His face turned red and he barked at his bailiff, "Arrest her."

———————

I sat in the back cell next to the judge's chamber for a good hour. A headache throbbed away as I waited on a cot that felt like a burlap sack.

I had thought that Hoover County had gotten lucky. Roscombe, I knew, hated the SYOA and was waiting for a case like this, and I'd thought it was just bad luck that he'd gotten it, but it wasn't luck. Instead, this had been a conspiracy. He and the DA sat down and tried to figure out how to get around a law they didn't like, a law that protected the most vulnerable in our society—children—from abuses of government power.

The monstrosity of this whole thing weighed on me like a roof slowly collapsing onto my shoulders, pushing me into the floor. It took effort to sit upright, so I lay down on the single cot in the cell and stared at the ceiling.

The door opened and the bailiff said, "The judge wants to see you."

I followed him out. Roscombe was still behind the bench but had taken his robe off. He looked at me. "I don't feel like having a bailiff babysit you overnight. You're free to go."

"Just for the record, you're supposed to have a hearing before finding me in contempt, Judge. I know you don't like to read the laws of this state, so I thought I'd tell you."

He leaned forward on his bench with both hands and inhaled deeply. "I would be very careful what you say and do right now, Ms. Rollins."

I shook my head. "You took an oath to uphold the law."

"*Just* laws."

"There's no mention of *just* laws. Only laws, all laws. Not only the laws you happen to agree with."

He raised his eyebrows and said, "Well, you have some options available to you. Do with them what you want."

I left the courthouse. The bailiff gave my phone back to me on the way out. Will had texted that he took Teddy around the corner to a café. There was only one café near the courthouse, and it was a trendy place with pictures of tribesmen on the walls, as though the café bought its bread directly from the jungles of Brazil instead of the Whole Foods down the street.

Will and Teddy sat at a table. Teddy had a ring of food around his mouth and was guzzling some red drink out of a plastic cup, further painting his face. I sat down across from Will and groaned.

"Just out of the big house, no big deal. Itching for some lovin' from a man, though. I haven't even seen a man in ages. Just lifting weights and sharpening toothbrushes for me."

He grinned. "Well, I'm sure there are plenty of gigolos who'd be impressed by that line."

"You think? I'll have to use it next time I'm picking up guys at the high school." He had the remnants of a personal pizza in front of him that had gone cold. I grabbed one of the slices and took a bite. It was rubbery and, Heaven forbid, I think vegan.

"Thanks for doing this," I said. "I'm sure you've got more interesting things to do."

"More interesting than watching you get arrested? I don't know."

"That judge is such an asshole."

"What made you lose it like that?"

150

"They planned this whole thing. I thought it was the county attorney's office being aggressive because they saw an opportunity to change a law that put a little limit on their power, but that's not what it was. They sat down with the judge beforehand and planned this. They colluded to get around laws written by the legislature. It's a total abuse of power."

He smiled.

"What?"

"It's just good to see you so passionate."

"Well, I can do without it. I don't think I'm qualified for this mess."

Gently, he took my hand and squeezed it before pulling away. "You'll do fine."

I looked at him for a long time. He was, in a lot of ways, a woman's dream. Wealthy from his own business, handsome, charming, nice, funny . . . I wondered what it was about me that didn't chase after him. Maybe because I grew bored of men so quickly and didn't want to get bored of him.

He rose and said, "I have to run."

I watched him leave and then turned to Teddy, who was shoving a giant slice of pizza into his mouth backward. I turned it around for him, and he giggled as he pushed half of it in.

"Buddy, I gotta ask you something and I need you to answer me, okay?"

"Okay," he said, through a ball of wet pizza.

"Where did you get that bag that we talked about? The night that you got to ride in the police car, do you remember? Where did you get that bag?"

His face went serious, and he wouldn't look at me. "I don't know, Danielle."

"Yes, you do. It's okay, you can tell me."

"Danielle, I don't know. I don't know, Danielle."

I sighed. "You lie about as well as I do, buddy."

I rubbed my head and looked out over the restaurant.

My next move would be filing a motion to quash the binding over, which basically meant I disagreed with the judge's ruling. The motion would go, again, to the same judge, because this was Hoover County, and he would decide whether or not he had made a mistake. Which had about as much chance of happening as a PhD being awarded to someone with the last name of Kardashian. But once I appealed the motion to quash, it would go to the Utah Court of Appeals and the hell away from Hoover County.

"You ready to go?" I asked.

Teddy guzzled the remains of his red drink and rose. I had to get a handful of napkins and wipe his face. As we headed out to the car, I texted Kelly. *Anything?*

No. Sorry. Nothing permanent anyway. Working on something.

I put my phone away. "Looks like you're staying another night with me, buddy."

"Can we get ice cream?"

I wondered if there were any bars that served ice cream.

27

I went into the office, Teddy sucking on an ice cream cone next to me, and was about to ask Kelly to watch Teddy when she said, "I got something."

"A home?"

"No. A school. When he turned eighteen, the school his parents sent him to required reenrollment, but his parents never reenrolled him, and all the deadlines have passed. But this is a special-needs school for adults who are out of high school. It's from nine to three every day, and his condition has to qualify. I need his guardians to sign some releases so I can send the school his medicals. I'll get it done today. I mean, if they are still his guardians. We might need to get you power of attorney over him to do it. I'll follow up on everything."

"I could kiss you right now."

"I told you I'd sue you for sexual harassment one day." She rose. "Teddy, come with me. We have to have your parents sign something."

Teddy looked at me and shifted awkwardly from one foot to the other. "It's okay," I said. "This is Kelly, and she's a good friend of mine." He smiled at her. "Hi, Kelly."

When they were gone, I collapsed into my chair and stared at the ceiling. This wasn't a case I wanted. I wanted guilty people. I wanted to go in and work out a plea deal and make them happy they didn't go to prison and then get on with my life and forget about them. Never, in a million years, did I think I would have a client living with me, and that I would be taking on an entire county and a district court judge.

I blew a raspberry at the universe in general, and then looked at my calendar. I had other hearings before Teddy's next one, but I didn't care about any of them. I didn't even want to think about them. I would likely get them all continued so I could focus on drafting that motion to quash.

I took a bottle of Johnny Walker Black out of the bottom drawer of my desk, poured a drink, and then opened the last motion to quash I'd written to use as a template.

———

I don't know how long I spent on the motion, but when I woke up, I was on my couch. I sat up and stretched my neck and back and then checked to see what I had. The motion was completed. I did a quick search for profanity and found "shit" twice, so I took those words out. Then I printed it and stuck a Post-it note on it asking Kelly to file it. Thinking of Kelly made me think of Teddy, so I texted her.

Where are you guys?

He fell asleep in my car. I'm at your house and just let him sleep. Got everything filed with the school. Waiting to see if Medicaid will cover the cost. Going down there tomorrow to get things moving quicker.

Fantastic! You're awesome.

Don't forget that when Christmas bonuses come around.

I left the office, thinking I would get over to the Lizard for a few drinks before trying to see Jack. I stopped before getting outside and thought a moment. The big question mark in this case was Zamora, and I hadn't spoken with him yet. He wasn't answering my calls. If only someone didn't care about the Bar ethical rules . . .

I hopped in the Jeep and drove to Richardson, after texting Kelly that I would be late.

Zamora's house was small and dilapidated. It looked like the type of place old rock stars went to die. I got out of the car and lit a cigarette, taking a few puffs while leaning against my Jeep and looking over the neighborhood. Not the worst place I'd seen, or even lived, but certainly not a place where it would be safe to look like a hapless visitor.

A pair of shoes with the laces tied together hung from a power line as a sign to addicts that there were several drug houses on the street. The color of lights on the porch told addicts what products they had. A red light was heroin, a blue light coke, a yellow light meth, a green light pot. That was the system now, but it would change in a few years. As soon as the narc units caught on, the dealers would change it up.

I tossed my cigarette onto the ground and headed up to the door. I knocked and put my hands in my pockets as I waited. Two men peeked out from behind the window curtains, and I smiled and waved. The door was unlocked, and one of them opened it. I could see the bulge of a gun underneath his shirt, tucked into his waistband right over his genitals. What was it with these homeboys wanting to blow off their own junk?

"Hola, amigo. Is Salvador here?"

"Who is you?"

"I've got some information for him. About the charges pending against him. He'll wanna hear it, trust me."

He looked me up and down. "Wait."

I looked back over to the neighborhood. No one was out. No kids playing, no elderly sitting on porches, no people. Everyone cowered inside their homes for fear of being caught up in something they didn't want to be caught up in.

The door behind me opened and a slim man with glasses and a tattoo poking out of his shirt onto his neck stepped out. I recognized Salvador Zamora from his driver's license photo and said, "Hi."

"What you need?"

"Man, is no one friendly around here? What happened to 'hello' and 'how you doing?'"

He spit on the porch near my feet. "What you need?"

"I need to talk to you about Teddy Thorne."

"Who are you?"

"Let's just say I'm an interested party."

"I ain't talkin' to no one." He turned to go inside.

"Hey, just one sec. Listen, we both know you and Teddy are getting it the worst. You really think three rich white kids are gonna go down for this? It's gonna be you and the black kid."

He stared at me. His eyes were unblinking, the eyes of a predator. I instantly didn't like him.

"Gimme five minutes. I think I can help both of you," I said.

He nodded. "Five minutes."

28

Salvador led me inside. The house smelled of South American cooking: fried beans and bread and some sort of corn dish. I saw an old woman at the stove stirring a mixture in a pot. Pictures of the Virgin Mary hung on most of the walls; there was a small bag of weed on top of a dresser.

We went into a room near the back. A water bed took up most of the space. Salvador sat and the bed waved up and down.

"So?" he said.

"Teddy didn't sell you those drugs. We both know it. What I don't get is why you're covering for Kevin. The guy's gonna screw you in the end."

He looked amused. "How you gonna help me?"

"I need to know what you know, first."

"Nah, it don't work like that. You tell me how you gonna help me, and I'll see if I wanna talk to you."

I put my hands on my hips and looked around the room. A large painting of an ancient Aztec warrior, the obligatory half-naked woman on his knee, hung above his water bed. "Kevin set up Teddy. I might be able to get the drugs tossed. You're all codefendants. If I get the drugs tossed, the case against you probably goes away, too. And like I said, they're gonna come after you. Nice boys from nice families, or you and Teddy? Who do you think will get thanked, and who's gonna get shafted? You'll do some time, for sure."

He shrugged as he lay back on the bed, his hands behind his head.

"You really think they'll let you off, with your record?"

He made a clicking sound against his teeth. "I ain't got no reason to talk to you. I'm getting me a deal."

"What kind of deal?"

"The none-a-your-business type. Time to get steppin'."

"Just tell me one thing and I'll leave—which cop was in charge of this bust?"

"The white dude. Not the other one. The *bolillo*."

———————

I left the house and looked up the file for the case. The white detective's name was Bo Steed. He had been the lead on the takedown operation. I texted Will and said: *I need you to get me everything you can on a detective with the Hoover County Narcotics Task Force. Bo Steed.*

A minute later, he texted back. *Your wish is my command.* I headed to the Lizard and the waiting drinks that would make me feel all warm and fuzzy for a while, before I had to go home to make sure Teddy was okay.

29

The Lizard was particularly empty, and Michelle wasn't there. One of the guys tending bar slid a beer and a shot over to me without being asked. "Am I that much of a regular?"

"Yes, you are."

"Shit. I better find a new place."

"Michelle would kill you."

I nodded as I sipped the beer. "She would. She's a jealous little shit."

I drank the beer and the shot. I wondered if I drank too much, so I ordered another beer and shot to forget that. I always knew when I started drinking too much because I would go for days wearing the same clothes, and then Will would mention something. It'd been a month since he said anything, so I must've not hit bottom yet.

On my second beer, I got a text from Will asking where I was. Half an hour later, he was sitting on the bar stool next to me. He tossed a file onto the bar in front of me. I opened it to the first page of the personnel disciplinary file for Detective Bo Steed.

"How the hell did you get this in three hours?"

"That's what you pay me the big bucks for."

"I gotta know."

"Got a contact at POST. I pay him . . . let's say a small bonus every time I need a cop's disciplinary record."

"Yeah, but I'm nowhere near your top priority."

He smiled shyly at me and said, "You are my top priority, lady. Haven't you figured that out yet?"

I lit a cigarette as I began flipping through the file. The guy had over a dozen complaints against him, ranging from excessive force to planting drugs. None of them stuck. Hoover County's Internal Affairs Division consisted of police officers who would no sooner take action against another officer than they would arrest their own mothers. Not a single one of the dozen complaints had gotten past the investigation phase.

"There are few things I hate more than corrupt cops," I said, blowing out a puff of smoke and squinting because the air-conditioning vent behind the bar just blew it right back into my eyes.

"What do you think this guy did, anyway?"

"I don't know. Nothing about this case makes sense. The county's doing something blatantly illegal to a kid who would normally be charged as a juvenile or not at all, and everyone who's more culpable than he is is getting a deal to testify against him. It's like they have some personal vendetta against him."

He shrugged. "I don't know. I'm getting worried about you. About how this is affecting you. The whole thing sounds like maybe you should withdraw."

"From the case?"

"You told me once you only focus on the guilty ones because nine times out of ten, you settle those. They don't want to go to trial knowing they did it. This kid might be innocent. Dani, I was all for this and I love the passion it's brought out in you, but maybe it's doing more harm than good. Withdraw, and let the next attorney have the headache."

I stared at his dilated pupils and the slightly pink hue to his cheeks. "Will, are you high right now?"

He hesitated. "That doesn't invalidate my argument."

I chuckled. "Since when are we toking on the job?"

"Since I'm almost retired and about to become a permanent fixture on a sandy beach." He put his arm around me and stared into my eyes like we were two lovers in Paris. "Come with me. Leave all this shit behind. Lay out on the beach all day. Write that novel you've always wanted to write. Forget Hoover County and Roscombe and all that bullshit."

"Wish I could, man. You have no idea how appealing that sounds. But right now, there's a hundred pounds of hipster teenager that prevents me from doing that."

He shrugged and put his hands on the bar. "Well, at least withdraw from this case. It's gonna give you an ulcer." He picked up the remnants of my beer and took a swig.

"I'm missing something in this. Something happened that no one's talking about."

"Well, there are always ways to get people to talk."

"How?"

"Leverage, my slightly dim Caucasian sister. Find something you can use to get some of these witnesses to tell you the truth for once."

Will, despite being high, had a point. The prosecution was fighting dirty, so why shouldn't I? There was one more thing to try before I went to the gutter, though: go to the top. I would meet with the county attorney tomorrow and see if I could talk some sense into her.

I polished off one more shot, and then decided to call it a night. Will was still drinking when I left, telling the bartender how he was leaving this nonsense behind for white sand.

30

When I got home, Teddy was awake again. He ran up to me and proclaimed, "I got to see a movie, Danielle."

"Really?"

Kelly said, "Yup. We did, on TV. What a lucky boy, getting to watch a movie today."

Teddy looked proud and held his chin a little higher.

"Can I watch TV, Danielle?"

"Of course." He smiled and ran off.

Kelly watched him and then turned to me and said, "It's really nice, what you're doing."

"What choice did I have? It was either this or drop him off back at the Road Home like his parents did."

"I met his parents today when I got them to sign the release. Teddy was in the car and they refused to even see him."

I lit a cigarette.

"So what's the plan?" she asked.

"What do you mean?"

"I mean this case isn't going to go on forever. What are you going to do when it's over? Is he going to live with you?"

The truth was, I hadn't considered it. I hadn't thought a bit about what would happen once it was over.

"I don't know."

"Well, you need to figure something out. He's a human being and deserves to have a say in where he's going to live."

"I don't have a clue, Kelly. I can't drop him off at the shelter, but I can't have him stay here long-term either. I couldn't take care of him."

"Couldn't or wouldn't?"

I shrugged as I took a drag of the cigarette. "He's a great kid, but he needs constant care."

"I think maybe you need to spend more time with him."

"Why?"

"Because he can do a lot more than you think he can. A lot of people probably make the same mistake about him, thinking he constantly needs someone else. If you give him a chance, he'll prove you wrong, I think."

"And how do you know so much about it?"

She sat down on my couch. "My brother lives with a disability. You met him once, remember?"

"Right," I said, kind of remembering a family reunion of hers I had received a pity invite to because it was Saturday and I had nothing to do.

"My mother was an alcoholic and couldn't do anything, much less take care of a disabled child, so I basically raised him. His whole life he got sympathy from people. They wanted him to be inspirational. Do you know how insulting it is to be inspirational to people because of your disability? He could function just like everybody else. He knew how to take care of himself. Knew a lot more than most other people I knew, actually. Teddy's the same way. He can grow if you give him the chance."

I looked back toward the bedroom. Teddy was shouting that the television wasn't working. "I'll have to think about it once this whole thing is done, I guess."

She rose and headed for the door. "Better run. Hot date."

"Thanks for doing this," I said.

"It was no problem. Good night, Dani."

"'Night."

I stepped out onto the porch and finished my cigarette before going back inside. Teddy sat on the bed, and the television was already on.

"I fixed it!" he said.

"Looks like it. You ready for bed?"

"I'm hungry."

"I'll see what I can do."

We ate mac and cheese and watched a Pixar movie. Teddy laughed through most of it, but he would cover his mouth as though he'd done something naughty. One time he snorted and then looked at me and we both laughed. When the movie was over, we did our jammies, our *SpongeBob*, and the whole shebang before I could finally leave him long enough to go sit on my porch. I took out my phone and called Stefan.

Peyton answered his cell.

"Hello, Danielle."

"Oh. Hi. So . . . how's it hanging?"

"Stefan's kind of indisposed right now. He's actually showering for me. I saw it was you calling, so I thought you'd want to know. Maybe he'll call you after we're finished in the bedroom."

That was the last image I needed right now: her plastic breasts and Botox-frozen face rubbing against the love of my life. I breathed out through my nose and said, "You already won. You got him. Do you have to be such a bitch about it, too?"

"Yes, Danielle. Yes I do. And by the way, I know it was you who stole my tiger head. I want that back."

"Don't know what you're talking about."

"I'm sure you don't. Oop, he's coming out. Need to get in the mind-set, so you'll excuse me. I think I'm going to ride him cowgirl tonight. What do you think about that?"

"Are you sexually attracted to animals?"

"What?"

"Just something I've been pondering lately. You seem downright obsessed with them, so the only thing I can think is that you must be turned on by them."

"Good night, Danielle. Sweet dreams."

She hung up. My heart raced, my stomach felt sour, and blood had rushed to my face. The skank had gotten under my skin. I didn't usually let people do that.

"You look like a woman who needs a drink," a soft female voice said. Beth stood on her porch next door. Though well into her seventies, she always struck me as having the spirit of a twenty-year-old and she looked it now with the wide smile on her face.

"And how, lady."

She went inside and came back with two tumblers of a brown fluid. We tapped glasses before she sat down and had a mouthful. I sipped mine. The liquor, probably brandy, felt warm and smooth going down. It had that quality that good liquor sometimes did when it warmed your stomach instantly.

"What's the problem?" she asked.

"The problem is that this is not where I pictured my life at this age."

"I think anyone can say that at pretty much any age, don't you?"

"I don't know. You seem pretty happy."

"I am happy. But that's because I've chosen to be happy. I've chosen to make my life what it is."

"You're a Jim Morrison."

"Who's that?"

"Google him. I think you'd dig his music." I took another sip. "It's hard to choose to be happy about your man marrying someone you despise."

"If he really does it, he was never yours to begin with."

"Ouch. That's harsh."

"You don't have time to spare feelings when you get older. Danielle, you need to move on. He's not yours anymore. He's hers."

"No, there's a part of him that doesn't want to be. I can feel it. I hurt him really bad, and he thinks this is what he wants, but it's just the pain doing the thinking for him. He always hated girls like her."

She took my hand and gave it a squeeze before finishing her drink. She grabbed my glass and finished that, too, before she rose. "You know what they say: you gotta get under to get over."

I chuckled. "What?"

"Go out and find some beautiful man, and make a memory with him tonight. Don't sit by and wait for someone who isn't coming back to you."

I watched as the little sage walked back to her house, humming. Though she was alone, and I never saw anyone over there, she was about the happiest person I knew. Maybe that was the key—solitude. No companionship, but no chance for others to hurt you either.

My phone buzzed. It was Stefan. I answered, thinking I'd hear Peyton again, and instead heard him. "You there?"

"Yeah. Sorry."

"Saw you called. What's up?"

"Just wanted to chat. You're not busy, are you?"

"No, not really. Just at book club."

Relief poured out of me. "Did Peyton have your phone?"

"Yeah, she dropped me off. I forgot it in the car but she brought it back. Did you need something, Dani?"

"No. I mean, yes. Kind of. No, no I just wanted to talk. When I felt shitty, you were the one I always went to to feel better. You and Will, I guess."

"You need to find someone else to do that now."

"So I've been told." I sighed. "Sorry to bug you. I'll let you get back to your manly book club. What are you guys reading, by the way?"

"Some detective novel. I don't know, I didn't read it. We usually just end up watching a game."

I grinned. "Have fun."

I hung up and stared at the passing traffic in front of my home, the headlights piercing the darkness like glowing eyes, the streetlamps lighting up patches of sidewalk and asphalt, and the moonlight raining down on it all. It was beautiful, if I stepped back and looked at it. People vaunted the beauty of nature, but I thought cities were just as beautiful. No one bothered to look at them in the same way because they saw them all the time. We took whatever we saw every day for granted, including people.

Will called me just then.

"I was just thinking about you," I said.

"Something naughty I hope."

"Will . . ."

"I know. Sorry. Why were you thinking about me?"

"Just that when I feel shitty, you and Stefan are the only two people I go to so I can feel better."

"Hey, wait a second, what do you mean '*Will*'? I'll have you know, missy, that I'm quite the hit with the opposite gender. A shitload of money in the bank will do that, I guess."

"No, you're sweet. That's more important and rarer in men."

"Wow. You must still be drunk to compliment me without sarcasm."

"Just in that type of mood I guess." I looked up at the sky. "What're you doing right now?"

"Mm," he said, clearly putting some food in his mouth. "Following up on a case. Nothing interesting, husband cheating on wife. Oldest story in the book. What're you doing?"

"Just sitting here on my porch. Thinking about moving back to LA."

A silence on the other end. "Still think that's a mistake."

"I told you I don't think I can handle seeing Stefan everywhere as a married man."

He chuckled. "Please. You know how many divorces I've seen happen because of my work? Everyone gets over it. It stings for a bit, but you get over it. You'll find someone else, and Stefan'll be a part of your past. Doesn't mean you have to stop caring about him, but he won't be the center of your life anymore." He paused. "Never know. Maybe a rich best friend might do the trick?"

"Shit. You *are* my best friend. How messed up is that?"

"I'm happy about it. I've never had a better one."

"You're a little charmer." I sighed.

"Indeed. Anyway, I just wanted to check up on you. Do you need me to come over?"

"No, I'm fine."

"You sure? You're sounding awful lonesome right now."

"I just want to sleep for two years. I appreciate you checking up on me, though."

"Anytime, m'lady. Call me if you need anything."

"I will."

I stared at my phone for a moment before slipping it into my pocket and going back inside.

31

Leverage. That was the only thing I could think about. After I woke up and helped Teddy dress in some clothes I'd bought him, I dropped him off at the school Kelly had found. Medicaid hadn't officially agreed to pay, but the school said as long as the application was in, they would take him for now.

His teacher was a woman with coal-black hair and she was wearing a plaid suit. She smiled and hugged him as a welcome. Teddy took a seat in front. His desk had a name plate with his name scrawled in marker.

"Tough gig," I said to the teacher. "I don't envy you."

"This is nothing. Attending here is optional, so I get to actually teach them things that matter. Like how to pay bills and balance checking accounts. When I taught special needs children in public school, I would have to teach them standard curriculum. Some of my kids didn't know the alphabet, and I had to have them write reports on *For Whom the Bell Tolls*. It was . . ."

"Soul crushing?"

She nodded. "I think that's the right phrase. But I got to see some of them flourish despite the system, and that made up for it."

"Is Teddy going to flourish?"

"I don't know. But I'll interview him and get a sense of where we are. I'm Rosalyn by the way. Um, and are you the mother?"

"No, no. I'm his lawyer, actually."

"His lawyer?"

I shrugged. "Long story."

I glanced at Teddy. A boy with Down syndrome behind him was speaking softly and then Teddy laughed at something he said, which caused him to start laughing, too. Both of them saw me noticing and then held it back as though it were a secret. He looked . . . perfectly normal. Like a teenager in a high school class. Kelly had been right: I didn't give him the credit he deserved.

"Can you do me a favor?" I said. "If Teddy ever mentions anything about the case he has pending right now, would you mind telling me? I can't get him to talk about it."

She nodded. "I guess I could do that. As long as he's okay with it. What type of case?"

"Oh, nothing big." I checked my watch. "I gotta run, but here." I handed her one of my cards. "Let me know if you need anything, if there's an emergency or something. His parents won't respond, so just call me."

"I will."

"Thanks again."

On the way out of school, I checked to make sure I had given her the right card. Every defense lawyer had at least two different business cards: one without their cell number, to be given to the run-of-the-mill clients, and one *with* the cell number to be given to the clients who you were billing hourly, or who had given you a sizeable flat fee.

I had five different cards: one with the cell number, one without, one that said I was a DUI specialist, one that said I was a violent crime specialist, and one that proclaimed me "Utah's Number One

Drug-Defense Lawyer." I had given Rosalyn the plain one with my cell number that I always kept near the back of my card wallet . . . I hoped.

———————

The Hoover County District Attorney's Office was about as ugly as I expected and gave off a real jail vibe. It made me uncomfortable walking inside, and the lighting immediately put me on edge—brighter than Walmart. I told the secretary I had an appointment with Sandy, then sat down and glanced at the magazines spread on the coffee table. Guns, hunting, fishing, guns, hunting, sports, guns, and bigger guns. It was like Peyton's Christmas reading list.

The conversation I was about to have kept running through my mind. Sandy Tiles had been the first woman elected to the position of Hoover County District Attorney. The county had a serious, macho, gun-culture, police-are-always-right attitude, so for a woman to climb over those types of men for the top spot meant she had to be tough as nails. I would probably only get one shot at a pitch, and I had to make it a good one.

I thought about going with the straight legal arguments, about how ridiculously illegal Teddy's entire prosecution was, but I had to believe she already knew all that. Trying to change the law by ignoring it, even in a county that cared as little about civil liberties as Hoover, was a big deal, and there was no way any of the line prosecutors would attempt it without running it by the big cheese. Especially Double D, who struck me as a bit of a coward.

"She'll see you now," the receptionist said.

I headed back to the large corner office. It was sparse and neat, only a few framed photos up on the walls: Sandy with cops at the shooting range or training sessions.

She didn't act as though she was doing something else, and she didn't feign inconvenience. She sat quietly at her desk with her hands neatly folded in front of her and stared directly at me.

"Dani Rollins," I said, extending my hand.

"Sandy Tiles. Nice to meet you. I don't shake hands." I lowered my hand. "I've heard about you."

I sat down. "All good, I hope."

She leaned back in the seat, but kept her spine entirely straight. "You know, it's customary to be invited to sit, and I didn't invite you."

"Would you prefer I stand in front of you? You would be vagina level with me, which really is my best angle."

Her lip curled slightly. This wasn't going as I had planned.

"Look, I'm sure your line guys have told you I'm shady and whatever other nonsense you guys tell yourselves to pretend you're the good guys, but I'm here about one case and that's all I want to talk about. Teddy Thorne."

"I know the case," she said with a sigh, as though we'd discussed it dozens of times before. "What about it?"

"I want you to meet him."

"Why would I even consider that?"

"Because if you met him, you would see that there is no chance in hell he committed this crime."

She smiled, and it was creepy, like a vampire smiling at a victim. "If I were to meet every defendant, I wouldn't be able to do my job. It would take up all of my time. The prosecution seems fair to me."

"It's not. Aside from the fact that it's blatantly illegal, which I'm sure you're already well aware of, he's not guilty. He can't be."

"We treat every defendant equally. You're free, of course, to pursue a not-guilty-by-reason-of-mental-defect defense, but every defendant is treated the same by this office."

"That's bullshit. Every person is different. The circumstances of each case are different. A blanket policy would lead to unequal outcomes."

She laughed. "Unequal? Are you basically telling me it's not fair? Are we twelve years old, Ms. Rollins?"

"Fairness *is* laughable in our criminal justice system, isn't it? I completely forgot, silly me."

"Mr. Diamond has made a reasonable offer on this matter. If you don't wish to take it—"

"Prison on a first offense is not reasonable. There is no other county in this state that does that."

"There is no other county in the state that has our unique crime problems."

"Every county everywhere has your crime problems. You just think you need to break the law in order to enforce it. It's the oldest belief in law enforcement, ever since the Sheriff of Nottingham tortured Merry Men to find Robin Hood."

"You're quite witty. I've heard that about you. I advise you to use it sparingly in front of a jury."

So much anger and frustration coursed through me that I didn't know how to contain it. I'd seen injustice before and I'd taken it in stride, but seeing it up close, seeing the face behind it, was monstrous. And the worst part was that this injustice thought it was justice.

"You guys suck," I blurted out as I rose and stormed out of the office like a teenage emo whose parents told her she can't go to the Morrissey concert.

32

"You said that?" Will asked as we sat in a café back in Salt Lake.

"I did."

"Just like that?"

"Just like that."

He raised his eyebrows, impressed. "I mean, it's childish and not creative, but that took some balls."

"It wasn't balls, it was just anger. You shoulda seen this sanctimonious tyrant. She had self-righteousness dripping off of her. I lost it, though. I got too pissed too quickly. If I'd kept my cool, maybe I could've convinced her."

He shrugged. "I doubt you could've convinced her of anything. She feels this case is worth fighting for. It's her right."

"I don't think this woman has feelings. I'm not kidding. She might be a block of ice in human skin. Maybe she's an alien. Isn't there some conspiracy theory about lizards taking the place of various leaders?"

"Lizard or no, you still got one helluva case on your hands. I hold to my suggestion to get out of it."

I shook my head. "Screw that. Now it's personal."

"Why? Because your charms didn't work on her and make her do what you wanted?"

"Hey, my charms are nothing to sneeze at."

"I'm not saying they are, but look at it from their perspective. They got a policy, they don't think your client is disabled enough to not be culpable, and, you know, there it is."

"You agree with them?"

He shook his head as he popped a clam into his mouth. "You don't have to agree with someone to see things from their side. I'm just saying, I'm worried about you. This case will pass, and you'll get others. The one thing I know for sure about life is that it always moves on."

"This is wrong, Will. This is so damn wrong. I can feel it in my guts."

"Wrong or no, it's just one case. And it's a case that a couple months ago you would've dropped like a hot potato. Let it go. There is no reason for all this aggravation."

I sat staring out the windows at the people passing by. There was something I was missing. I had to go back into the files. "I'm gonna head to the office."

"Now? We just sat down."

"I'm not hungry."

He grabbed my hand, preventing me from leaving. "Danielle, I've known you a long time. Do you trust me?"

"Of course."

"So take my advice. We can find another great lawyer and make sure Teddy's taken care of. Don't let this case eat you up."

Lost causes. I thought about that phrase as I drove back to the office and rode up the elevator. Was this a lost cause? Was I bashing my head against a wall, and the change in the statute was inevitable? I didn't know. But I had a feeling the answer was buried deep in the files, somewhere.

I told Kelly I didn't want to be disturbed, and took out the Teddy Thorne file. Not just the stuff I got from the prosecution, but the stuff Will had gotten me as well: the disciplinary records of the officers, dispatch call logs, video interviews of the witnesses—I was particularly interested in watching Freddy's interview—and all the other stuff the prosecution didn't think was relevant and didn't always send along to the defense attorneys. I opened the first file and began to read.

I read for over two hours, every page, several times. I read carefully, one word at a time, as though the misspelled grammatical nightmares that were police reports were the deepest of poetry and each syllable needed to be contemplated. I learned absolutely nothing I hadn't known before.

I leaned back in my chair and my head hit the headrest. From this angle, I had a good view of the ceiling, made of wood that had faded from old water leaks, cracked and dotted with rusty nails. I hated bland rooms with no character.

I lifted Will's additions to the file and flipped through them again. Nothing there either.

As I was about to toss it back on the desk, I noticed something in the dispatch logs. It was just a feeling in my guts, a slight tick. If I hadn't been so desperate for anything I could use, I would've completely missed the feeling.

The dispatch logs went through all the calls to 911 and the police dispatch in a case. Here, the detectives had called into dispatch, logging the times they did certain things—when people showed up to the scene, time of the deal, time of the handoff, time of the takedown. I hadn't noticed before that a patrol officer had called in, offering to assist. Detective Bo Steed had refused his help and said they had all the men they needed. Two other patrol officers in the area had responded after this, however, and they *weren't* called off.

Nothing ground shaking. The detective might have thought they had enough men at the time and then changed his mind, or just didn't pay attention to the other officers coming to the scene. Still . . . he'd turned one cop away and allowed two others onto the scene. I had nothing else to go on, so I might as well look at it.

I popped in the audio CD of the dispatch logs and skipped ahead until I found the right part.

"This is unit 262, I'm about five minutes away."

Bo Steed came on and said, "Negative, Stu. We got it covered."

"You sure?"

"We're good. We got enough uniforms to cover."

"Roger that. Good luck."

Unit 262. I texted Will *Get me the name and badge numbers of the police officers in unit 262 for Hoover County.*

He texted back a second later. *Give me an hour.*

33

When Will got back to me, he had not only the badge number and full name of the cop—Stuart Lively—but also his address and disciplinary record, as well as his schedule. I would miss Will like hell when he left. How would I find someone else that efficient? Then again, I didn't think I was going to practice law in Los Angeles. Maybe I'd work in a coffee shop or paint or something.

I got into my car and headed to Richardson.

Stuart Lively wasn't on duty right now. He worked primarily night shifts, and I guessed that he was at home sleeping. I went to his house, the south unit of a duplex, and parked out front. A police car was in the driveway and I peeked inside as I walked past. Immaculately clean. No fast-food wrappers or empty cans of Red Bull.

A lot of cops didn't like defense attorneys, and one showing up unannounced at their house could really spook them. After I knocked, I took a few steps back to give him space and seem nonthreatening. I put my hands in my pockets, then thought that looked like I was concealing something, so I took them out and put them at my sides. I thought I looked like a creepo stalker, so I put them on my hips. I thought this was too aggressive, so I put them back in my pockets.

A black man in a tight shirt with a crucifix around his neck answered the door. He looked at me with a modicum of surprise. He was chewing, and I guessed I had interrupted his meal before he headed out on patrol.

"Officer Lively?"

"Yeah."

"I'm Dani Rollins. I'm an attorney on a case that you were tangentially involved in. I was hoping I could have thirty seconds of your time."

"Tangentially?"

He spoke with a smooth, deep voice, and I didn't get any hint of aggression from him.

"It's Teddy Thorne. He's the disabled kid who was charged with distribution. I don't know if you've heard about it, but—"

"I've heard about it." He looked me up and down. "What do you want to know?"

This was good. He didn't swear at me, pull out his gun, or crack a joke about hunting defense attorneys. "Just had some quick questions is all."

He hesitated. "Better come in, then."

The home smelled like warm cinnamon. Seated at the dinner table were a woman and a small child. I waved to them, and only the child waved back. Stuart took me to his home office, away from the dining room. He sat in the chair behind the desk, and I took a spot on a couch against the wall.

"I don't know nothing about that case. I wasn't involved in it," he said.

"I know. But you were, like, five minutes away and were heading down to assist. Is that pretty common for officers on patrol?"

He shrugged. "It depends. We were busy that night, and they only had six guys there and five perps. I thought they could use a hand."

"Did you help them?" I asked, feigning ignorance.

He thought for a second and I could tell he was weighing how to answer. "No. No I didn't."

"Why not?"

"They didn't need me."

I leaned forward, my elbows on my knees. "Officer, I know all about the brotherhood of cops. You guys look out for each other. I get that, and I'm not looking for you to betray anybody. But we both know they purposely didn't want you to show up. After Detective Steed told you not to come, they let two other officers come. Why those two but not you?"

He folded his arms and didn't respond. We held each other's gaze a second and he looked away first.

"Do you know anything that can help?"

"I told you, I don't know anything. I wasn't there."

"Why didn't they want you there?"

He exhaled through his nose. "I got a kid. And I'm scared for him. Scared for the world he has to grow up in."

"Crime's never been this low. Statistically, this is the safest period in history to be alive."

"I'm not talking about criminals."

We held each other's gaze again. "Cops. You're talking about cops."

He ran his hand over his head. "Read this story on the news. Twelve-year-old kid got shot by the cops because he was holding a stick and wouldn't drop it. Shot him seven times. Black kid, white police officers. I look at my son and I don't know how to explain to him that that's a hard fact of life." He looked down at the floor. "I don't know how to explain to him both how to protect himself and why I wear the uniform."

"They didn't want you there because you're black? Why did that matter?"

He didn't answer me.

"Oh," I said, a giant lightbulb going off in my head. "They chose Teddy out of everyone there because he's black. But they didn't count on his disability, did they?"

Why hadn't I seen that before? Hoover County was hard-core hillbilly country. A black kid was far more likely to be convicted by a jury there, whether he did it or not. They had chosen Teddy because of the color of his skin.

I knew a lot about how blacks were treated in our system. Once, in a moment of drunken honesty, I'd even had a police chief of one of the largest cities tell me, "If you follow a black guy until he commits a traffic violation and pull him over, you're gonna find something. Pot, or a gun, or something. Not every time, but nine times out of ten. That's how we keep our numbers up."

"He's just a kid," I said. "Not that much older than your boy out there. But your boy can at least explain himself. Teddy can't. He doesn't have the capacity. And he's gonna go away for life unless you can help me."

Stuart looked at me and shook his head. He rose from the desk and got two bottles of water out of a small fridge and handed one to me before sitting back down. He opened his and took a long drink before speaking.

"If I tell you, it don't leave this room. I got four years until my pension vests, and I'm not looking to get fired now."

"It won't leave this room. You have my word."

"The word of a defense attorney don't mean much to me. You're gonna have to do better."

"How?"

"I want you to call my cell phone and leave a voice mail. Say it's a shame I wouldn't meet with you, and that you might subpoena me anyway even though I refused to talk to you. That way if you say anything, I have that and can deny it."

I took out my phone and did as he asked. When I was through, he said, "I just heard rumors. They don't tell me anything."

"I'll take rumors at this point."

"They've been looking to change that law for a long time. Looking for the perfect case to do it with. So when they found a black kid with three white kids willing to testify against him, they jumped on it. Black kid with three white accusers don't stand a chance with a jury here."

"A gambler's jury."

"What?"

"A gambler's jury. A little nickname for these by defense attorneys— a jury with a case where any rational person would acquit, but they might convict because of race. You're gambling by taking the case to them."

He nodded.

"Why are they trying so hard to change the law? What do they care if they can prosecute juveniles for drug crimes or not?"

He shook his head. "That I don't know. I just heard that they found a case they wanted to use and told Steed to make sure the witnesses cooperated."

"Did they set Teddy up?"

"I don't think they went that far. I think it just fell in their laps."

I leaned back and spun the water bottle in my hand, staring off into space. Why would they care so much about being able to prosecute juveniles with no oversight? It didn't make sense.

"Is there anything else you can tell me that would help?"

"Don't think so. That's all I know."

"You did the right thing."

I rose and set the unopened bottle on his desk. Before I left, he said, "Counselor, we're not all like Steed."

"I know. But the reason people like Steed are able to pull this shit is because people like you don't stand up to him." I opened the office door. "Thanks for your help. I'll keep it between us."

34

Teddy had been placed in a program called "extended day," and as I headed to his school to pick him up, I thought about Bo Steed. He'd chosen Teddy because he was black, and they knew they could get a conviction. But the conviction wouldn't matter because we wouldn't get that far. I'd filed a motion to quash after the preliminary hearing, and as soon as Roscombe denied that, which of course he would, I would file an interlocutory appeal. The appeals court would hear this case long before a jury. There was no way they'd let Hoover County get away with this. Sandy was smart enough to know this as well as I did. So why bet on a gambler's jury?

I went into Teddy's classroom, where the teacher was sitting at her desk.

"Hey," I said.

"Oh, hi. Teddy's in extended day down the hall."

"How'd he do today?"

"Excellent." Rosalyn flipped through some papers. "Look at this."

I took the paper she held out. It was an intricate pencil drawing of a young boy with a straw hat on a raft with a guy lying on his back. The guy's skin was colored in.

"Huck Finn and Jim," I said.

"Wonderful, isn't it? Did you know he had talent like that?"

"Not a clue."

"You can hang on to that. He was quite proud of it."

"Thanks."

I headed out of the classroom and found Teddy. He sat in the center of the floor with five other teenagers, and they were playing some game where they tossed a hacky sack around and then laughed hysterically when someone dropped it. A teacher in the corner asked, "Who are you here for?"

"Dani!" Teddy squealed before I could respond. "Did you see my drawing?"

"I did, buddy. It's amazing."

"It's Huck Finn, Dani. He's on the river."

"I got that. Since when can you draw like that?"

He smiled shyly. "I don't know."

I thanked the teacher and we headed out. I was helping him buckle his seat belt when my phone buzzed. It was Stefan.

"What'd he do now?" I said as a greeting.

"Who?"

"Jack. That's why you called, isn't it?"

"No. I called to check up on you."

I grinned. "Reallllyyy?"

"This was a mistake. I knew you'd read too much into it. I'm hanging up."

"No, no, don't hang up. I'm just surprised is all."

"I just . . ."

I sensed something in his voice. A slight pullback, maybe. Like he wanted to tell me something but didn't know how to say it.

"What's wrong?" I said.

"Nothing. Why?"

"Like I don't know you. Something's clearly wrong, so what is it?"

"I don't know . . . It's just . . . I don't know."

Please, for the love of all that's holy, let it be second thoughts about the wedding.

"Any subject in particular bugging you?" I asked.

"No," he said, his voice just a little too high to be casual.

"I think I've got beer and condiments at my house. Me and one of my clients were just about to grab some dinner out. Come with us."

"One of your clients?"

"Long story. Teenage kid, disabled, with nowhere else to go so I've been letting him crash with me. So you coming or what?"

I expected an excuse or a lecture about how we're not that way anymore. Instead, he just said, "Okay."

———————

I picked a sushi place in Cottonwood Heights, about fifteen minutes outside of Salt Lake City. I knew sushi was Stefan's favorite, and I wanted him away from Peyton the Bambi Killer's neighborhood. Teddy and I grabbed a table, and he immediately pulled out the chopsticks. He saw how some people at a table nearby were using them and tried to imitate them. The chopsticks kept falling out of his hands because he kept rubbing his fingers together.

"I like Chinese food, see," he said. "My mom used to get Chinese food for my birthday because I like Chinese food."

"Yeah? What's your favorite Chinese food?"

"I like sweet and sour chicken, see. With the red sauce. Like Jell-O."

"Yeah, I guess it is kind of like Jell-O. We'll see if they have some now."

Stefan came in through the doors and headed for our table. Teddy started clapping, which made Stefan smile. He sat down and said, "How are you?"

"Can you do magic? Please please please!"

I grinned. "That's Will that knows magic, buddy. This is my friend Stefan."

"Okay, yeah. New magic trick from Will. That's a good trick. A new one."

Stefan looked at me. "What?" he said.

"What?"

"You're giving me this dopey teenage girl look."

"I am a dopey teenage girl."

He chuckled. "Do you remember that time Jack hit his head at the bookstore? When he was so excited he found a Captain America book that he tripped and cut his head open on that shelf?"

"Yeah, I thought I might faint when I saw the blood."

"It was actually amazing. You scooped him up without hesitation and ran out of the bookstore and we sped up to the hospital. You didn't say anything, you just had this look on your face like nothing in the world was going to stop you. I thought that woman could conquer the world. I miss that woman sometimes. But that was another life, Dani."

I nodded. "I know. I miss that woman and that life, too."

He leaned back and said, "I could really use a beer."

"Your wish is my command," I said, signaling to the waitress.

We ate and laughed and drank beer. Stefan wanted to see Teddy draw after I told him he was a virtuoso, so we got a pen from the waitress and he drew a swirling Chinese dragon on one of the paper menus. It was one of the best I'd ever seen. Each line came out of the pen as expertly as though it had just been waiting inside, and Teddy was only letting it fall out. The tic of rubbing his fingers together disappeared and his eyes managed to focus on the drawing. No darting around the room, no exaggerated lifting of his eyelids or excessive blinking. He was completely focused.

"Here Stefan, you can have it. It's for you."

Stefan picked up the drawing and stared at it. I thought his eyes got a little moist when he said, "I love it. Thank you."

Teddy hummed to himself as he dug into his food. I sipped the beer I'd ordered and watched Stefan. I hadn't seen him eat since . . . a long time. The last actual meal we'd had together was breakfast as a family. He had been quiet the entire time, distant. Jack and I had joked and talked about what we were going to do that day, but Stefan just ate in silence. When breakfast ended and Jack went off to school, he pulled out the divorce papers and laid them on the breakfast table.

"So what's going on? Really?" I said.

"I don't know what you mean."

"I'm sure you don't. A gal you divorced over breakfast was number one on your speed dial when you're feeling blue."

"What makes you think I'm feeling blue?"

"I could always tell when you're depressed. You never hid it well."

He shrugged. "Maybe if you'd applied that laser observation to yourself, you could've realized what was wrong before letting another man . . ."

"Easy, the boy has sensitive ears."

He sighed and dropped his fork onto the plate, burying his face in his hands.

"What is it?" I asked.

"Peyton and I got into a fight."

"A fight with the Deer Terminator? No way."

He gave me a hard look.

"Sorry," I quickly added. "What happened?"

"So, you know how my dissertation's almost done?"

"It is? I thought you had like a year of classes left."

"It's been a year, Dani. Two semesters."

"Oh. Okay, yeah, what about it?"

"Well, Peyton's paying for everything right now because I'm just working on this and I want to hurry and finish to get back into the workforce and start standing on my own feet again. But she doesn't want me to finish."

"Why not?"

"She says there's no point having me devote myself fully over the next several months, or even a year, to a dissertation. Her family gives all the kids half a mil when they marry and pays off their debts as their wedding gifts. That, and she makes crazy money managing a division of a hospital . . . I don't know. She thinks I should just focus on Jack."

I laughed. "She wants you to be a housewife?" When Stefan only gave me a rigid look in return, I stopped laughing and cleared my throat. "Sorry." I sipped my beer. "Did you ask her why?"

"She said she doesn't think it's proper for both people in a marriage to be working outside the home."

"Doesn't think it's *proper*?"

"She just says that someone needs to focus on raising children."

"Children? Plural?"

He nodded. "She wants to have kids as soon as possible."

I drank down the rest of my beer, trying not to imagine Stefan in a hospital catching some baby who would be born wearing camo with an NRA sticker on its butt.

"Oh," I managed to say.

"It just feels weird, you know? Like . . . I don't know. Marriage is one thing, you can divorce online in a couple of hours, but kids . . . Two people have kids together, and they're bound for life. You can't get out of that. Ever."

"So, you're not gonna have kids with her, then?"

"I don't know. I don't know. She has just . . . a really old-fashioned view of things. It's actually charming in a lot of ways, but really idiotic in others."

"Let's cut out the parts where you compliment Peyton, can we? You're killing my libido."

"Danielle . . ."

"What? It's true. You know I can't control myself around you."

"Take a cold shower or something."

I leaned forward. "If you have doubts, you go with your gut."

"My gut's telling me my brain doesn't know what's good for it."

"Have you talked to anyone in your family about it? Your sister always gave good advice. You talked to her?"

"Yeah, I did. She says not to marry her, and that I should've worked it out with you."

I had to suppress a smile. I had always liked his sister. "So she wants one way and you want another. Seems like something newlywed couples fight about until they get used to each other."

"I love my work. Being a history professor is everything to me. I want to get back to it. But if she thinks staying home is best, maybe I should listen."

"You don't have to listen to her."

I watched as he played with his food, making a design of some kind and then taking a little nibble before he pushed it away.

"You remind me so much of Jack right now," I said.

"Why?"

"I don't know. Something in the way you move. I dig it all, handsome. The whole package."

"That's very sweet of you, Dani, but unnecessary. I'm going to be fine."

"You sure? No mention of calling off the wedding in this little spat?"

"No. Despite all her bullshit, she would never say that. She's crazy in love with me."

I sipped my beer. I knew the feeling.

I walked Stefan to his car, and Teddy followed behind, playing a game on my phone.

"Thanks for this," he said. "I needed it."

"I'm always here. Well . . . actually there was something I should tell you: I'm moving back to LA."

"When did you make that decision?"

"Little bit ago." I put a cigarette in my mouth and this time lit it. "If I can't be with you, so be it. That's my fault. But I can't live in the same city with you and your wife. I gotta go and start over."

"If you think that's best," he said.

"Like I told Will, what the hell do I know about what's best?"

"And what are we gonna do with Jack?"

"I'm not going through a custody fight. I think we should ask him who he wants to stay with."

"Ask him? No, Danielle, we don't need to ask him. Clearly he needs to stay here."

"Clearly? Why clearly? I may suck at a lot of things but I try with everything I've got to be a good mom."

"That's not it. I don't want a son raised in Los Angeles. Have you seen what LA does to its men? It hates its men. It teaches them to treat women like . . . things. Teaches them that their only worth is their looks or their bank accounts. I don't want him there."

"I don't know if I buy that. Kids are package deals. I think maybe they come with the wiring already in place."

"You weren't a guy growing up in LA. I was. If you weren't the best looking, or the one getting laid the youngest, or the richest, or the one doing the most drugs, you were nothing. I was considered uncool in elementary school because I hadn't had sex yet. We're talking twelve years old. I would sit by myself in the hallway and eat lunch so I wouldn't have to hear what the other guys were saying about me. Maybe it's like that everywhere now; I don't know. But I just can't let him do it." He shook his head. "No, he is not being raised in that. He's at a good school; he has good friends; he lives in a good neighborhood. I'm sorry, Danielle, but if you move, you're moving alone."

This wasn't a fight I wanted to have right now, so I decided to wait until the shock had worn off and he'd had some time to think about it. "Well, I guess we can talk about it more later. Um, look, take care of yourself, all right?"

He drove off. I waved and he waved back. I watched the taillights disappear in the darkness.

"Hey, Danielle?" Teddy said.

"Yeah, buddy?"

"I think he likes you."

I grinned. "Let's go home. *SpongeBob* awaits."

35

That night, after putting Teddy to bed, I lay on the couch and flipped through television channels. It didn't matter what was on as I wasn't really watching, so I stopped on a sitcom. I muted the volume and stared at the screen. A couple kissed. I wondered if the actors ever felt it was real, or if they felt like frauds displaying care for a person they didn't really give a shit about.

I heard someone fumbling with the back door in the kitchen. I listened for it again, and I heard the chain on the door sliding off. I rose slowly. I didn't have a gun, but I did have a baseball bat in my hallway closet. I grabbed it. Peeking around the corner, I saw a figure at the door, fumbling with the lock.

My heart raced. I thought about running out the front door, but there might be someone there, too. My cell phone was in my bedroom. Maybe I could ease back in there and call the police. I wished I had a gun and decided right then I would be buying one the first chance I got.

Then it hit me that the figure was trying to get out, not lock the door behind him.

It was Teddy. I lowered the bat and leaned it against the wall.

"What are you doing, Teddy?"

He didn't respond. He undid the lock and tried to open the door, but he hadn't unlocked the lower lock on the door handle. I approached him and he shouted, "Don't touch me!"

I held up my hands and took a few steps back. "Easy, buddy. What's going on?"

He turned back to the locks and couldn't figure out why the door wasn't opening. "I'm going home."

"You can't."

"I'm going home, Danielle."

I sat down at the table and watched him. The lower lock had a trick to it: you had to push and twist at the same time since it had rusted. Teddy was getting more frustrated and mumbling to himself.

"Teddy, you can't go home. I'm sorry."

"I want to go home, Danielle!"

I rose slowly and approached him. He stopped fumbling with the door and turned to me, his eyes on the floor, his fingers furiously rubbing together.

"Take it easy, buddy."

"I am not . . . I am not your buddy! I want to go home. I want my mama."

I shook my head. "I'm sorry, Teddy. You can't go home."

"Why not! Why not, Danielle! I want to go home."

I exhaled loudly through my nose and watched him as he shifted his weight from foot to foot. "They won't take you back."

"No!" he shouted, his movements gaining speed. "No! That's not true, see. That's not true. You're keeping me here. You're keeping me here, Danielle, and it's wrong. I want to go home. I want to go home!"

"There's nothing there for you anymore, Teddy."

"I want to go home!" he screamed.

There was no use fighting this. I figured it was best he see for himself.

I dressed and we got into my Jeep. We drove to his parents' house. A light was on in the upstairs bedroom though it was nearly eleven o'clock. We parked by the curb, and he jumped out and ran to the door. I got out and leaned against the hood of my car. I wanted to turn away.

"Mama!" he shouted. "Mama, open the door. Mama!"

Another light went on, a hallway light. Then another in the living room. The curtains in the living room opened and Riley stood there. Teddy saw her and squealed, "Mama!"

Riley hesitated. The two of them watched each other, and Teddy jumped off the porch and pushed his way through the bushes to get to the window his mother was standing behind. He put his hands over the glass, as though trying to touch her. Riley watched him for another few seconds, and then the curtains closed.

"Mama!" he screamed. "Mama, open the door. I wanna come home. Mama I wanna come home!"

I couldn't watch. I looked at the pavement instead, and the way the glass that had been crushed into it glimmered in the moonlight. A car drove past as Teddy screamed and pounded on the window. Then he went back to the door and tried opening it, then he tried hitting and kicking it. The light in the living room went off, then the light in the hallway, then the light upstairs. The house was dark.

"No! Mama, please. Mama, I wanna come home. Please!"

I got off my car and went to Teddy, who was now pounding so hard on the door I thought he would break his hands. I came up behind him and wrapped my arms around him. He struggled against me, kicking and spitting and screaming.

"No, Mama, please! Please. I wanna come home. I wanna come home! I'll be a good boy. I wanna come home."

I pulled him off the porch, and he collapsed onto the grass, crying so uncontrollably that strands of drool hung from his mouth. I held him in my arms and eventually he turned to me and wrapped his arms around my neck as he wept.

"Why doesn't she want me, Danielle? Why doesn't she want me?"

I couldn't get any words out, though I wanted to say something. Something that would make him feel like he mattered, like he was a human being . . . but nothing came out of my mouth.

I felt the warmth of tears on my own cheeks as I said, "I don't know why, buddy."

36

I was about to drop Teddy off at school several days later. We sat in the Jeep for a second and he rocked slowly back and forth. We'd been talking the past couple of days about what happened at his mother's house, but I'm not sure he fully understood. I hadn't told him anything about my past.

Finally, I swallowed and said, "My mama left me, too. I was younger than you. She said we were going to Disneyland and then dropped me off at a girls home. I've never seen her again."

"Do you miss her?"

"I don't know. I don't really think about her. That's what happens, Teddy. You'll have your own life and your own family."

He sat quietly for what seemed like a long time and then said, "Okay, bye, Danielle," and left. I watched him go to the teacher and she waved to me, letting me know she had him. After he was gone, I sat a minute longer before driving off.

I had the hearing on the motion to quash today. I had a few other things scheduled as well, but I sent out some text messages to defense attorney buddies of mine and had them cover those. I didn't want to think about any other cases right now.

I drove to Richardson without music and rolled the window down to get some air. Halfway there, I stopped at a Chick-fil-A and got a sandwich and a Sprite.

The courthouse parking lot was full and I had to park across the street. I finished my sandwich while leaning against the hood of my Jeep and watching people pile into the building. People going into court always looked nervous, and people coming out usually looked devastated. I had yet to leave a court without seeing someone crying in the parking lot.

One couple was arguing. The male was dropping the female off at work. They were yelling about a bill that hadn't been paid or something along those lines. I remembered the ridiculous arguments Stefan and I used to get into. Most of the time, I couldn't even remember what they'd been about five minutes after they happened. So much useless aggravation and fighting. I couldn't see the big picture then.

Will texted me. *Good luck*. He was always looking out for me, and it made me smile.

When I walked into Roscombe's courtroom, I immediately knew something was wrong. Double D sat at the prosecution table and was laughing at something the public defender sitting next to him had said. When he saw me, he stopped laughing, sat quietly, and faced the bench. I sat down at the defense table. The public defender cleared his throat and gave me a sad little grin as he walked by. Whatever the problem was, apparently he knew about it, too.

The bailiff said, "All rise," and Roscombe came out. He glanced at me and said, "Counsel, where is your client?"

I rose. "Your Honor, Mr. Thorne had school today, so I would ask that his appearance be waived since his presence is not required for this hearing."

"State?"

"No objection," Double D said without looking at me.

"His appearance is waived," Roscombe said as he put on his glasses and opened a folder. "After having reviewed both the motion and the response from the State, I feel this case should be bound over as I originally found at the preliminary hearing. As laid out by supreme court precedent, the evidence at a preliminary hearing must be viewed in the light most favorable to the prosecution, and I feel there is enough evidence to presume that each element of the sole count is established, and that a crime was committed and that the defendant committed it. Multiple witnesses testified as to the defendant's involvement in the sale of narcotics, and, though the question of credibility is one the trier of fact must analyze in a broader context of the case at trial, I found them sufficiently credible for this stage of the proceedings. I am therefore denying the defense's motion to quash bind over."

"Thank you, Judge," Double D said. "We did have one more item to address in this case." He rose and cleared his throat, hesitating a second. "We believe the defendant is a threat to the community, and since the preliminary hearing has now concluded, we would like to readdress bail."

"What?" I said. "Your Honor, he's not a threat to anyone. And he's staying at my house. Where's he gonna flee to, my backyard? We don't need another bail set in this case."

Double D looked down at the table, running his fingers along the edge. Without looking up, he added, "We would be asking for a no-bail warrant to issue."

I nearly shouted, "Are you shitting me?" I looked to Roscombe. He was writing in the folder in front of him as if I hadn't said a thing, then closed it and looked at me as he took his glasses off.

"Your Honor, do I even have to address that? He doesn't need to be in custody."

"Based on the recommendation of the State, I am issuing a no-bail warrant for the defendant in this matter, to be executed by the Hoover County Sheriff's Office forthwith."

I stepped around the defense table so there was nothing between me and the judge. "That's ridiculous. Even if the allegations are true, he was a juvenile when he committed them. He doesn't need to be locked up."

"I disagree. Now is there anything else?"

Double D said, "A new date for the post prelim arraignment, Judge."

"Wait a second," I said to Double D. "You can't think this is a good idea. He doesn't need to be in jail. If you're seriously worried about him, put him on a GPS ankle monitor if you have to, but there's no reason to have him locked up." He didn't say anything and still wouldn't look at me. "Is this Sandy?" I asked. "Did she tell you to do this because we're not bending over and taking it from you?"

"Counsel," the judge bellowed, "I will not have talk like that in my courtroom. I have made my ruling and that's that. If you want to save your client an arrest, have him self-report to the jail, but he is going into custody." Roscombe leaned forward and stared into my pupils. "He is going to jail because I said so, and there is nothing you can do about it." Then he leaned back again and looked at his computer screen. "The arraignment will be set for tomorrow morning at nine a.m. Make sure your client is here—if he is not in custody."

"Your Honor, I will be filing an interlocutory appeal along with a motion to stay."

"The trial is set to begin Friday at eight a.m. Please have—"

"Are you fucking shitting me!" I nearly ran to the bench and jumped over. The bailiff must've sensed it because he stepped between me and the judge.

"Ms. Rollins," the judge said with a chuckle, "if you ever swear in my courtroom again, I will lock you up and throw away the key. Do you understand?"

"Did you not hear what I said? I'm filing a stay on this case."

"So file it. The trial is in three days. I'm pretty sure the court of appeals won't be able to look at it by then. So you'd better prep the case."

"I won't do it. I won't go forward with trial. This is a gross violation of my client's Fifth and Sixth Amendment rights, and over two hundred years of precedent. I won't do it."

"Very well, I will have you removed from the case and appoint the public defender. Is that agreeable?"

I hesitated, but only for a second. Will's voice echoed in my head: *Get out of this case.* If I was going to do it, now was my chance. But the public defender wouldn't go to trial. He would make Teddy plead guilty the first chance he got. Sandy would pressure the PD into doing what she wanted.

"No," I said, the fire leaving my voice. "No, I'll do it."

"Excellent. Please be here at nine a.m. tomorrow for the arraignment and eight a.m. for the trial on Friday. You are excused, Counsel."

I followed Double D out of the courtroom. My insides felt like they had been tied into a knot. I grabbed Double D the second we stepped out into the hallway.

"What the fuck, Jasper? What was that in there?"

He shrugged. "This isn't my case or my concern anymore. Sandy is personally taking it over. I was just following orders."

"I think that excuse has been used in history a few times. Let me think. Where have I heard that? Oh, right—Nuremberg."

"I'm just doing my job, Danielle. You got a problem, take it up with the boss."

He turned away and I grabbed his arm again. "Jasper, please, just tell me what is going on. Why have you guys lost your minds over this case?"

He sighed. "Talk to Sandy."

I watched him get on the elevator, and I was left alone in the hall.

I shot over to the Hoover County District Attorney's Office and went up to Sandy's office. The secretary said something about having an appointment, and I rushed past her before she could get up from her seat. Sandy was sitting at her desk, speaking on the phone.

"What the hell was that about today?"

The secretary came in behind me and said, "Sorry, Sandy."

"Let me call you back." She hung up the phone. "It's all right, Wendy. I'll speak to her."

Wendy shut the door, and I stood in front of Sandy's desk. "You didn't need to take him into custody."

"I say we did. Who knows what he's capable of?"

"Bullshit. What's going on? Why are you doing this?"

"What makes you think I'm doing anything?"

"Please. Roscombe would want to do this with your approval, for appearance's sake if nothing else. Why are you so eager for this to go to trial?"

She stared out the window. "When my parents moved here from Wisconsin, do you know what the crime rate was? Single digits. Almost nonexistent. Now, just forty years later, we are one of the most crime-ridden counties in the western United States. There are many factors, but I think it's interesting that the black and Hispanic populations of the city increased in parallel with the crime rates."

"So what? That's not Teddy Thorne's fault."

"No, it's not his fault. Not his exactly."

She stared at me. Without a word, I knew what she was telling me.

"You're banking on him being convicted because he's black, and you need a conviction because you *want* someone to appeal this. You've got someone on the court of appeals ready to rule for you, just like Roscombe."

"I didn't say anything, Ms. Rollins."

"I don't get it. What does it matter to you if you can charge juveniles as adults? What does that do for you? If anything, it's more work."

She leaned forward. "I'm quite busy. Please leave now. And I'll see you in trial on Friday."

"He doesn't need to be in custody. Ask that the warrant be withdrawn."

"No."

"He's a disabled kid. He can't be in jail without anyone looking out for him." I had to swallow my pride, and it felt like fiery poison going down. "Please. I'm asking you as a favor to me: please do not take him into custody."

"Good-bye, Ms. Rollins. I will assume you know the way out."

I stood over her desk awhile longer, but she was already back on her phone.

I turned and left the office in a haze. I didn't know what to do. I could take Teddy and stash him somewhere, but that would only make things worse. When he was eventually picked up, they would hold him in custody until the trial, which would be reset to a lot more than three days away. There was always appealing and trying to push it through on an emergency basis, but if my gut was right—and it usually was—this plan had been in motion for a while, and Sandy had already cleared it with at least one or two members of the court of appeals. They likely wouldn't be granting any stays for me.

I got the impression suddenly that I was a mouse in a very elaborate trap that had been set a long time ago.

37

I drove up to Salt Lake and told Kelly to cancel anything I had today. I couldn't think. My brain felt like mushy oatmeal, and the only solution on my mind was to drink until I felt better. I called Will.

"What's up, my snow-colored sister?"

"Sandy Tiles cleared the Teddy Thorne case with people on the court of appeals and probably the Utah Supreme Court, too. I need to know who."

"Whoa, whoa, whoa, girlfriend. That's a serious accusation. You got any proof?"

"None."

"Hm. Didn't think so." He sighed. "Fine, I'll look into it for you. What makes you think this, though?"

"They're way overconfident. They wouldn't do this if they knew the higher courts were just gonna smack them down. This was planned out, and I'm just the mark."

"All right, let me see what I can find. I'll call you back."

I drove over to Will's condo instead.

He answered the door in a robe, though it was the afternoon. I guess being rich, you could wear a robe whenever you wanted.

"What's going on?" he said.

"I'm sorry. I didn't . . . I feel like shit right now and didn't have anywhere else to go."

He hesitated a second before opening the door and letting me in.

He sat me on the couch and got me a drink. The cushions were plump and soft, and I sank into them like warm sand. "So, how much money do you make at this little private investigator firm of yours?"

"A lot," he said from the kitchen as he got us two beers. "Growing up poor gives you drive like that."

He sat across from me on another sofa as I explained what had happened in court.

"Just like that?" he asked after hearing the whole sordid tale. "They're just going to take him to jail over nothing?"

I nodded. "It won't be pleasant for him either. Hoover County Jail isn't like other jails. There are a lot of hard mofos in Hoover County."

"Well, you gotta decide: If you're gonna keep the case, you gotta do something. If you think this case is taking too much outta you, we gotta find someone else today. Someone good. Either way, you have to do something."

"I am, I'm drinking."

"I'm serious."

"Hey, you got any ideas? I'm open to suggestions. But I don't understand it. Why do they care if they can send juveniles to jail instead of detention?"

Will was silent for a second. "You said she mentioned blacks and Hispanics specifically."

"She did, but I always guessed she was racist. That's not a surprise—she wants a gambler's jury so she can be guaranteed a conviction and guaranteed an appeal."

"It sounds like she meant more than that. I mean, think about it. If the Serious Youth Offender Act is overturned, she can get them when they're young and lock them away for as long as she wants, right? I mean, in detention they'd get out at eighteen, but not in jail, right?"

I stared at him. Holy shit.

At first I'd thought this was about Teddy's disability, then about his race, but it was about neither. This was a program. Sandy had been telling me in her office, and I'd been too upset to listen.

"This isn't about this case at all," I said, barely able to control the rising surge of adrenaline. "It's about social engineering. She's lined up the judges to give her the power to lock kids away until they're much older. To get them out of society."

Will stared at me. "Creepy."

It wasn't enough that over 80 percent of blacks across the nation received harsher sentences when convicted for the same crimes committed by other races. She wanted to control the children. She could get them off the streets in droves and lock them away until they were in their twenties and didn't know anything else. They would become lifelong criminals and end up convicted felons in the revolving door of prisons. An entire underclass of citizens would be marked, as children, to fail in society, and therefore be removed from society entirely. It would drop the crime rate in suburbs, and force them into ghettos when they finally got out of jail or prison. They could be controlled and monitored and away from everyone else: segregated.

"I'm gonna need another drink."

38

I wouldn't have the strength to go drop Teddy off at the Hoover County Jail after I picked him up from school. I'd let them take him into custody tomorrow after the arraignment. Maybe Roscombe had some heart left under all the bitterness. It would be harder to lock Teddy up if Roscombe had to look into his eyes while the bailiffs slapped the cuffs on.

Will and I sat in the Jeep outside of the school until Teddy came out with his backpack and gave his teacher a hug. He waved to us and then ran over. He got into the backseat and said, "Hi!" to Will.

"Hi yourself, Teddy."

I said, "How was school?"

"Good. We learned about checking accounts."

"Checking accounts? Wow, that sounds fun."

"No," he said simply. "It wasn't."

We drove down to a burrito place I liked and sat in a booth and ate. Will cracked jokes and showed Teddy various apps on his phone. I couldn't do it. I couldn't do anything but sit there and stare at Teddy. He had been a mark even more than I had.

After we ate, we drove Will home, and I stopped near the curb. He stared at the building for a second and said, "You can't control the system. You can only do your best with what you're given."

"That doesn't cheer me up, somehow."

"Hey," he said, lightly touching my arm, "keep your chin up."

I watched him leave, and Teddy said, "Bye Will!" through the window. He turned and waved and gave me a little smile.

———

We spent the evening watching movies. I was impressed by Teddy's ability to consume movie after movie without the slightest decline in enthusiasm. I think as a kid I had that, too, and about more than just movies. I could spend hours watching bugs crawling around in the dirt, or clouds floating in the sky, or the way people interacted in public together. It was all . . . magic. As an adult, I lost that sense of magic somewhere along the way.

After our nighttime ritual, I sat in a chair close to his bed and knew I had to say something.

"Buddy, something's going to happen tomorrow, and it's not going to be fun for a while. You're going to have to go away for a little bit."

"Go away where?"

"To a place by the court. The judge is ordering that you go there. They're going to take you tomorrow. You've been there before. The jail."

"But I want to stay here."

I nodded, staring at the carpet. "I know. It'll just be for a little while. I'll get you out of there as fast as I can. There's going to be some nice people in there and there's going to be some mean people, and you won't be able to tell the difference. The mean people will act like nice people at first. So I want you to do something for me; just keep to yourself. Do you know what that means?"

"Don't talk to anybody."

"That's right, don't talk to anybody. Don't hang out with anybody, don't do anything. Just keep to yourself and know that I'm going to get you out. Be alone. Okay? Will you do that for me?"

"Sure, Danielle."

I stood up, my eyes never leaving his. "All right, get some sleep."

"Danielle?"

"Yeah?"

"Can you read to me, please?"

"Um, sure. *Huck Finn?*"

"Yes."

I sat back down in the chair and picked up the book—his only possession in the world. I opened it randomly and started reading:

"Now she had got a start, and she went on and told me all about the good place. She said all a body would have to do there was to go around all day long with a harp and sing, forever and ever. So I didn't think much of it. But I never said so. I asked her if she reckoned Tom Sawyer would go there, and she said not by a considerable sight. I was glad about that, because I wanted him and me to be together . . ."

I kept reading until he fell asleep. I closed the book and set it on the nightstand. He looked like a child, free of worry and regret and malice. It was hard to understand that there were people in this world who looked specifically for those traits, the best traits in us, so that they could exploit them. Worse still were those who did it in the name of justice.

I rose, shut his door behind me, and sat on the couch and drank until I was too tired and drunk to do anything but sleep.

39

The next morning, I got Teddy ready and buckled him into the car. I called his parents. They didn't answer, so I left a voice mail.

"Hey, it's Danielle Rollins. I don't know if you even care at this point, but the judge is taking Teddy into custody today. I don't know how long he's going to be in there, but if you could visit him or . . . something. If you could just drive down and visit him . . ."

I hung up. There was nothing to say.

We didn't speak on the way down. I felt sick. Teddy listened to a classical music station. "My mama used to play music like this," he said. It was the only thing he said to me all the way down to Richardson. He could tell something was wrong, and he put his hand over mine at one point. I thought how screwed up the world must really be if he was comforting me at this point.

We parked and went up to the courtroom.

It was already packed, and the attorneys lined the seats behind the tables, waiting for their turn to speak to the prosecutors. I sat Teddy close to the front and took my spot.

Attorneys called their cases, and we ran through the court's calendar. I could have gotten up a couple of times, but I didn't feel like it.

Then again, maybe Roscombe would be more merciful in a courtroom full of people. Or maybe he would use it as a chance to teach everyone that he couldn't be trifled with. I didn't know what to do, so I just sat quietly until all the attorneys were done.

It was customary for the people without lawyers to be called alphabetically when no more attorneys rushed to the lectern, but the judge didn't do that. He called me first.

"State versus Theodore Thorne," Roscombe said.

I rose and waved for Teddy to join me. He got up and came and stood at my side. My eyes locked onto Roscombe's and neither of us moved.

"Mr. Thorne," he said, "you have been bound over on one count of distribution of a controlled substance, a first-degree felony, punishable by five years to life at the Utah State Prison. How do you wish to plead?"

"Not guilty," I said. I couldn't get the words "Your Honor" out.

"So entered. The issue of bail was addressed yesterday, and a warrant was issued for your arrest, Mr. Thorne. I am ordering that you be taken into custody pending the outcome of your trial. Bailiff?"

The bailiff came over and grabbed Teddy's arm. Teddy tried to pull it back behind him and shouted, "Hey!"

The bailiff pinned him against the lectern.

"Get the fuck off of him," I said, shoving the bailiff. The other bailiff came running. The one I had pushed grabbed Teddy and twisted both arms behind his back like a pretzel and Teddy screamed. Without a thought, I swung. I swung harder than I've ever swung in my life, and I nailed the bailiff square on the jaw. It was almost comical. He stumbled and fell across the defense table where three attorneys sat with their mouths open. I'd caught the bailiff completely off guard. The other bailiff whipped out a Taser and shot before I could do anything.

It slammed into my upper arm and shoulder and sent me back onto the prosecution table, where Double D jumped away. Three other bailiffs were swarming the courtroom. Two of them tackled Teddy.

"Leave him alone," I gasped, convulsing on the floor.

I was pinned to the floor by a meaty bailiff who stuck his knee in my back. I could hear Teddy's screams. "Don't touch me! Don't touch me! Danielle. Danielle!"

I felt a palm against my face as the cuffs went around my wrists, and I was lifted into the air.

40

I lay on the cot in the cell nearest to the judge's chambers. My home away from home, apparently. Teddy was supposed to be here, too, but they had taken him to a different holding cell.

My bicep was the color of an eggplant, and my shoulder hurt so much I couldn't move my left arm. My back ached from Bigfoot's knee, and the side of my face felt burned from being pressed into the courtroom floor. The worst pain was in my right hand—I thought I might've fractured it on the bailiff's jaw.

I heard boots in the hallway coming closer with each step. Tilting my head, I saw Tommy, a bailiff I had always joked around with. He came up to the bars and shook his head at me.

"You shouldn't have hit a bailiff, Ms. Rollins. That's not good."

"It wasn't exactly my plan. He okay?"

"He's fine. Just embarrassed is all. I think he's lookin' to kick your ass."

"Tell him to take a number." I sat up with a groan and electricity seemed to shoot through my shoulder. "Do you know where Teddy is?"

"They already took him down to the jail." He paused and looked around the cell. "You need anything, Ms. Rollins?"

"Some ice and an ibuprofen would be heavenly."

He nodded and turned away. I said, "Tommy?" He turned back around. "Thanks for treating me like a person."

"You one of my favorite people, Ms. Rollins. It ain't nothin'."

I don't know how long I sat in the cell. There were no meals. At least there was a single steel toilet in the cell.

Two bailiffs finally came and got me. They stared at me for a second before opening the cell, and I knew they were contemplating getting a few more shots in before letting me out. I just turned around and put my hands behind my back. They had badges and guns; it was hardly a fair fight. If they were going to hit me, they didn't deserve to hit me in the front.

No blows came, though, and they just took my arms and pulled me back to the courtroom. It was evening, and the court was empty except for the judge and Double D. The bailiffs stood me at the lectern and left the handcuffs on.

"Ms. Rollins, you should know they will be citing you for assault over that little temper tantrum."

"I wouldn't expect less, Judge."

He nodded. "The offer still stands: I will withdraw you from the case right now and give Mr. Thorne a public defender. Get out of this case, Ms. Rollins. There's no reason for you to pursue this. You're too . . . emotional. Too involved. Women always are. Withdraw now, and maybe Mr. Diamond would consider not filing those charges. If the bailiff you struck approves, of course."

What an odd thing for a judge to say. I looked at Double D, who couldn't even meet my eyes. I turned back to the judge. "I'm good. And your mother was a woman. Maybe a little respect is in order. Assuming you have a mother."

He shook his head and folded his hands in front of him. "You are a stubborn one, aren't you?"

"I once played Halo for ten hours just to find this little bastard who hit me with a grenade. I sniped him while he wasn't paying attention. One of the finest moments of my life."

He leaned back in the chair. "I'm releasing you to complete the trial. The issue of your custody will be addressed after the trial is completed."

The handcuffs were taken off. I looked at Double D, who kept his eyes on the floor, before I left. Outside the door, the bailiff I had hit sat with an ice pack pressed firmly against his swollen jaw.

"Hey, sorry, man," I said. "No hard feelings?"

"Fuck you."

"Alrighty then. Take care."

I got out into the parking lot and couldn't get into my car. Every muscle ached and the thought of driving back to Salt Lake right now sounded awful. I put my arms on the hood and my face between them.

"Danielle?"

I turned and saw Double D approaching. He stood a few feet away and licked his upper lip while he thought. I could almost see the words forming in his head, and I knew he felt bad for what had happened. The judge hadn't been moved by taking Teddy into custody, but someone had.

"I'm sorry," he said. "Good luck in the trial."

"What they're doing is wrong, Jasper. I know you didn't become a prosecutor to do shit like this."

"Yeah, well, sometimes it's just not in our control."

"You could stop this if you wanted to."

He shook his head. "I couldn't." He hesitated a second longer. "Take care of yourself."

After he left, I looked at the courthouse: an ominous building that was like some tyrannical weapon of war. Eight men and women on a jury would be deciding how this was going to turn out, and I had no idea what I was going to say when I stood in front of them. A diminished-capacity defense would be my normal course, but it was unlikely Roscombe would allow me to enter existing doctors' reports or IQ results. Teddy would have to be evaluated by new experts, mine and the prosecution's, and we'd have motions and hearings on it. Meanwhile, Teddy would be sitting in jail, his life at risk. Do I leave him there in the hopes of putting together a stronger defense that might not win at trial anyway, or go ahead with the trial and hope for the outcome I wanted?

I sighed and got into my Jeep.

41

At home I lay on the couch with a bag of frozen peas on my hand. I wished I had some painkillers. I had just decided to take a nap when my doorbell rang.

"It's not locked."

Will walked in and shut the door behind him. He stood in front of me and said, "What the hell happened? Kelly said you got into a fight."

"I got tased by this big bastard in Richardson."

"You're kidding. Why?"

"Doesn't matter. The trial's the day after tomorrow. Tell me you have something."

He sat down at my feet and looked me in the eyes. "I have something. So get this. Sandy Tiles is married to Richard Tiles, who is the brother of Randy Tiles."

"Lovely. What's this got to do with my case?"

"Randy Tiles, as in the state legislator Randy Tiles. And get this, lady—I checked out his voting record and the bills he's proposed. Just a gut feeling, right? Two years ago, guess what bill he submitted? HB 1105. Wanna take a guess as to what the bill contained?"

"Will, normally I love guessing games, but my hand feels like it's been raped by Thor's hammer. Can we just get to it?"

"HB 1105 tried to abolish the Serious Youth Offender Act and give prosecutors the discretion to charge any juvenile as an adult for any crime."

"Whoa."

"That's not even the best part. Guess who . . . oh, sorry. One of the supporters who testified at the capital on the bill's behalf was someone you are somewhat acquainted with: Patrick Howell. As in chief justice of the Utah Supreme Court Patrick Howell."

"You're shitting me."

"I shit you not." He squeezed my thigh. "You wanted to know how far the rabbit hole went; now you know. This was in the works for a long time, my friend. Your poor client just couldn't have picked a worse time to get busted for something like this."

I put my arm across my face and groaned.

"I'm, ah, leaving in four days. You need anything before then?"

"You're leaving now? I need you, Will."

"Hey, man, the place is rented. I got a condo waiting for me in Fiji. There's nothing I can do. I mean, unless you really want me to stay."

He gave me a look that told me he wanted me to convince him to not go. But I didn't have the strength to think about it right now. I'd be lying if I said I hadn't thought about what a life with him would be like—a life with a man who would treat me like a queen. Right now, though, the only thing I could think about was the hot, piercing pain in my shoulder and hand.

"I think I'm done with law, Will. After this, I'm done."

"Really?"

"The fix is in, brother. I won't keep bashing my head against a wall. Eventually these tyrannical shits will get what they want, neighbors spying on neighbors and secret police."

"Well, maybe that's why you gotta stay in it? Someone has to fight them."

"It ain't me."

He folded his hands and stared at me. "I know a lot of attorneys, Dani. A lot. I turn most of them down, and they could pay five times the hourly rate you pay me. You know why I keep you around?"

"Because of my ocean-like eyes?"

"Aside from that. You care. Most attorneys wouldn't cross the street to spit on their clients if they were on fire. As much as you put on this front that you're some sort of rogue hellion, you care about these people."

I sighed and looked at him. "And what's it gotten me, Will? I'm lonely all the time; I spend my days getting yelled at by judges and condescended to by prosecutors; I'll get cases dismissed and my ungrateful clients will be mad that I didn't do it fast enough; the public thinks I'm a scumbag for defending criminals . . . What's it gotten me?"

"Your soul, young lady. You get to keep your soul when a lotta people lose theirs." He slapped my leg. "Cheer up, pal. Tomorrow's a better day. It always is."

I tried to nap, but thoughts kept rushing through my head about the trial. I kept seeing Teddy's face as the jury read the verdict of guilty. He wouldn't understand what it meant. He wouldn't know why he was behind bars, potentially for life.

My phone rang. The ID said *Salt Lake Tribune*. I answered.

"This is Danielle."

"Ms. Rollins?"

"Yeah."

"It's Clay with the *Trib*. How are you?"

"Actually, not too hot, Clay. Mind if I call you later?"

"Just wanted to talk to you about this whole Teddy Thorne case."

"Thorne? Since when do you care about cases in Richardson?"

"I'm expanding my horizons. I was looking at some of the notes in the docket, and it just doesn't make sense to me. Is it true it's a juvenile case they didn't even get certified?"

"It is. They're using this case to cut the balls off the SYOA. And there is some shit going on, Clay."

"Like what?"

"This was fixed from a long time ago. The judge is in on it, a justice on the supreme court, the cops . . . everyone was lined up to find a case just like this."

"Hm. Well I'd love an interview after the trial."

"The trial starts the day after tomorrow," I said. "Why don't you be there?"

"Yeah, I was planning on it. Interview right after?"

"Sure."

"All right, take care."

I hung up. Crime-beat reporters were a dying breed. Everything was blogs now. An actual, paid, crime reporter going out and looking for interesting stories almost didn't exist, except in the largest cities for the largest papers. They were invaluable in defending the rights of the average citizen, since the one thing the corrupt didn't want was exposure. With their extinction, the justice system would look a lot different.

I had planned to go to the media at some point, but it was smarter to wait until after the trial. Roscombe might back down if I went public, but he might go even harder—he might reschedule the trial two months out, hoping the attention would die down, and keep Teddy in custody the whole time.

But having Clay at the trial wouldn't be a bad thing. If he could draw enough attention to the case, maybe the higher courts wouldn't uphold it on appeal for fear of public outrage.

I got up and hobbled around the house until I found half a bottle of Jack. Then I drank, listened to Depeche Mode, and fell asleep on the couch.

42

The next day, I prepped the best I could. I read the reports several times and then made an outline of the topics I wanted to hit. What a witness would say at trial was always unpredictable anyway, so the dominant trait of every good trial attorney was an ability to improvise. Intelligence, experience, book smarts, law school grades, knowledge of the case . . . none of that mattered. Only the ability to improvise, and whether or not the attorney cared about their client. I don't know how juries did it, but they could always smell when a lawyer didn't care.

The one issue in this case that hurt us more than anything was that we didn't have a single witness in our favor, not even the defendant. He still hadn't told me what he remembered from that night, and I had no idea what he might say. The only witness that might help was Freddy, but the video of the interview, which I had watched last night at two in the morning, was ambiguous. The police certainly didn't follow correct interview procedure with a minor, but they did it in such a subtle way that a jury probably wouldn't be able to tell. And if Will was right and Freddy was going to renege and say the police didn't lead him, then we didn't have anyone to get up there and contradict what the government was saying.

I prepped for a few hours and then made the drive down to the Hoover County Jail to visit Teddy.

A few dark clouds drifted across the sun as I drove, giving me a disorienting feeling, as if I were watching some sped-up film of alternating day and night. The guards at the jail were extra rough and groping while searching me—a little payback for hitting one of their own. As long as I didn't get tased or shot, I considered it a win.

I sat in the attorney's visiting room and waited for them to bring Teddy in. When they finally did, I wanted to turn away. His black-and-white striped jumpsuit didn't fit him well and the cuffs around his wrists rattled as the guard sat him down. The guard glanced to me before leaving.

"Are you okay?" I said softly.

"I don't like it here, Danielle. But I'm doing what you said. I'm not talking to anybody."

"Good, buddy. You keep that up, and I'll get you out of here, okay?"

He nodded. "Okay. Where's Will? I like Will. He's funny."

"He didn't come with me. Maybe he'll be there tomorrow." I paused and looked over at the door. The guard was staring through the glass window. "Teddy, it is very important that you tell me what happened that night. The night you rode in the police car. Where did you get that bag, and how do you know Salvador Zamora?"

He shrugged.

"Teddy, look at me . . . If we lose this trial tomorrow, you will be in a place like this for years and years. A long time. You have to tell me where you got that bag."

"Kevin is my friend."

"I know he's your friend, but you need to tell me if Kevin gave you that bag. Did he tell you to give it to Zamora? Is that what happened?"

He didn't answer. I reached out and held his hand. "Teddy, do you want to live here for the rest of your life?"

He shook his head.

"Then you need to tell me what happened. Did Kevin give you that bag?"

He shook his head.

"You have to tell me, buddy."

He began to rock back and forth. "Kevin is my friend . . . and, and he said I could play games with them."

"Was the bag yours? Can you at least tell me if the bag was yours?"

He hesitated, and then shook his head. "No."

"Then listen to me: Tomorrow, I'm going to put you in front of people in the courtroom. You're going to say exactly what you just told me. I don't want you to be scared that other people are there. They want to hear what you have to say. So just tell the truth, okay?"

"Okay, Danielle."

"A woman named Sandy is going to ask you questions after I do. You just have to answer them honestly. Just be honest and say what happened. Yes or no. Easy peasy. Okay? You won't get nervous?"

"Okay. I won't get nervous."

The truth was, I knew he wouldn't give much on the stand. That's not why I needed him up there. I needed the jury to see that he had a mental disability, and the only way to do that was to put him up there and show them.

He hadn't said anything about it, so I figured neither his mom nor dad had been to visit him.

"I'll see you tomorrow, Teddy. Don't talk to anyone, okay?"

"Okay."

As I left the jail, I wondered if I should've spent more time prepping him, making sure he understood. On the one hand, it might take care of his jitters, but on the other, he could inadvertently tell the jury how much we prepared or that I told him to say something. That would definitely kill his credibility. Better not to risk it. I wanted the jury to see him confused, to see what his mental capacity was, exactly.

A Gambler's Jury

Driving back to Salt Lake, I headed to the Lizard. It was well past lunch, but there was still a crowd there. Inside, the tables were taken up with construction workers and politicians, teamsters and police officers. I sat at the bar away from everybody, and ordered a sandwich and a beer. Michelle came out of the back room with a few people and said good-bye to them. They looked like mob types, though anyone who did *anything* shady liked to pretend they were Al Capone, so I could never really tell. Michelle saw me and came over. She had a despondent look and sat down with a groan.

"Rough day at the office?" I asked.

"Old business associates. One of them, that tall one there, he's missing his daughter." She shook her head. "Twenty years old. Ran away from home with a pimp she thinks she's in love with. He was asking if I'd seen her. These pimps, Dani, they convince these girls online to come out to see them, and the girls never go home."

I didn't respond. I didn't have the capacity to deal with any more tragedy right now, so I just stared at my drink.

"What's wrong, Butterfly?"

"This case. The one I told you about. They're making me go to trial on it tomorrow."

"Making you?"

I nodded. "They took my client into custody. If I take more time, he might get hurt in there. He can't defend himself. And I'm scared about what a jury's going to do."

"You told me juries are unpredictable."

"They are. That's what's scary. They can't be trusted to do the right thing."

She put her hand on my shoulder. "Hey, I've never known you to lose when you really wanted a win. You want it, you'll get it. Oh, hey, I meant to tell you—remember you asked about this cat Zamora? I found something else out."

"What?"

"Check this out; he's not just a snitch, he's a life snitch."

"What do you mean?"

"I mean one of my buddies with the Salt Lake PD said this guy's been working with them and Hoover County Narcotics for over four years. He sets up busts. They're called life snitches because they've done so much dirt they gotta snitch for life to get a pass."

"Four years? Why would . . ."

"What? What's wrong?"

I threw a twenty on the counter and ran out of there without explaining.

43

I raced down to Richardson. Will got me Jasper Diamond's home address. Prosecutors, unlike judges, didn't usually take any steps to hide their personal information. Jasper didn't live very far from the courthouse.

His house was far nicer than a government employee should've been able to afford, but I wasn't surprised. Richardson had some of the lowest home prices in the state. A large house, it had a big front lawn and a three-car garage. I parked in the driveway and hesitated a second before going up to the door. I listened to see if I could hear anything, but I couldn't. I rang the doorbell.

Double D answered in a robe and smoking a pipe.

"What are you, Hugh Hefner?"

"What the hell are you doing here?"

"I need to talk to you."

"It can wait."

"It can't . . . please."

He sighed and opened the door wider. The house looked like a museum for cowboy memorabilia. Paintings of horses, bears, deer, and old Mexican-style towns were crammed onto the walls. A rough-hewn table in the front room was made out of some fallen tree, and the fireplace had two old rifles crossed above it.

"Did you buy Billy the Kid's house or something, Jasper?"

He sat down in a worn leather chair with a bearskin over it. "Just tell me what you want."

"Zamora's a life snitch for the narcotics task force. Did you know that?"

He stared at me a second. "Yes."

"And you didn't think to tell me?"

"I was instructed not to."

"By who—Sandy? It's a *Brady* violation. I have a right to know if one of the witnesses against my client works for the damn state, Jasper. You've pulled some shit before, but nothing like this. How the hell did you go along with it?"

He tapped his fingers against the chair. "I've . . . I don't know. You start doing things, and it gets easy and then you don't stop. I gave in a little here and a little there, and before I knew it I was doing . . . this."

"So quit."

He shook his head and stared off into space. "Five years away from my pension, so no, I won't be doing that."

"You gonna be happy spending that pension knowing you put an innocent disabled kid in prison?"

"Who said he's innocent? Even if Zamora is a snitch and set this whole thing up, your client did everything willingly."

"Jasper, if you do this, you will never forgive yourself."

He looked away and tapped the chair again. "I think you should leave, Danielle."

"Talk to Sandy. She'll listen to you. Don't put that kid on trial for this."

He led me out of the house and then stood on his porch a short while as I headed to my Jeep. I sat in the driver's seat and looked back at him. I could almost see the struggle going on inside him. I almost felt bad for the guy. Almost.

I started the car and drove to my office to draft a new motion.

44

I wished I could've driven Teddy to court the next morning. On the way over, we would have gone through a few questions and I would've practiced cross-examining him. Sandy, if she were smart, would try to paint him as both more intelligent than he let on, and angrier.

At the courthouse, I saw potential jurors and cops, prosecutors and judges, piling in. I always felt alone on the day of a trial: me against a machine that was set up to crush me. A trial was a battle, originating in trial by combat between nobles. Eventually, the nobles got sick of killing each other and hired people to fight in their stead. The ancestors of the modern trial lawyer were mercenaries. I took a deep breath and went inside.

Sandy and Double D were seated at the prosecution table, beside Detective Steed. The prosecution got to have their lead detective as a case manager, who got to remain in the courtroom through the entire trial—even though it could clearly sway his testimony. I had no such luxury or witnesses. I tried to clear my head and calm myself. Trials had never bothered me before. I could walk in and wing it on a moment's notice and not even elevate my heart rate. But right now my palms were sweaty, and my heart was trying to break out of my chest.

I looked over to the prosecution table to see if Sandy felt anything, but she just stared straight ahead and didn't speak to anyone. The woman might've been a robot.

"All rise," the bailiff said. "Second District Court is now in session, the Honorable Mia Roscombe presiding."

We got to our feet. Roscombe sat down and let out a quiet burp as he booted his computer. He glanced over at me and then to the prosecutors and said, "Both parties ready?"

"We are, Judge," Sandy said without rising.

"Yes," I said.

"Then we'll bring out the defendant."

"I did have one thing," I said. "May I approach?"

"You may."

Sandy and I went to the judge's side. I flopped my *Brady* motion onto his bench, and he picked it up and scanned it. It was only a page and a half, as I stated that I would need an evidentiary hearing to further develop the issues.

I handed a second copy to Sandy, who read it much more carefully.

"Your Honor," she said, without taking her eyes off the document, "this is clearly a substantive motion and the rules are plain: they must be filed at least seven days before trial. I'm not prepared to argue this today."

"There's an exception," I said. "It must be raised seven days before trial if practicable. I only found out about this yesterday. I'm as prepared to argue it as she is. I think the appropriate thing to do would be to either have the hearing right now, since the only two witnesses I'll be cross-examining are Detective Steed and Mr. Zamora, who are both here. Or we could continue the trial and set a hearing date. I would only agree to that if my client could be released, though. He can't stay in there."

"I would object to both," Sandy said. "I think the motion should be ignored due to untimeliness, and Mr. Thorne's subsequent counsel should seek an appeal based on ineffective assistance of counsel since Ms. Rollins didn't do an effective investigation to discover this before today."

"You gave Zamora a deal so he wouldn't want to talk to me. How the hell was I supposed to find out he's a snitch?"

Roscombe watched me to see what I did. I may have shown a glimmer of hope that he would either have the hearing or let Teddy out. I got the feeling he enjoyed seeing that the way a child enjoys seeing an ant climb onto his foot, the ant unaware he's about to be crushed.

"I agree. The motion is untimely. Back up and let's put it on the record."

"They hid evidence, Judge. It's untimely because they lied to me in clear violation of every rule of discovery ever written. It's their fault, not mine, and I think the proper remedy is to let my client out and give us all a chance to prepare."

"I disagree."

I chuckled. "You would disagree with that."

Oh shit.

"It appears," he said quietly, "that you would like to spend more time in my cell." He looked at Sandy and then back to me. "Now step back while we bring the defendant and the jury panel out. Your motion is denied due to untimeliness."

I went back to the defense table. A bailiff came out of a side door, with Teddy in front of him. Teddy waved to me and smiled. He wore the clothes I had brought him, slacks and a shirt and tie. He was sat down next to me with his handcuffs still on. "No cuffs," I said.

The bailiff hesitated, then removed the cuffs. Teddy immediately began tugging at his tie, unable to make himself comfortable.

"Let me," I said.

I loosened the knot so it wasn't touching his throat, and he seemed to calm.

"Hi Danielle."

Despite where I was and what I was doing, I couldn't help but smile at him. "How are you, buddy?"

"I watched TV last night, Danielle. Um, *Spider-Man*. They let me watch *Spider-Man*. Have you seen *Spider-Man*?"

"Haven't seen it. Was it good?"

"It was really good. I like it because he can jump far, see. He can jump far and fly."

The bailiff said, "All rise for the jury."

I stood and helped Teddy to his feet. Nearly thirty potential jurors walked in. I scanned their faces, hoping to be able to tell something about them from nothing more than a glance. Every lawyer did the same thing when a jury first walked in. Of course, we couldn't tell anything. Jury consultant firms, charging a thousand bucks an hour, had elaborate algorithms and statisticians working the data to try to predict which way a juror would find on a case, and they were wrong a little over 50 percent of the time. They picked slightly worse than random selection. Humans are just too complex to predict how we feel at any particular moment.

"Please be seated," Roscombe said.

His entire demeanor had changed. His face, usually looking like a wrinkled statue, had softened. He even grinned, or at least tried to as he began reading his stock instructions and introductions to the jury panel. The entire process of jury selection would be quick. Roscombe was known for allowing the lawyers to question the jury panel for fifteen minutes each, not a minute more for either lawyer.

"Will the lawyers please introduce themselves?" Roscombe asked in a voice kinder than I'd ever heard him use.

Sandy rose. "My name is Sandy Tiles and this is Jasper Diamond. We represent the state of Utah in this case. Our witnesses are Detective Bo Steed, Mr. Salvador Zamora, Kevin Simmons, Clint Andrews, Freddy Willmore, and Dr. Harold Coltrane with the Utah State Crime

Lab." Roscombe would be asking if any of the jury knew any of the witnesses, so they were introduced whether they were present or not.

I stood and faced the panel. A few of them glanced at Teddy. I could tell what they were thinking: Just because Teddy sat in that seat, their hindbrains assumed he was guilty. Oh, they would try to fight that idea as well as they could; people hated to think they couldn't be impartial. But the subliminal suggestion of guilt was always planted the moment the jury saw the defendant behind that table.

"I'm Danielle Rollins, and this is Teddy Thorne."

Teddy waved to them, and I saw several looks of confusion. I wanted to grab them by their collars and scream: *This kid is innocent, and you have no fucking idea what the government is doing to your rights!* But that wasn't allowed. Instead, I just said, "I'm helping Teddy today."

No one on the panel knew any of the attorneys or witnesses. We then went into the mechanics of trial, when the jury would be getting breaks, that they were not supposed to talk about the case while outside of the jury deliberation room, and a thousand other things that judges thought were somehow necessary for a person to think clearly.

Sandy went up to the lectern and silently flipped through her five pages of questions before she began on number one. How many of them had ever been arrested for possession of illegal narcotics? How many had general criminal histories or had family members who had criminal histories, and how many had used narcotics and blah-blah-blah. In my experience, no one was going to be honest to a roomful of strangers about Uncle Billy's meth habit.

She grilled the jury for the full fifteen minutes, glancing back once at Roscombe to ensure she had his full attention when she asked, "Can you convict a person and uphold your oath under the law even if you feel sorry for them?" Sneaky sneaky.

It was my turn. I handed Teddy the iPad I'd brought for him. I didn't stand at the lectern but went up close to the jury. I stared at them.

They stared at me. An uncomfortable silence passed before I asked my first question: "Do you or anyone in your families have anything against the mentally disabled?"

I didn't care much about the question, because someone who hated the disabled wouldn't be honest about it. I just wanted to get into their minds that Teddy couldn't be held to the same standard as everyone else.

"Could you really be impartial, knowing my client is mentally disabled? Do any of you view a mental disability in a light that would make it hard to judge the innocence of my client? Do any of you have family members who suffer from disabilities and are not able to think on the level of an average person?"

I must've said "mentally disabled" in every sentence for fifteen minutes. No one answered yes to any of my questions, so there was no need to explore their answers further.

When I was done, I thanked the jury and sat down. I got little information from them, but that wasn't terribly important. I couldn't possibly guess how they would find even if I spent a year asking them questions. I just hoped I had planted in their heads that Teddy needed to be held to a different standard than people who were not mentally disabled.

After the questioning of the jury panel, the judge went over another half hour of instructions, and then we took a break. I turned to Teddy, who was smiling at the iPad, and saw the bailiff make a motion toward it.

"It's gotta go," the bailiff said.

"If you want him calm and quiet, he needs it," I said.

"We can make him calm and quiet."

I stared at the bailiff for a second and then reached across and lowered the iPad. "You have to concentrate on what's going on, buddy. They won't let you have the iPad."

"But I wanna play games, Dani."

"I know. Just for the trial, though. I'll get you your own iPad afterward, and you can play as much as you want." I looked at the bailiff again, who was smirking now. "I have to go to the bathroom, Teddy. Do you need to go?"

"No. Um . . . no."

"Okay, if you need to go, just tell me."

I walked into the bathroom and vomited into a toilet.

45

After a ten-minute break, Roscombe droned on and on about procedure and rulings and how sometimes the lawyers would have to discuss something out of the earshot of the jury and that they shouldn't take it personally. Usually, whatever was withheld from the jury was the information they most needed to know.

The jury selection for a felony trial allowed four peremptory challenges, meaning the defense and prosecution each got to strike four potential jurors. I didn't have much to go on, so I struck the people who were staring at Teddy as though they didn't like him. The prosecution really aimed for anyone who might be in danger of actually weighing the evidence and making a fair ruling.

No black jurors, no liberals, no one who read anything but the local papers.

When it was over, we had our eight jurors: three women and five men, all white, all blue-collar. All small-town folks who probably only saw black people on television. One of them was wearing a sweatshirt with a deer in crosshairs.

Across the courtroom by the bailiffs hung a small poster of a dog sitting on a stand and a jury of cats judging him with the caption, "Does this seem like a jury of his peers? Make sure the process is fair."

It almost made me laugh.

"It is now time for opening statements," the judge said. "The attorneys will each have an opportunity to address you. Please bear in mind that what the attorneys say is not evidence, and only meant to inform you of their theory of the case. Mrs. Tiles?"

Sandy rose, moving like a robot, keeping her limbs unnaturally close to her body. She stood at the lectern and read a prepared statement.

"The evidence in this case is clear as day. Mr. Thorne is a troubled young man, but a young man who decided the best way to earn money was to sell cocaine."

Double D lifted the gym bag again and stacked the cocaine on the prosecution table so the jury could see.

Sandy continued. "Mr. Thorne was contacted by his next-door neighbor, Kevin Simmons, about playing video games with two other boys you will hear from today, Clint Andrews and Fredrick Willmore. The boys informed Mr. Thorne that they were going to another friend's house and that he was welcome to come along. Mr. Thorne informed them that he would like to, but that he needed a ride to Richardson first. Mr. Simmons thought this unusual but had an affinity for the boy and agreed."

Affinity? I thought. There is no way half the jury knew what "affinity" meant. I wondered if Sandy borrowed parts of an opening statement she found on Google.

"Mr. Thorne brought with him a blue gym bag, that gym bag right here on the table, and would not inform the boys why he had to travel to Richardson—not until they arrived there. Mr. Thorne directed the boys to the home of Salvador Zamora, a confidential informant working with the narcotics task force. Mr. Simmons will tell you today that he didn't feel comfortable allowing Mr. Thorne to go by himself, and followed him up to the porch. Once Mr. Zamora came to the door, he exchanged a plastic bag filled with thirty thousand dollars in cash, only about one-sixth what the cocaine was actually worth, for the gym bag with the cocaine. Unbeknownst to the boys, this deal had been set up by the Hoover County Narcotics Task Force. Mr. Zamora had been cooperating with us in finding drug suppliers in the Wasatch Front, and Mr. Thorne took the bait."

That was interesting. Usually, prosecutors didn't burn CIs in court. Their identities were only released to defense attorneys with a protective order, meaning the defense attorney couldn't reveal the name to anyone. Putting his name on public record in court meant they wouldn't be using him as a CI anymore. Maybe this bust had earned Zamora his freedom.

"Mr. Thorne is charged with distribution of narcotics for the selling of this cocaine. It is important for you to understand that no one forced him to commit this crime. No one put a gun to his head to sell cocaine, and the involvement of the police was minimal. Mr. Thorne chose to sell that cocaine, and he must face the consequences himself."

Sandy sat down. No mention of his disability. This was such a farce I could hardly stand it. Instead of a proper trial, I had been manipulated into a corner and forced to put the fate of my client into the hands of a jury who wouldn't even hear about his disability other than from me, and from what they could pick up while he was on the stand.

I looked at Roscombe, who sat patiently and waited for me. Slowly, I rose and stood in front of the jury. I looked each of them in the face. The words wouldn't come out of my mouth. I kept picturing Teddy in prison, abused by the other inmates, alone, hurt . . . a sick, gray weight sat in my gut and I couldn't shake it.

"Teddy Thorne . . . When I was twelve years old, I lived with a foster family who had taken me in primarily for the monthly check they would receive. They had three children of their own and didn't have the time or the patience to spend on me. One of the children was a girl my age who didn't like that a new girl had come to town. Any chance she got, she would blame me for anything she did. If something broke, if she ate something that her father had been saving for later, if the dog got out and ran away . . . she would blame it on me. And her parents would take her word for it every time. No matter what I said, they never believed me, because they had already made up their minds that I wasn't believable.

"Teddy is here because the government has made up its mind that he isn't believable. You'll hear from him today, and you'll know, you'll *know*, that there is no way he committed this crime. Kevin Simmons is the one who went down there to exchange the drugs for money, and he and his two friends have stuck to the same story from the beginning, protecting each other. Zamora, to protect himself and stop being a confidential informant, blamed Teddy, too, since that became the official explanation. If you want to get your sentence lowered by informing on others, it's pretty difficult when you say something that goes against three other witnesses. So he just went along with what everyone else was saying—that Teddy was the mastermind behind this whole thing.

"Teddy, because of his condition, was chosen as the scapegoat. All I'm asking from you is that you please listen to him, and not make up your minds that he isn't believable before you even hear him out."

I sat down. I couldn't think of anything else to say. Without an expert to lay the foundation for discussing Teddy's disability, I didn't know how much Roscombe would let me say about it.

I glanced behind me and saw Clay from the *Salt Lake Tribune* sitting in the back row of the courtroom. Part of me wanted to run over and tell him everything that was going on, but if that all came out now, Roscombe would declare a mistrial—based on the fact that I might have tainted the jury if they read anything about it—and that meant more time for Teddy behind bars. I couldn't risk it. My only hope was that the jury would acquit him.

"Mrs. Tiles," Roscombe said, "your first witness, please."

46

Sandy stood at the lectern while Clint Andrews took the stand. The boy wore a button-down and had his hair slicked back. An older man I'd seen in the courtroom a few times, no doubt the boy's lawyer, stood in the back and watched the proceedings with his hands in his pockets, occasionally taking out his phone and checking email or texts.

Clint looked nervous. He cleared his throat and couldn't look at the jury. Sandy asked him his name and where he lived, how he was connected to this case, and Clint stuttered a few times.

"Do you know the defendant in this case, Theodore Thorne?"

"Kind of," he muttered. "He lives next to Kevin. I've seen him a few times."

"Tell us what you remember about the night in question, Mr. Andrews. April second of this year."

He swallowed. "It went quick. Like, we were playing games and Teddy came over to Kevin's house. We were leaving to go to my other friend's house, Eric, who lives in Roy. And Teddy said he wanted to come. I didn't really want him to come, but Kevin said we had to be nice to him, 'cause, I mean, you know. He's, like, retarded. And so he came."

"So what happened after you allowed him to come?"

"We drove down, and he'd brought this bag with him. This gym bag."

"This bag right here?" Sandy asked, picking the gym bag up off the table.

"Yeah, that looks like it. So he says we have to stop somewhere, and Kevin asks him where. And Teddy says he can't tell us other than it's Richardson."

"Did you find it strange that he wouldn't tell you?"

"Yeah, I mean, yeah, it was weird. But I just thought it was because he was retarded."

Sandy held up her hand. "Let's leave him being special off the table for now, Mr. Andrews, and stick to what happened. Now, did you drive him to where he wanted to go?"

"Yeah, he said that he had to go, and then he started kind of wigging out about it. So we drove him, and he kind of told us where to go. Like he'd been there before."

"What happened then?"

"We got to this house in this really shitty—sorry, crappy—part of Richardson and he said he had to go in but he was scared. He didn't want to. So Kevin said he would go with him. So the two of them went up to the porch."

"And what were you doing at this time?"

"Just sitting in the car with Freddy."

"Could you see the defendant and Mr. Simmons clearly?"

"Yeah, I mean, they weren't that far."

"Okay, so what happens while you're sitting there?"

"They talked for a minute, and Teddy handed the dude at the door the bag. And then it was just crazy. Like all these cops swarmed everywhere. One of 'em put a gun to me and pulled me out of the car and we were arrested."

"Mr. Andrews, did you know it was cocaine he had in that bag?"

"No, I mean, yes. Kind of. He said that's what he had, but no one believed him. And I didn't see it. I thought he was just messing with us. No way I would've gone down with him on something like that."

"And you're certain it was Mr. Thorne's bag?"

"Yeah, he ran back to his house, and I saw him come out with the bag in his hands. It was the same bag he gave to the dude in Richardson."

"Thank you, Mr. Andrews. That's all I had."

I stood up and looked at Clint. He poured some water out of a jug in front of him into a paper cup and took a swig. "They charged you with distributing narcotics, too, didn't they, Mr. Andrews?"

"Yeah."

"What kind of deal did they offer you for testifying against my client?"

"They said they would drop the charges."

"Drop the charges. Just like that?"

"Yeah. I didn't do anything."

"Hm. How long have you and Kevin and Freddy been friends?"

"Long time."

"Like, two years, five years—what?"

"Like ten years. We were in elementary school together and just kinda stayed friends."

"You care about them, don't you?"

"Yeah."

I stepped closer to him. "And they care about you?"

"Yeah."

"Would you say they're your best friends?"

He nodded. "Yeah. They're my boys."

"And as best friends, you guys look out for each other, don't you?"

"I guess."

"You guess, or you do look out for each other?"

"Yeah, we look out for each other."

"And if you knew one of your buddies was in trouble, I mean *real* trouble, being a good friend like you are, you'd be there for him, wouldn't you?"

He shrugged. "Yeah. I guess."

"You'd say anything to protect them?"

"Not anything, no."

I took a step closer and could see that he grew more nervous the nearer I was to him. "So you just said they're your best friends, right?"

"Right."

"And that you'd protect them if they were in trouble, right?"

"Yeah."

"So if one of your buddies was looking at going to prison, you'd want to protect him from that, wouldn't you? Otherwise you wouldn't be much of a friend, would you?"

"Um . . . Yeah, I guess I'd want to protect him."

"Now, you said my client was, in your word, 'retarded,' right?"

"Yeah."

"What did you mean by that?"

Sandy stood up. "Objection, Your Honor, Mr. Andrews is not an expert on mental conditions."

"No," I said, "I was denied an expert because my client would sit in jail while I got one, so this kid's what I've got."

Roscombe said, "Counsel, approach."

I went up to the bench, and he hit a button in front of him that sent static through the speakers of the courtroom so no one else could hear what we were saying.

Sandy whispered, "She hasn't laid foundation as to his condition, I would ask that any mention of it be excluded."

"You gave me three days to prepare a defense. You cut my arms off and sent me into a fistfight, Judge. And now you're both complaining that I want to tell the jury about my client's obvious condition? And she opened the door anyway by letting the witness say he was retarded."

Roscombe said, "Ms. Rollins, what you need is to stick to the facts of this case and not conjecture on ideas that haven't had foundation laid."

I wanted to turn away and ignore them both, but I couldn't. Before I could stop myself, I blurted, "And what you need is a sane judge so you can see what one looks like."

His face went slack, and he glanced at Sandy before saying, "Perhaps more time in my cell *would* do you some good, Ms. Rollins."

I walked away and went back to the lectern. "You never talked to Teddy before that night, did you, Clint?"

"No."

"Never spent any real time with him?"

"No."

"So you couldn't say what type of condition he has or how severe it is, could you?"

"Um, no, I guess not."

"And you couldn't say if he has the mental capacity to understand what he was doing?"

Sandy shouted, "Objection!"

"Ms. Rollins," Roscombe said, trying to keep his voice calm in front of the jury, "we discussed this, and I have made my ruling. Move on."

It didn't matter what he said. As long as I kept hammering into the jury's mind that Teddy was disabled, they might be thinking about that when they went back for deliberation, and why I was denied a chance to present it to them.

"You just said Teddy told you Richardson. Do you recall that we had a conversation at your school a bit ago?"

"Yeah."

"And you told me that you didn't hear Teddy ever mention Richardson, is that right?"

"Um . . . I don't remember. I don't know."

"Seems like an important thing to remember doesn't it? Whether he actually said Richardson or Kevin did."

"I don't remember if I heard Teddy say it or not."

"You don't remember," I said. "Thank you."

I sat down, and Sandy gave me a hard look before she said, "Fredrick Willmore, please, Your Honor."

Clint was taken out and Freddy came in. He was dressed in a suit and wouldn't look at us. He took the stand and was sworn in and then kept his gaze on Sandy as she looked through her questions.

"Please state your name for the record," Sandy said.

"Fredrick Taylor Willmore."

"And where do you live, sir?"

"Salt Lake County."

"Do you recognize the defendant in this case, Theodore Thorne?"

"Yes, ma'am."

"Where is he in the courtroom?"

"He's sitting down at that table," Freddy said, glancing at us quickly. "In the shirt and tie."

"When was the last time you saw him, Mr. Willmore?"

"In, um, April."

"April second?"

"I think so. Yeah."

"Describe your interaction with him at that time."

He inhaled deeply. There was a pause. The words weren't coming easy to him; he didn't want to do this. Maybe if I could push him enough he would say something Sandy didn't want him to say.

"We were at my friend Kevin's house—"

"Kevin Simmons?"

"Yeah. We were over there. Me and Kevin and Clint. We were playing video games. Just hanging out. Teddy came over. Kevin let him in and let him sit down. He took my seat, actually."

"Why do you say that?"

"I mean, Kevin was just really nice to him. He told me to move so Teddy could sit there."

As Fredrick was testifying, I noticed movement to the side of me. Teddy had begun rocking back and forth. He wasn't looking at the stand; he was staring down at his fingers, rubbing them together. Slowly, not at the furious pace I'd seen him do when a situation overwhelmed him. But the intensity only increased as the testimony went on.

"Teddy played games with us for a little bit. He asked if we could give him a ride somewhere, and Kevin said sure, and then they didn't really talk about it again. Then Clint got a call from his friend Eric who told us to come over, some girls were coming to his house. Teddy asked if we could give him a ride first."

Sandy leaned her elbows on the lectern, attempting to look casual and instead appearing like a wooden doll straining for a position its stiff joints were fighting against.

"Let me stop you there one second, Mr. Willmore. Are you saying the defendant asked for a ride first? Before he knew where you were going?"

"Yeah."

"You're sure of that?"

"Positive. I remember because I thought it was weird that Kevin didn't ask him where he wanted to go. He just said he'd give him a ride. I think Kevin felt bad for him because he's retarded."

Sandy opened and then closed her mouth. I nearly laughed. She had almost objected to her own witness. Once she had reached the status of district attorney, she became an administrator and stopped being a trial lawyer. Trial law was a skill that needed to be sharpened every day or it dulled immediately. Eventually, it would rust and you'd be back to square one, forgetting everything you had learned, losing the comfort you felt in court.

I looked over at Double D, who was watching Sandy with an oh-shit look.

"So he asked for a ride. What happened next?" she asked, hoping the jury had missed the part where her second witness had contradicted her first about when my client asked for a ride.

"We told him, or Kevin told him anyway, that we were going to Roy, and Teddy said he had to go to Richardson. It's close, but it's still, like, ten minutes away, and I said I didn't want to go that far. But Kevin said we'd do it."

Son of a bitch. The little turd really did change his story. He had clearly told me he never heard Teddy say Richardson.

"Did Mr. Thorne say why he needed a ride?"

"No."

"So what happened then?"

"Then Teddy ran back to his house and came out with that blue gym bag that's on that table."

Sandy went over to it and lifted it. "This one?"

"Yeah."

I stared at the bag, noticing the small FHY symbol on it, a symbol that wasn't in any of the photos the police took. I remembered that Teddy's father worked at FHY. So the gym bag wasn't Kevin's. But it would make sense for Kevin and the boys to have Teddy grab a gym bag out of his own house rather than one they owned.

"You're positive this is the one?"

"Yeah. It had that logo on the side."

"Did you ask him what was in the bag?"

"No."

"Did he tell you?"

Freddy shook his head. "No. Kevin didn't even really ask until we were in the car."

"So you guys get in the car to drive to Richardson. Tell us what happened then."

"We just drove down. We listened to music. I don't remember what it was. But Kevin only asked Teddy a couple times what was in there, and Teddy wouldn't tell him. But I really wanted to know now. I figured it had something to do with his being retarded but—"

"Mr. Willmore," Sandy interrupted, "let's refrain from using that particular term, shall we? Especially since you're not a psychiatrist and can't speak to what Mr. Thorne's condition is."

He shrugged. "Okay."

"So you're driving down. Did you ever find out what was in the bag?"

"Not until we were there. We sat outside the house, and Teddy kept rocking back and forth and just saying, 'I don't want to do it, I don't want to do it . . .'"

Freddy looked over at Teddy and then immediately back at Sandy.

"So what did you do when Mr. Thorne was doing this?"

"Kevin did the talking. He kept telling him that he could trust us and tell us what was in the bag. Finally he did. He said it was drugs."

"Drugs or cocaine?"

"No, just drugs."

"You're sure about that?"

"Positive."

Little bastard. I could've punched him in the balls.

"What did you do when you found out he had drugs in the bag?"

"I didn't believe him. I mean, none of us did. Kevin kept trying to see inside the bag, but Teddy wouldn't let him. He just kept saying that he didn't want to do it, and Kevin said, 'Do what?' and Teddy was, like, 'I have to give the bag to the man.'"

"What man?"

"I don't know. I don't think Teddy knew his name. So Kevin said he would do it with him. I mean, none of us thought he had drugs, so Kevin was just playing along. And then he went up to the porch, and this guy came to the door. They talked for a second, and then Teddy handed the bag to the guy and the guy gave him a different bag back. Then there were cops everywhere."

Sandy nodded. "Thank you, Mr. Willmore."

I stood up before the judge could give me permission and said, "Do you remember talking to me at your school, Freddy?"

"Yes."

"Do you remember telling me then that you never heard Teddy say he needed to go to Richardson?"

"Um, I don't remember that."

"You don't remember saying specifically that Teddy never mentioned Richardson?"

He looked down. Clearly, he was scared of something, and I wondered what Kevin's family lawyer and Sandy had cooked up to get this kid to lie under oath. "I don't remember that."

"Do you remember saying that Teddy never mentioned there were drugs in that bag?"

"I don't remember that."

"You don't remember or you didn't say it?"

"I don't remember saying it, no. What I just said was the truth."

He couldn't even look me in the eye. I wished like hell I had recorded that conversation earlier.

"You called him retarded, Freddy. Why did you say that?"

Sandy stood up with a sigh. "Your Honor, we've already been through this."

"I'm not asking about whether he is or is not mentally incapacitated, Judge. I'm asking why Freddy said that. What behaviors did he observe to make him say that? He can at least testify as to what he saw, can't he?"

Roscombe thought for a second and said, "I'll allow it."

I looked back to Freddy. "Why did you say that?"

"Because he is. I mean, I'm not a doctor or anything, but he's clearly retarded. And I don't mean that in a bad way. I don't know if that's the proper term for it anymore, but he doesn't get things very easy."

"How do you know that?"

"You can just tell. I mean, he didn't want to deliver that bag, but he couldn't form the words to tell us why."

"Did it seem like he was being pressured to deliver that bag?"

"Yeah."

All good stuff. But if I confronted him and said that Kevin had forced Teddy to sell the coke, Freddy would deny it. I'd just save it for my closing argument to the jury.

"Did Teddy ever mention Salvador Zamora by name?"

"No."

"Did he ever mention anybody who lived in that house by name?"

"No. I don't think he knew their names."

"So it seemed to you that someone had forced or pressured him into delivering that bag to a man he didn't know, is that right?"

"I think so. I mean, he looked really scared. I don't know. I've only seen him a few times so I don't know, but he seemed like he didn't want to be there."

I sat down and Sandy stood up and said, "Redirect, Your Honor?"

"Certainly."

She stood at the lectern again, her back stiff and straight, her butt cheeks clenched so hard I could see the outline through her suit pants.

"Did anyone else take responsibility for the cocaine that night?"

"Umm . . . no."

"Has anyone, that you know of, come forward and claimed this cocaine?"

"No. Not that I know."

"Did Mr. Thorne ever mention any other person who would be getting any proceeds of the cocaine sale?"

"No."

"Thank you, Mr. Willmore."

The judge looked at me and I shook my head. Better to quit with a few good statements than risk Freddy saying something new against us.

"You are excused," the judge said. "Next witness, Mrs. Tiles."

The next witness was a lab technician by the name of Coltrane. He was a small, white, nerdy guy who looked like he might pass out as he was being sworn in. He didn't look like a Coltrane.

Teddy leaned over to me. "I have to go to the bathroom."

"Can you hold it just a little longer?"

"No. I have to go to the bathroom now."

I rose, cutting off Sandy. "Your Honor, would it be possible to take a quick bathroom break?"

"Ms. Rollins, I would expect you to take care of those necessities on proper breaks."

"It's for Teddy, Judge." I never called a client by the term "defendant" or by their last name in front of a jury. I always used their first names and the prosecutor was always the "government's attorney"—a little trick to establish the power dynamic in the minds of the jurors.

He sighed. "Very well. Mrs. Tiles, let's take a quick ten-minute break before continuing with Dr. Coltrane."

The bailiff helped Teddy, and I went out back for a smoke. I sat on the edge of a large, solid-cement planter and lit a cigarette. I took out my phone and dialed Jack's number, but he didn't answer. Stefan answered when I called him.

"Hey," I said.

"Hey."

He sounded sad and I said, "What's going on?"

"What do you mean?"

"I can tell, Stefan. What's up?"

"Do you ever think maybe people don't want to discuss every detail of their lives with you?"

"Easy. Who took a dump in your Cheerios?"

I heard the phone click as it was dropped or thrown, and then Stefan got back on. "Sorry. Not in the right mental place right now."

"What's going on?"

"Nothing."

Marital discord in the Rollins home?

Shit. I needed to change my name. My maiden name had been Danielle Evelyn. Too bad—I liked Rollins. It rolled off the tongue easily.

"Come on, what is it?"

"We came to a compromise. I'll be halting my doctorate until Jack's out of the house. Then I'll be going back to school. I mean, it's the best we could both agree on, but I'm pretty bummed about it."

"So don't do it. Just finish."

"That's one thing I don't think you ever understood about marriage, Dani. It's a compromise. If you're gonna make it, it's a compromise." He sighed. "So, how's it going, anyway?"

"Shitty, Stefan. It's going shitty. You should see the way some of the jurors look at Teddy. They're supposed to be presuming he's innocent but that certainly doesn't apply."

"No one said the system was fair, Dani. Just that we're forced to live in it."

I inhaled a puff of smoke and let it out through my nose. "It'd be nice to have you here."

"Why?"

"I don't know."

We sat silently on the line—one of those awkward silences where you both have something to say, but neither person wants to be the first to speak.

"I better go," he said.

"All right. Tell Jack to call me when you see him."

I stomped out my cigarette, glanced at my reflection in a window to make sure I looked halfway presentable, and headed back into the courthouse.

47

Teddy had already sat down when I came back. He was tracing his finger along a carving on the tabletop that someone, probably in his spot, had whittled into the table: a heart with a knife through it.

"Can we go home now?" he asked as I sat.

"Not yet, buddy. Almost. This shouldn't last longer than today."

"And then we can go home?"

I stared at him a second and then cleared my throat and pretended to be looking at something on the legal pad in front of me. I scribbled a few notes and then pushed it away from me.

Coltrane would just establish that the drugs were in fact cocaine.

The next witness was Kevin and then Zamora, and the entire case hinged on what Zamora said. I slid something out of my bag and put it in my breast pocket. I tapped my pen against the table for a second and then rose and went over to Sandy and Double D, who didn't seem to have moved at all during the break.

"I wanna talk to him."

"To who?" Sandy asked.

"Zamora."

She shrugged. "Feel free. He's outside with a sheriff."

I went out and looked around. Zamora was just stepping off the elevator followed by a sheriff's deputy. I stood in front of the doors of the courtroom and folded my arms.

"I wanna talk," I said.

"Don't matter to me."

I opened a door to one of the attorney-client conference rooms and held it for Zamora. He went inside and the deputy stayed out. I was relieved, because he wasn't a client and the deputy had no duty to leave us alone. I shut the door behind me and sat down.

"What're you gonna say up there today?"

"Why don't you wait and see?"

"Why don't you just tell me?"

He grinned. "Nah, see, this time the law's on my side. I'm their star witness against your boy."

"You don't feel any guilt that an innocent person might get convicted for something he didn't do?"

"Shit, I don't care if he did it or not. I'm getting cut a sweet-ass deal. Witness protection, the works, baby."

"Witness protection? Not just for this case. Who else you ratting on?"

"Don't worry 'bout it. Ain't up to you."

I nodded, looking down to his shoes—alligator leather, expensive, and without a scuff on them. My shoes looked like they had been on a marathon through a forest. Whoever said crime didn't pay didn't get out much.

"You and I both know he's innocent, Salvador. Don't do this to him."

He rose. "Shit, girl, it's done. Don't care if he's innocent."

I waited until he was out of the room, took the digital recorder from my breast pocket and hit the "Stop" button.

After Coltrane, whose testimony only lasted ten minutes since I wasn't denying the drugs were cocaine, Kevin got up there. I didn't want a repeat of his emotional outburst at the preliminary hearing, so I kept my cross-examination minimal. A few questions about the gym bag and Teddy not playing sports: since Sandy hadn't drawn much attention to the FHY logo, I treaded lightly. A few more questions about Kevin's marijuana use, which he fully admitted and which caused Sandy to look like she was going to kill him. Guess she didn't cover that little tidbit in his interviews.

After ten minutes I sat down. Kevin was too believable to allow him much more time with the jury.

After Kevin, Salvador was sworn in. He had the goofiest grin up there, as if he were the Lord's chosen, doing God's work here on Earth. He felt self-righteous about this whole thing, and that was the worst part of it: he thought he was doing good.

Sandy asked his name and background and then paused a moment before going into the case. She was debating something, deciding which line of questioning to follow, and I didn't know why. The events of that night were straightforward; what topics did she have to stay away from?

"Describe the events of April second, Mr. Zamora."

"Yeah, it's really simple. Like that dude, Teddy, called me up and said he had a bag for me. I told him cool and that was it. Then I called Detective Steed. I told him I had someone doing a sell, and he said he was interested in being there."

"How did you know what Teddy was talking about when he called you?"

"He done it before."

"How many times?"

"Five, six times I think."

How could someone get up there and lie with a straight face like that about a kid? I wanted to run over and punch him in the liver. Instead, I had to do what I told my clients to do when they were upset and a jury was watching their every move: scribble down cuss words on the legal pad in front of you.

"So you knew him as someone who frequently sold narcotics to you?"

"Oh, yeah. Always coke. I told him we needed other shit, but he never messed with that stuff. Just the coke."

"How did he make contact with you?"

"He'd call me."

"Do you have evidence of these calls?"

He shook his head. "Nah. It wouldn't do nothin', anyway. He'd call from libraries or from like, 7-Elevens and shit like that."

"And what did he say when he called you that night, April second?"

"Um, he just said how many kilos he had and that he'd find a ride down that night. That was it."

"He didn't say anything else?"

"Nope. That's how it always was, though. He don't talk much."

"Do you remember the dates of the previous purchases of cocaine you made?"

"Nah. Like, every three months or some shit."

Sandy, I could tell, grew uncomfortable with the profanity. Her back stiffened and her jaw muscles flexed. I wondered if I could get Salvador to explode on the stand in a flurry of expletives and make Sandy squirm.

"What would you do with the cocaine?"

"We had a guy who had the hookup in Phoenix. A stash house is what you'd call it. He'd take the dope and spread it around. I was just the delivery boy between Teddy and the guys. That's it. I never sold the shit myself."

"Did Mr. Thorne ever explain to you where he was getting the coke from?"

He shook his head. "Nah. I didn't ask, neither. He would call, say how many kilos he had, and then tell me when he was gonna drop it off."

"Mr. Zamora, we have charged Mr. Thorne with a serious crime. Your testimony here is helping our case against him. Are you absolutely certain it was Mr. Thorne who called you and told you he had the cocaine to sell?"

"Yeah, I recognize his voice from the other times."

"And are you certain it was Mr. Thorne who showed up with the bag of cocaine on April second?"

"Yeah. Him and this other dude. But Teddy was holding the bag with all the coke."

Sandy lifted the gym bag. "This bag?"

"Yeah."

"Did you see the cocaine he was going to sell you?"

"Yup, the cops opened up the bag and I saw the bricks."

"And is this," she said, waving her hand over the bricks of cocaine, "the cocaine Mr. Thorne was going to sell you that night?"

"Yup, looks like it."

"Thank you for your cooperation in this matter, Mr. Zamora."

Sandy sat down.

So . . . that was what she'd been debating. Not a single question about how Salvador and Teddy had come into contact the first time.

I rose. "Mr. Zamora, how did you and Teddy first meet?"

"I don't remember."

I stepped between him and the lectern and stared into his eyes. "You're a drug smuggler, right? Not a drug dealer?"

"That's right."

"Pretty successful drug smuggler, from what I hear."

"Yeah, I do a'ight."

"How many times have you smuggled drugs to that stash house in Phoenix, do you think?"

"I don't know. Too many to count." He was almost glowing with pride.

"Would you say you're the most successful drug smuggler in this state?"

You could always rely on pride to give you the answers you were looking for.

"Most def."

"What were your impressions of my client the first time you met him?"

"Don't know. Nothin' really."

"Nothing stuck out to you about him?"

"I thought he might be retarded."

"You thought he might be retarded. So, how does someone who is mentally incapacitated to the level of a child meet up with the most successful drug smuggler in the state?"

I sneaked in the "to the level of a child" and was waiting for the objection, but it never came.

"I don't know," he said. "I don't remember."

"Oh, but that seems like such an interesting story. You don't think it's odd that you don't remember how you met the one mentally disabled kid in the country who magically has access to dump-truck loads of cocaine?"

"Objection, Your Honor," Sandy said.

"Sustained."

I moved closer to Zamora. "What are you getting in exchange for testifying against Teddy?"

He looked toward Sandy.

"Don't look at her. I asked you the question. What are you getting?"

Out of the corner of my eye, I saw Sandy give him a slow nod.

"They dismissing my case and putting me in witness protection."

"Wow. A free pass for the most successful drug smuggler in the state. That is quite a bargain for testifying against a handicapped kid, isn't it?"

He didn't say anything, though he certainly looked like he wanted to. He had probably been instructed that he couldn't discuss anyone else he would be testifying against.

I'd played with him enough. Time to pull out the big guns.

"Mr. Zamora, you know my client is innocent, don't you?"

"I don't know that."

"Really? You've never said to me that he's innocent?"

"No."

"We just had a conversation outside, do you remember that conversation?"

"Yeah," he said, shifting in his chair. "You asked me a buncha questions and I said I didn't know."

"That's it? That's all you said?"

"Yeah."

I took out the digital recorder from my pocket and hit "Play."

What're you gonna say up there today?

Why don't you wait and see?

Salvador looked like he needed a new pair of underwear.

"Objection!" Sandy shrieked. "Approach."

I stopped the recording and we came up in front of the judge. Sandy started in without taking a breath.

"Your Honor, she recorded a conversation with my witness without telling me and without telling him. I need a copy of the recording and notice of her intent to use it, at the very least. She can't just spring it on the jury out of nowhere."

"It's impeachment evidence, Your Honor. I can spring it anytime."

Roscombe thought about it a moment and said, "It is impeachment evidence if he contradicts his earlier testimony. And I'd like to hear it myself. I'll allow it."

Whoa. Did hell finally have a snowstorm? Did piggies finally join the ranks of their fowl brethren? I couldn't quite believe he'd actually ruled in my favor on an issue. I turned back to the jury and hit "Play" again.

The rest of the recording played out to them, and when it was over I turned to Zamora and said, "You know this boy is innocent, and you're still testifying to put him away. Hope the witness protection is worth it."

I sat down. A little more dramatic than I normally liked, but it served my purposes. Besides, Zamora never actually said Teddy was innocent: that's just how I liked it framed for the jury. Really all he did was hint that he knew more than he was letting on, so I didn't want to overplay my hand.

I glanced at Sandy, who sat there staring into Zamora's eyes like a witch about to cast a curse. I couldn't even imagine the hell she had in store for him when this was over.

She rose. "You never actually said he was innocent, did you?"

"No," Zamora said. "Because he's not. I was just playing with that attorney. She came to my house and pissed me off. I'm telling you, though, that dude, Teddy, called me up a bunch of times and said he had coke. I don't remember how we met. I think it was through one of my guys who works in Salt Lake at a lab or some shit. But it was him."

Sandy slowly looked back at me. "No further questions, Your Honor."

I watched the jury. They didn't like Salvador.

I looked at Teddy who was staring down at his shoes and rocking back and forth restlessly. I put my hand on his back and for the first time in the trial felt like we might actually have a shot at this thing.

48

We took a break for a late lunch. We had blocked out two days for this trial, but it looked like it would finish by this afternoon, which wasn't unusual on a Roscombe jury date. The one thing I could say about Roscombe was that he was efficient.

I bought a sandwich from a café up the street and sat at the counter by myself. I didn't feel like eating, and just stared at the tuna fish in my sandwich and wondered what the little guy had been like in life.

The trial had gone as well as could be expected. I caught their star witness lying on the stand. He didn't exactly say what I made it sound like he said on the recording, but he certainly didn't say Teddy was guilty either. Hopefully, it would be enough to raise reasonable doubt with the jury. But it was never certain: he was a black kid being tried by an all-white jury in a county known for racial tension. We were playing roulette justice.

I pushed the sandwich away and wished I could have a beer instead. Then my phone rang. It was Jack.

"Hey," I said.

"Hi, Mom. Dad told me you called."

"Yeah, I just wanted to hear about your day."

"It was fine."

"That's it? It was fine?"

"Yeah, it was fine."

I put my elbows on the counter and, for the first time that day, actually relaxed a little. "So what's going on with you? How's soccer?"

"Boring. I like baseball."

"I like baseball, too. It's relaxing. Why don't you play baseball?"

"Maybe, I don't know. They practice, like, every day after school."

"So what? It'll be fun. You gotta follow what you love. Be a Jim Morrison."

"Who?"

"Never mind." I waved to the cashier behind the counter and pointed to a bottle of Sunkist. She popped it open and slid it in front of me. "So what else is new?"

"Nothin'. We're going to the mall, Mom, so I gotta go."

"What do you guys do at the mall so much?"

"Nothin'. Just hang out. Get something to eat."

"Well, how about me and you get something to eat tomorrow? I'm free all day."

"Maybe."

"I'll take a maybe." I paused. I wanted to tell him that, after the wedding, I would be moving, but the words wouldn't come out. "Jack, I just want you to know you're the best thing in my life. You're my knight in shining armor."

"Don't be weird, Mom. I gotta go; they're gonna be here soon."

"I love you."

"Love you."

I hung up and noticed I had a smile on my face that hadn't been there before.

I still wasn't hungry, but I sipped at my drink slowly. I didn't feel like being anywhere near a courtroom right now, and the thought of Teddy sitting in a holding cell eating whatever the guards could scrounge from the cafeteria wasn't helping my appetite.

Eventually I had to suck it up and go back. I rose from the stool at the counter and noticed for the first time that four of the jurors were sitting together at a booth. They smiled at me and I smiled back. I once had a mistrial declared because I had said hello to some jurors walking down the hall. This time I was extremely careful and hurried past them.

When I got back to the court, Sandy wasn't there but Double D was. He was flipping through some pages when I sat in the chair next to him.

"I can't do anything," he said, not taking his eyes off the page. "I already told you."

"She's not a trial lawyer, Jasper."

"So?"

"So she looks to you for advice. If you told her you guys were losing and to give my boy a misdemeanor with no more jail, she would do it."

He sighed and leaned back, tossing the paper on the tabletop. "We are losing, aren't we?"

"Your star player just broke his ankle. He got caught in a lie and the recording made it sound like he knew Teddy was innocent. Get me a misdemeanor. Everybody's happy."

"I can't."

"Why not? I mean, at least bring it up and see what she says."

He shook his head. "She's taking this one seriously. I don't know why."

"Shit, I know why."

He looked at me, and I saw genuine surprise on his face. He didn't know the Führer's master plan to craft a pure race, from childhood on. It surprised me that Sandy hadn't trusted him with that knowledge. Or maybe she had, and he was just too dense or naïve to realize what she was saying.

"Why?" he asked.

"You should ask her. Frankly, you wouldn't believe me if I told you."

He picked up his paper again. "I know how bad she wants this. I'm sorry, but there's nothing I can do."

I let out a long breath and stared at him, disgust rolling up and down my body like the shockwaves of an earthquake. "Do you know that the Nazis didn't have high suicide rates?"

"What?"

"The Nazis. After the war ended, they didn't have high suicide rates. All the horrible shit they did, and they could still live with themselves. You know who *had* high suicide rates? The civilian contractors who collaborated with the Nazis. The guys who never fired a single shot in the war. They couldn't live with themselves. You wanna know why?"

"I'm sure you'll tell me."

"They couldn't live with themselves because inaction is action, Jasper. God won't forgive you for sitting one out. They could've done something to stop the injustice they were seeing and they didn't, and they couldn't live with themselves, and you won't be able to either."

I went back to my table, unable to look at him. I kept my head down over my phone and reviewed the notes I had made about my closing arguments. Sandy came in a few minutes later, and Teddy was brought in a little after that. He had Jell-O smeared on his face, and I asked the bailiff for napkins and wiped it off. He said, "I had a hamburger and applesauce and Jell-O."

"I can tell, buddy. It's all over your face."

I tossed the napkins in the trash as Roscombe lumbered into the courtroom. The sadistic bastard was humming something. He actually looked happy. Happy to be in a courtroom where someone's life was at stake and he had rigged the odds to give him such an uphill battle that it matched Custer's Last Stand. Actually, Custer could have run away at any time. Teddy's situation required him to just sit there and take it.

"Okay," Roscombe said, "looks like we're all back. Did we have any preliminary matters to handle?"

"Your Honor," I said, rising, unable to hold it in. "I would renew my objection to this entire proceeding. This court does not have jurisdiction over my client, and the law and procedure required by the *Rules of Juvenile Procedure* were blatantly ignored. I was not allowed sufficient time to explore defenses for my client, most notably a mental health defense. This entire case is a gross miscarriage of justice violating the Fourth, Fifth, and Sixth Amendment rights of my client."

"So noted," he said, putting on his glasses without looking at me.

"That's it?"

"Excuse me?"

"You're not going to justify all this to me or try to say it was all in accordance with this or that case?"

"No, Counsel, I will not. I am the judge here, and you are a guest in my courtroom. I do not have to explain anything to you."

"Judge," I said, anger rising in me, "look at him. Just fucking look at him! He doesn't belong here. Somewhere under your Frankensteinish exterior I know is a human being. You can't let this happen to him."

He grinned and slowly removed his glasses, placing them on the bench. "Counsel, if your client didn't want to be in this spot, maybe he shouldn't have sold drugs. Now, are we ready to call in the jury?"

Nothing. It was like talking to someone who'd had his empathy surgically removed. That was the most frightening type of person: someone who had conclusively made up his mind and refused to be persuaded any other way.

On the verge of tears—something I sure as hell wasn't going to show Roscombe—I said, "You're right. How silly of me to believe fairness has anything to do with a court of law. Hey, drinks on me after this, Judge. I mean, after we firebomb a black church or something. Maybe burn a few crosses on lawns. Is that still a thing? Because the cross seems so Middle Ages. We should update it to something else, iPods or something."

"Counsel, you must really enjoy the holding cell."

"Actually, it's better than my first apartment."

He flexed his jaw muscles and said, "Sit down."

I didn't obey. Fuck it. Everything was rigged against me anyway. Maybe it was best to go out in a blaze of glory and get into the papers as the lawyer who got arrested during a trial for nailing the judge in the head with her purse. It would at least call attention to Teddy's case.

I felt a hand on my arm, a soft touch. Teddy looked up at me with his big eyes and said, "Sit down, Danielle."

If I exploded, I wouldn't suffer. I'd be in the holding cells maybe one night. Teddy's trial would be declared a mistrial, and new counsel would be appointed. The new lawyer would have to catch up on the case and then would probably plead him the first chance he got. Teddy would be held in jail, and then transferred to prison within a few months. The only person who would truly suffer for my actions was Teddy.

I sat back down.

"Now," Roscombe said. "I have here the jury instructions both parties have agreed to. Are there any amendments or corrections I should be aware of?"

"No, Your Honor," Sandy said.

"No," I said, unable to look at him.

"Excellent. Now I believe, Mrs. Tiles, you have one more witness, is that right?"

"Correct."

"And Ms. Rollins, will your client be taking the stand today?"

"Yes."

"Okay, then I anticipate," he said, looking at the clock on the wall, "that we will take a quick recess after these two witnesses and then start into closing arguments. I prefer to give the jury over to deliberation before dinner." He looked to the bailiff. "Please bring out the jury."

The bailiff shouted for everyone to rise for the jury and we all stood. When we sat back down, Sandy called Detective Bo Steed, who strolled to the stand like a man who had just eaten Thanksgiving dinner and needed a place to lie down. He was sworn in, gave his name and how long he'd been with the sheriff's office, and then went into a résumé-reading frenzy. He went through every qualification he had and every seminar he'd ever attended. Normally I would stipulate to his credentials to get him to shut up, but it was taking so long that the jury looked annoyed, so I let him keep going.

Sandy finally asked her first question. "Tell us what you remember about April second, Detective."

Steed went into detail about getting the tip on a buy between Zamora and Teddy. He said Zamora had been working with them, and had said that Teddy had made frequent sales of cocaine to him before.

"We were positioned around the home and listening on microphones secreted throughout the porch and on Mr. Zamora's person. Once we had notification of the exchange, we moved in and made the arrests."

"But you arrested Mr. Zamora, too, correct?"

"Correct. It's customary to arrest CIs on a bust so that suspicion isn't immediately thrown on them."

"I'd like to play a video for you, Detective Steed. Please narrate it for us."

The video showed the interviews with all three boys. Kevin, Freddy, and Clint all pointed the finger at Teddy. Steed explained what he was doing throughout the video, why he asked the questions he did, and the jury looked attentive for once.

I was really interested in the video with Freddy, but not one of the jurors reacted in any way. They didn't see that the detective was subtly leading him in his questions. I would get up and point it out to the jury, just in case, but I knew they couldn't see it. Steed was too good at covering it up.

Next, Sandy said, "And you have another audio recording of the exchange, is that right?"

"Yes."

"Your Honor, for this recording, I've marked it 'plaintiff's exhibit four' and would move for its introduction."

"No objection," I said.

The audio was of the actual exchange. I'd already heard it a couple times. You could barely hear what was said, and someone sounding like Teddy said something like "here," and then Zamora said "thanks." But it could've been Kevin, too. The audio just wasn't clear.

All in all, Steed's testimony hadn't really added anything. I debated whether to question him at all, but then I rose and said, "You admitted today that Mr. Zamora is a confidential informant, is that right?"

"Yes."

"And Detective, it's customary not to use confidential informants once their identities have been revealed in a case, correct?"

"That is correct."

"So we can assume that Mr. Zamora is no longer working as a CI?"

"That's correct."

"How many cases did he work on with you?"

"Over the years Mr. Zamora and I worked together, I would say about thirty."

"Thirty cases, and now he's done. Each case a CI works is dangerous for that CI, isn't it?"

"It is, yes. They're dealing with individuals who typically don't hesitate to use violence against those who testify against them."

"So a CI wants to stop working with you as quickly as possible, right?"

"I guess so."

"'I guess so' or 'yes'?"

"Yes."

"So Zamora just had to wrap this case up and he'd earned his freedom, so to speak?"

"I wouldn't know about that. As I said, he informed us of a frequent buyer, and we moved on the information."

"Did he have any evidence of these frequent buys?"

"Such as?"

"Any text messages, voice mails, photographs . . . anything corroborating his story that he'd bought from my client several times before?"

"No, nothing like that, ma'am."

"So it's just his word that these previous transactions took place?"

"Correct."

"The word of someone who gained his freedom as a CI by setting up this deal?"

"I wouldn't characterize it that way, but yes, that's essentially correct."

"Mr. Zamora ever lie to you?"

Steed hesitated and glanced at Sandy. I got between them, so he was forced to look at me.

"Umm, yes, ma'am."

"What did he lie about?"

"There was a previous incident where he had accused someone of purchasing narcotics from him, and it turned out to be false."

My heart raced. One member of the jury shook his head. I moved closer to Steed. "Who?"

"I don't recall his name. Monty something or other."

"What did Zamora say?"

"Basically that this person was a frequent drug buyer and had bought from him recently. We tracked the man down and found that he had left the state for work and had been gone about three weeks. He couldn't have purchased drugs from Mr. Zamora."

"Did you figure out why Zamora lied?"

"He admitted that he was incorrect. I couldn't say why he did it."

"He did it to impress you, right? I mean, you said CIs want to be done working with you as fast as possible."

"I guess that's accurate, yes."

"And after you knew that this CI was a flat-out liar, you continued to use him?"

"I didn't say he was a flat-out liar."

"What would you call it, Detective? I mean, you saw him lie on the stand today, right?"

"He was mistaken back then." He hesitated. "Frankly, I believe he was high when he was speaking to us. Mr. Zamora had a drug problem himself."

"What was his drug of choice?"

"Heroin."

"How often would he use?"

"I couldn't say."

"Were there other times he called you while high?"

"I don't believe so, but I can't say for certain."

"Can you say for certain he wasn't high when he called you about Teddy and claimed Teddy set this whole thing up?"

"I . . . can't be certain. No."

I turned and looked at Sandy. "Are you aware, Detective, that the State did not give any of that information over to the defense in this case?"

"Objection," Sandy said. "That's a discovery issue that has nothing to do with the jury."

"Overruled."

Two objections overruled in my favor was a new record in Roscombe's courtroom. When this case eventually went up on appeal, a couple of objections in my favor would make it look like he was actually hearing me out, so he had an incentive, but still. I would take what I could get.

I turned back to the detective. "A lying drug addict. Perhaps you should choose your CIs more carefully, Detective."

He didn't say anything.

"One more thing, Detective. Do you know an officer Stuart Lively?"

He glanced to Sandy. "I do, yes."

"He was just a few minutes away from this bust, wasn't he?"

"Yes, he was."

"Every other officer in this case that came to help was much farther away, right?"

"I don't recall."

"But Lively was on his way down when you told him that it wasn't necessary. Do you recall that?"

"I do."

I stepped close to him. "Officer Lively is black, isn't he, Detective?"

"That had nothing to do with—"

"The one black officer nearby and you tell him to turn away but accept two white officers farther away helping you on the case. Seems odd, doesn't it?"

"I . . ."

He didn't know what to say, and it confirmed what I suspected: Stuart Lively had been turned away because of his race.

"You were gonna get the one black kid in this whole thing and Officer Lively might've gotten in the way of that."

He turned a shade of light pink. "I didn't care about his race."

He said it just a little too loud, a little too forceful. I glanced to the jury and they were all staring at him. I figured I'd gotten as much mileage out of him as I could.

I sat down. Sandy stood. "Did Mr. Zamora have an opportunity to lie in this case?"

"No, ma'am. After the mix-up before, we made sure to monitor everything. I saw the defendant with my own eyes carry that bag up to the porch and hand it off."

"Thank you, Detective, no further questions."

Roscombe said, "You may step down, Detective Steed. Any further witnesses, Mrs. Tiles?"

"No, Your Honor. At this time, the State would move to introduce the additional exhibits, and rests."

"Any objection?"

"No," I said.

"Okay, the time is now yours, Ms. Rollins."

I looked at Teddy. He was playing some game with his fingers and smiling to himself.

"You ready to tell them what happened, buddy?"

He looked up and around the courtroom and then whispered to me, "I don't want to, Danielle."

"Why not?"

"I'm scared."

"I'll be with you. Right next to you, I promise."

He swallowed and looked around a little more before nodding his head. I helped him to the stand and then stood in front of him.

"Spell your name, Teddy."

49

Teddy looked like he might pass out. I stepped closer to him and wished I could reach out and hold his hand, but I had to look dispassionate. Jurors didn't like to see lawyers who cared too much about their clients; they had to care just the right amount. I had always thought that was a good policy—why would you want to listen to someone who had their feelings wrapped up in a case?—but now I saw how ridiculous that was. Why would you want to listen to someone who could be a robot and detach like that?

"Um, Teddy Thorne," he said. "I'm Teddy Thorne."

I nodded and he smiled. "Teddy, do you understand what's going on here today?"

"Um . . . yeah. Yeah I'm friends with Kevin, see. I'm friends with Kevin and Kevin's in trouble."

"Is Kevin the only one in trouble?"

He glanced away from me, as though embarrassed. "No. No I'm in trouble, too."

"What are you in trouble for?"

"For the bag."

"What bag?"

He lifted his arm and pointed to the gym bag on the prosecution table.

"What was in that bag?" I asked.

"Bad things."

I leaned forward on the banister in front of him. I wanted to be as close to him as possible. "What bad things?"

He shook his head. "I don't know."

"You don't know what was in there?"

"No. Just bad things, see."

"Who gave you the bag with bad things?"

He didn't answer me, just began rocking back and forth.

"Teddy, please, who gave you the bag?"

He kept shaking his head and the rocking motion was getting worse. I might've made a mistake putting him up here, but the jury had to hear it from him. They had to see that he wasn't capable of this.

"Teddy," I said, swallowing. It felt like hot lead going down my throat. This was definitely not something I wanted to say, and I debated not saying it, but then I remembered what was on the line. I had hoped against hope that he would tell me who gave him the bag. Without that, I had only one tactic left: show the jury Teddy didn't have the mental capacity to do this.

"Teddy, you're not like other boys, are you?"

"What do you mean, Danielle?"

He wasn't going to make this any easier for me. "You have a certain condition, don't you?"

He looked down, probably at his shoes, as he continued to rock. "I'm just like everyone else. Everyone is different, Danielle."

"I know, Teddy. I know everyone is different. But can you talk about why you're different?"

"I . . . I talk slow. And I can't do things some people can do, but my mama said there's things I can do that other people can't do, see. There's things I can do."

I folded my arms, fighting back the emotion that choked me like a lump of clay. "Teddy, you're not very smart are you?"

The pain of having to say that stung like a hot needle going into my heart. I didn't have a choice, and I knew that, but it didn't make it any easier.

"I'm smart," he said. "I'm smart, Danielle."

"Not smart like other people are smart, though, right? What's the capital of our state, Teddy?"

"I'm smart," he said, staring right at me. His eyes glimmered off the tears forming, and I wanted to turn away from him, but I didn't let myself do it. I had to stand there and look him in the eyes. I deserved this pain for what I was about to do. "I'm smart, Danielle."

"Teddy, what's your favorite movie?"

He paused a second, and the pain was replaced with a slow smile. "I like *George of the Jungle*. I like *George of the Jungle* because he can swing into trees and he swings on the trees and hits them and it's so funny."

"*George of the Jungle*'s a kid's movie. But you're not a kid, are you?"

His lips moved as though an answer was coming out, but nothing came. He didn't understand what I was doing. I couldn't have prepared him for this; if I had, the jury would've seen through it. The pain he felt had to be genuine . . . and I'd never felt like more of a piece of shit.

"Who's the president of the United States, Teddy?"

He didn't answer at first, and then he looked at me, almost pleadingly, and said, "I don't know, Danielle."

"If you drank one third of a glass of water, how much would be left in the glass?"

"I don't like water from a glass."

"What size shoes do you wear, Teddy?"

"Um . . . Thirty."

"That's not a real shoe size. You don't know anything about numbers, do you, Teddy?"

"I can count, Danielle. I'm smart like everyone else."

274

"What city are we in right now?"

Sandy stood up. "Your Honor, I don't understand how any of this is relevant."

"She's accusing my client of being a drug mastermind. My client doesn't even know his shoe size or that people can't really swing into trees without getting hurt. I have a right to explore his mental capacity."

Roscombe shrugged and said, "I'll allow it, but I won't allow exploration into actual mental health disorders as no foundation has been laid."

I turned back to Teddy, who was still staring at me with his large brown eyes. "What's two hundred plus ten, Teddy?"

"It's . . . It's three hundred, see. Because three hundred is bigger than two hundred. It's three hundred."

"It's not three hundred. It's two hundred and ten. You can't add or subtract large numbers, can you?"

"I'm good," he said, furiously rocking back and forth now, nearly stuttering, "I'm good at a lot of things, see. There's a lot of things I'm good at, Danielle."

"You don't know what city we're in, do you?"

"Stop it," he said.

"Teddy, what city are we in?"

"I know where we are, see. We're in court. We're in court because you said we're going to court and I have to wear a tie. I have to wear a tie."

I stepped closer to him. "What city are we in right now?"

"Stop it, Danielle."

"Teddy, what city are we in?"

"Stop it!"

"What city, Teddy?"

"I don't know! I don't know, Danielle. I don't know. I'm not smart. I'm not a smart person. I don't know things and I get confused and I forget things. I'm not smart, Danielle," he said, crying now. "I'm not smart."

Tears streamed down his cheeks as he continued to rock. I turned away from him as I wiped the tears away from my own eyes, and sat down. "Nothing further for now, Judge."

Sandy stood up. She waited a moment. "Did you give this bag full of bad things to Mr. Zamora?"

He was silent a long while. "Yeah. Yeah I had to give the bag to him so I did."

"And he gave you a bag full of money?"

"Yeah, I had to get the money, see. I had to give him the bag and get the money."

"Did Kevin give you this bag?"

"Kevin's my friend, see."

"Thank you. No further questions."

I stood up again for redirect and said, "Teddy, answer me honestly. It's very important: Who told you to give that bag to Mr. Zamora?"

He shook his head. "I gave him the bag."

"Who told you to do it? Where'd you get the bag?"

Please answer me.

He shook his head again and said, "That was not nice, Danielle. You're not being nice to me."

I had to put my hands on the table to keep myself up. "Teddy, please, please tell these people who told you to give that bag to Mr. Zamora."

He stuttered out a few words and then said, "I gave him the bag, see. I gave him the bag and I had to get the money."

It hadn't worked. I was hoping he would say everything I needed him to say, but, even after all this, he still wouldn't betray someone he thought was his friend. I turned to the audience. Kevin was still there. I stared him in the eye and he looked away.

I sat back down. "No further questions."

50

I had no more witnesses. I had no evidence. I had nothing to present to the jury that would scream in their face: "This kid is innocent! There's no way he could've done this. He's clearly covering for his shit-bag friend."

After Teddy got off the stand, Roscombe said, "I'd like to take an hour dinner break before we come back for closing arguments. At that point, we'll be turning over the case for your deliberation, ladies and gentlemen. So please be back in an hour, and do not talk to anyone about this case while outside of this courtroom. All rise for the jury."

We rose as the jury filed out. I kept my eyes down on the table. I couldn't look at them, or at Teddy, or at anyone. I felt like guzzling a bottle of whiskey and crawling into my bed and never coming out again.

I watched as the bailiff took Teddy away. He didn't look back at me.

I turned to Sandy and said, "Have dinner with me."

"You want to have dinner together?"

"Yes. And I promise I'll be civil."

"Sure. Why not?"

This was the last chance I would have to convince Sandy to give me a palatable deal. Once the case went to deliberation, she wouldn't budge.

We chose an Italian restaurant up the block and I met her there. We sat at a table in the center of the restaurant, away from the windows, and we both ordered water. When the waiter left, she said, "You went after him pretty hard."

"I wasn't left with much of a choice. Roscombe didn't allow me to defend him."

She shrugged. "I guess that'll be decided when this case is appealed."

"Guess so."

She looked around the restaurant. "I'm surprised you'd want to sit with me. I assume it's to try to get me to make a better offer. It's not happening, you know."

"You saw him up there. He doesn't know anything. He's clearly covering for Kevin."

"If it's that clear then the jury should see it."

"Juries see what they want to see. I have no idea what they're going to do. But neither do you. Give us a misdemeanor with no more jail."

She shook her head. "No."

"Why? Because you have some master plan, and you need this case appealed? I know you have connections on the appellate court and the supreme, but I don't give a shit about that. I just want this kid to have a life."

"The parole board will see his condition and let him out the first chance they get."

"His '*condition*'? You agree with me that he's too disabled to do this?"

"I never said that. The mentally disabled are capable of a lot more than we give them credit for, good or bad."

"I still don't understand why you're doing this. I've had cases far worse than Teddy's get settled by your office without you guys putting up any fight. Is it really like you said—having control over juveniles? What do you think that's going to get you? You'll just be creating new felons, so unless you want that sort of thing there really isn't a point."

She stared at me. "Why would I want new felons?"

The way she said it made it clear that she did. She wanted me to know it without actually saying it. I didn't understand at first. She *wanted* new felons? Hoover County was gun country and felons wouldn't be able to own guns, which meant a loss of revenue to the NRA and voting and . . .

My stomach suddenly churned and something was pushing its way up into my throat. I had to swallow to make sure I wouldn't throw up.

"Voting," I said, the word escaping my lips like poison. "It's voting. If they're tried as adults and get convicted of felonies, they can't vote when they turn eighteen."

She looked completely impassive, neither moving nor speaking, just calmly staring at me.

"You don't want blacks voting. Their numbers are starting to grow, and that has you and your buddies scared."

"Don't act so shocked. Our entire justice system is set up as a tool to be used to maintain order. This is how you maintain order. Why do you think possession of narcotics wasn't a felony until the Civil Rights Movement? Why does it continue to be a felony when no one but the user is harmed by its use?"

"I thought this was about cleaning up the county, but this is about voting," I said, my mind reeling. "You don't want a large black population to have political power because they'll vote you and people like you out of office."

She leaned back and glanced around the restaurant before resting her eyes on me again. "They can't be trusted. They think only in the short term, only for the immediate future. It's much better this way for everyone."

"This isn't for their good, it's for yours."

"You're blaming me for something that I inherited. Do you know we're the only advanced society on the planet that doesn't allow their inmates to vote? Why do you think that is? It's because we're the only society that has an entire community descended from slaves. It's those rotten genes, community zeitgeist, whatever you want to call it, but they can't be trusted to vote for their own good."

She seemed so normal when you looked at her, like a soccer mom driving her kids to school, volunteering for the PTA, recycling . . . Innocent. And there she sat, saying some of the most evil things I'd ever heard anyone say—a Nazi with a Chanel purse and a Fitbit on her wrist.

"They're people, Sandy. They're fucking *people*. You're purposely making it so you take their right to vote away when they're children."

"It's how it's always been. Possession of crack is punished ten times as severely as possession of cocaine, even though the only difference between them is baking soda. Crack is a black drug, cocaine is a white drug. Our system is predicated on certain people not being able to assert power based on choices they've made. Like I said, drugs weren't felonies until the Civil Rights Movement. They weren't even illegal until after Prohibition. Then we had hundreds of unemployed federal agents and didn't know what to do with all of them. So the government pushed for more illegalization. That's our system, Danielle. The powerful pull the strings, and the weak dance. I didn't invent it. I wouldn't have wanted to invent it. But it is what it is, and I have to do the best I can for my community."

"This has nothing to do with choices they've made. You're judging them on the basis of their skin color."

"Call it what you want. The problem with you bleeding-heart types is you just don't have the spine to do what's necessary to make this country great again."

"We don't need to make it great again—it's always been great. Not because of people like you, but in spite of people like you. And when that jury acquits my client, we're gonna file a lawsuit so big against the county and against you personally that you'll be working a century to pay it off."

"Do your best," she said with a little shrug.

I rose to leave.

"What about dinner?" she said.

"I lost my appetite."

51

I sat outside the courtroom doors, eating a granola bar from a vending machine and staring at the tiled floor. There was no one around, and the courthouse had an eerie, haunted-house type of feel to it when it was quiet. I pictured how many people had been sentenced to death here. How many people took their last steps as free men before being shackled for the rest of their lives? How much pain had these walls absorbed, and was the taint still in them?

I had stopped at a copy shop to print a photo, and I took it out of my pocket and stared at it for a second before slipping it back in.

The elevator opened and Will stepped out. I hadn't told him to come; he just showed up on his own.

He smiled at me as he came and sat down. I could smell his cologne—the same one he had worn the entire time I knew him. I put my head on his shoulder.

"I'm glad you came."

"I thought maybe you could use someone in your corner. Besides, my other clients don't count when it comes to you."

"I'm sure you've got better things to do than sit here with a washed-up defense lawyer."

He looked at me, really looked at me. "There's no place I'd rather be than next to you."

"Will . . ."

"I know," he said, holding up his hands in surrender. "I know. We're best friends and maybe something else, too, but we're not sure what. I get it. But I need you to know . . . I love you."

"Will—"

"No, let me say it. I have to say it just once. I love you, Danielle. I have loved you from the second I met you and it's never stopped. If Stefan doesn't realize what he's missing then forget him. I will worship the ground you walk on for the rest of your life, if you let me. Relationships, the ones that last, don't start with good looks and sex. They start with friendships. And you are the best friend I've ever had. I'm your soul mate, not him."

A long silence passed between us, and he finally said, "Glad that wasn't awkward."

I lightly punched him in the arm. "Why did you have to say that, you big dummy?"

"Because it's true."

Did I feel the same? I didn't know. I couldn't think about that now. Instead I stared down at the floor. "I can't even think right now, Will."

"How's it going in there, anyway?"

"Good as can be. Their star witness might look like he was lying. That Perry Mason shit never happens, but this might've been one of those moments if the jury buys into it."

"So you think an acquittal?"

"I don't know . . . I don't know. The deck is so stacked against us. But I guess you never know with a jury."

He put his hand on my back and gently rubbed, something he'd done a million times before during trials he helped on because he knew I didn't have good posture and my back frequently ached. "Where's he gonna live when he gets out of this?"

"I don't know. Maybe I can try and get him—"

The doors to the courtroom opened. The bailiff pressed the door-stops down with his boot and said, "The judge is back."

"I can't stay too long," Will said. "But I'll be here when you need me."

We filed inside. Will sat in the back of the courtroom. Sandy and Double D were already there. It always bothered me that prosecutors were allowed to use the same entrances and exits as the judges and clerks. It gave court a real "them vs. everyone else" feel. I sat down at the defense table while Roscombe wrote something in a file and handed it to the clerk. Teddy was brought out. I tried to smile, and he didn't smile back.

"That was mean, Danielle," he said as he was seated next to me.

"Buddy, I didn't mean any of it. I had to do it in front of the jury. We have to play pretend that you're not smart. That way they'll feel sorry for you and might let you go. Don't you want to come home?"

He nodded. "I miss *SpongeBob SquarePants*."

"Yeah, I miss watching it, too."

"Both parties ready to proceed?" Roscombe said.

"Yes, Your Honor."

"Yes."

He nodded to the bailiff, who said, "All rise for the jury."

The jury filed back in. The judge said, "Ladies and gentlemen, you have under your seats a copy of the jury instructions. Please review them with me as I read aloud."

We went through each instruction. It was honestly the most painful part of a trial for me. The instructions in this case had been whittled down to fifty-two, and Roscombe read each one—enunciated each word, each letter, as though the jury were a bunch of children. By the end, some of the jurors looked like they had headaches. Although Roscombe took half as much time as any other judge.

After twenty minutes, he said, "Ladies and gentlemen of the jury, it is now time for closing arguments. As I stated previously, closing arguments are not evidence, and are the opinions of the attorneys in relation to the evidence presented today in court. You may give whatever weight to the attorneys' statements you feel appropriate." He looked at Sandy. "Mrs. Tiles."

"Thank you, Your Honor," she said, getting up and approaching the jury. "And thank you, ladies and gentlemen of the jury. We appreciate your service here today in this important matter." She stepped to the whiteboard near the jury and uncapped a marker. She drew a puzzle piece in the center of the board. "This case may seem like disjointed facts, and it's easier to think of those facts if you look at them like a puzzle. Each fact is a piece of that puzzle, and if we take them as a whole, the entire picture becomes clear."

She drew a puzzle piece in the corner and wrote inside it: *Four Witnesses.*

She proceeded to summarize the testimony of Kevin and his friends and Detective Steed. "Now, you also heard from Mr. Zamora, who counsel claims was caught being dishonest with you. Unfortunately, that is simply the nature of the confidential informants we deal with. If they were honest, they wouldn't be criminals."

This got a slight chuckle from the jury. How adorable.

"But just because he was dishonest about one thing doesn't mean he was being dishonest about the transaction, especially since so many other people saw it take place. You also heard the audio recording of the handoff itself. The fact is that the evidence is overwhelming."

She drew other puzzle pieces and wrote inside them: *Gym bag, Money received,* and *Audio recording.*

"All these pieces, taken independently, may not amount to the standard of 'beyond a reasonable doubt' that the judge explained in the jury instructions. But," she said, holding up a finger as though she were lecturing, "taken together . . ." She drew a square and wrote *Guilty* in the center. "Taken together, they all add up to one thing: Mr. Thorne sold those drugs to Mr. Zamora. He did it, and we all know it. I would ask you to do the only thing that justice demands, and that is find him guilty."

She sat down. She didn't even address his mental status. She didn't have to. Prosecutors got rebuttal time after a defense closing, which meant they could save their big guns for when I couldn't respond. I took a deep breath and stood up. I looked at Teddy, and then removed the photo I had printed at the copy shop from my pocket. I approached the jury and held it up so they could see it.

"This is George Stinney Junior. Young black kid, not unlike Teddy. George is the youngest person we have ever executed in this country: fourteen years old. He was accused of killing two white girls. The evidence against him was that he talked to the girls on the day they were killed. The jury was all whites, since blacks weren't given the right to be on juries at the time. Three detectives took the stand and testified that George had confessed to the crime. George's public defender was a tax commissioner in the middle of a reelection campaign. He didn't ask a single question, even though George insisted he had never confessed. The jury's deliberation took minutes. The trial lasted one day, and he was executed two and a half months later.

"When he walked into the execution chamber, he was carrying a Bible, and he had to use the Bible as a booster seat because he didn't reach the electrodes. After the first shock, the face mask slipped off, revealing his tear-filled eyes and the saliva dripping from his mouth. They secured it to him again and again shocked him, and then the child died.

"Some decades later, a white man from a rich family confessed to the crimes, to his family on his deathbed. George's only crime was being a black kid who had talked to two white girls, and the government— your government, in your name—killed him for it." I looked at Sandy. "Would we be here right now if Teddy Thorne was white? This case has nothing to do with facts; it has to do with the color of a man's skin. Blacks in this country are convicted at four times the rate whites are for identical crimes. The death penalty is given to black defendants at five times the rate as white defendants for identical crimes. But the law says that punishments must be determined based on the circumstances of a case, not the color of the defendant's skin."

I pointed to Teddy. "You've got a mentally disabled black kid with three white accusers against him, three white accusers who have been friends forever and would cover Kevin's butt, since he's probably the one who actually got the drugs and set up the deal. And let's not forget the sleazy confidential informant who got up there and lied to your faces. We can't believe a single word that scumbag said, and yet the prosecution joked about CIs being untrustworthy as though it has no implications. The implication is that Teddy could go away for the rest of his life based on the color of his skin and the word of a known liar. And you know what the government is banking on? Your inherent prejudice. That Teddy's got the right skin color for you to convict without looking too hard at the case."

I stepped close to the jury and looked as many of them as I could in the eyes.

"So I'm asking only one thing from you: Pretend my client is white. Because the only way you could find this boy guilty of this crime—when his main accuser is a known liar and three boys banded together to point the finger at him, three boys with their full mental faculties blaming a boy who's mentally disabled—is if you think he has the wrong skin color. So I'm asking you, I'm begging you, please, when you go back there and discuss this case, please pretend that Teddy is white."

I sat back down. Some of the jurors couldn't look at me. I could see the guilt in their eyes when they would glance up. They knew I was right and it shamed them—some of them, anyway. Some of them stared coldly at me and Teddy like we were soldiers from an enemy army.

A few of the jurors were staring at Teddy, who was running his fingers over the carving in the table. The judge asked Sandy for a rebuttal. She got up, spoke for exactly five minutes, and said the same things she'd said before. It was known as "hammering home" the facts she wanted the jury to keep in mind during deliberation, a technique taught in trial advocacy classes in law school. I had discovered juries just found it annoying and repetitive.

When she was done, the jury was excused for deliberation. We all stood as they filed out, and my stomach dropped. I usually had a sense for how juries would find. I couldn't really read this one, but I couldn't believe they would find him guilty. Not when the CI was a known liar and Teddy was disabled. They had to see he'd been set up.

"We are excused for deliberation," Roscombe said, hitting his gavel against the sounding block.

Teddy was taken by the bailiffs. "Can we go home, Danielle?"

"Almost, buddy. Little longer."

"Can I get Jell-O?"

I turned to the bailiff. "Can you get him some?"

"We'll see."

Once Teddy disappeared into the bowels of the court, I collapsed into my chair. I got a text from Will that he had to run for a minute but would meet up with me later.

Trials, even just a one day, took it out of me, physically and emotionally. I rubbed my head and then rose to leave. I saw Stefan sitting in the audience seats. I smiled and sat next to him.

"That was good," he said. "Hit them in the white guilt."

"White guilt only works if they feel guilty."

He looked out over the courtroom. "You all right?"

"Yeah. No. I don't know."

"Wanna drink? I'm buyin'."

"I would love to."

52

There was a bar not far from the courthouse. We sat and ordered two beers and didn't talk for a minute.

"You haven't seen me in trial in ten years," I said.

"I know. You've improved. I remember your first trial. You were so scared your hands were trembling. You won that one, do you remember?"

"Yeah. I think the jury just felt sorry for me. I threw up before the trial, did I tell you that?"

"No. When?"

"Right before. I asked for a two-minute break to return an emergency call and then puked my guts out in the bathroom." I shook my head. "My client didn't even thank me after. That should've been a sign that I was going into the wrong profession."

"I don't think it's the wrong profession. You're good at what you do."

"Pablo Escobar was good at what he did, too. I wouldn't have recommended he continue."

He smiled before taking a long drink of beer. "Not the same." He paused, staring into the amber fluid. "You really gonna move to LA?"

"Yeah. Soon as possible. I miss California. I miss the ocean. Maybe I'll open a little burrito shack on a beach somewhere. No stress, no mess, just sunshine and drinks and the sound of the waves all day."

"Sounds like paradise."

I nodded and gazed at my beer. "I am so in love with you."

He stared at me a second. "Dani, I—"

"You don't have to say anything. I just wanted to say it one more time." I looked at him. "You really gonna marry her?"

He hesitated and then nodded.

I took another sip of beer and stood up, laid a ten on the bar, and kissed his cheek before heading back to the courthouse.

———

I lay on one of the benches outside Roscombe's courtroom and covered my face with my forearms, protecting it from the brutal lighting. I dozed off for a while before I felt someone near me. I peeked through my fingers and saw that it was Mia Roscombe, standing in front of me with his hands in his pockets, wearing a sweater-vest and tie with Dockers.

"Little rest, Counselor?"

"You have to sneak them in where you can."

He nodded. "You certainly do. I recall, when I had my own firm some forty years ago, that I would sleep on the couch because it would save time that I could bill rather than driving all the way home."

"I didn't know you had your own firm. Defense?"

"Some. I had to take whatever came through the door. Lawyers back then didn't really specialize. You had to know how to set up a trust and conduct a breach-of-contract trial in the same day."

"Sounds stressful."

He shrugged. "No malpractice lawyers around back then either," he said with a grin.

I sat up. "Can I ask you something? Between me and you?"

"I don't know if that's appropriate."

"Judge, this entire trial is inappropriate and you know it." He didn't say anything. "She wants to lower the number of black voters in this county. If a juvenile is tried as an adult for a felony, that felony follows them into adulthood and they can't vote. That's what this whole thing is about. There's been a surge of black and Mexican voters, and she wants to make sure she and her friends don't get overwhelmed at the polls. Did you know that?"

He looked down at his shoes, staring at a scuff mark on the toe. "Those in power have only one goal: to stay in power. That shouldn't surprise you."

"That doesn't surprise me. What surprised me is how many judges they have going along with this. You and at least one on the court of appeals. Probably one on the supreme court. You and I disagree on your sentences and your manner on the bench, but I never thought you would do something so blatantly wrong."

He inhaled deeply. "The DA should have the power to decide if a juvenile is tried as an adult. I cannot tell you the number of cases I had as a prosecutor where I just knew the juvenile was going to go on to become a monster, but there was nothing I could do. The Serious Youth Offender Act is a mistake. Our prosecutors should have that power. So to that end, I agree with her."

I didn't attack him. There was no point. He was a true believer in his own crusade. Instead, I lay back down and stared at the ceiling. He shuffled into the courtroom. We'd had a chance to see each other as human beings rather than enemies, and seeing him for who he really was was worse. I preferred not knowing.

I heard the elevator doors open. Will stood there smiling at me and I smiled back. Before I could say anything, the clerk came out of the doors. "They have a verdict."

53

It'd taken this jury an hour and forty-seven minutes to decide Teddy's fate. Everyone trickled back into the courtroom. Teddy came out with Jell-O smeared on his shirt. He sat down. "They gave me Jell-O, Danielle. They gave me grape and strawberry see, but I like grape. I like grape Jell-O, see."

I couldn't breathe. My chest tightened and my vision was constricting into a gray tunnel. I had to close my eyes and suck in some deep breaths before I could open them again and take in what I was seeing.

Once the bailiff seated the attorneys and everyone in the audience, Roscombe said, "Bring out the jury, please."

We stood up and sat down again and I barely noticed. My brain was a goopy mess, unable to hold a single thought for more than a second or two. I watched the jury file in and tried to predict what they had done. I couldn't tell anything from the way they moved.

"Ladies and gentlemen of the jury," Roscombe said, "it's my understanding you have reached a verdict. Will the foreman please rise and address the court?"

A pale man with a thin mustache stood up at the end of the first row. "I'm the foreman, Your Honor. And yes, we've reached a verdict."

"Please pass it to my bailiff."

They gave the verdict form to the bailiff, who walked over and handed it to the judge. The judge read it and handed it back.

"Will the defendant please rise?"

I helped Teddy to his feet. My hand slipped down to his, and our fingers interlaced. He rocked back and forth silently.

"What say you in this matter?" Roscombe said.

The foreman began reading the verdict form. "In the matter of the state of Utah versus Theodore Montgomery Thorne, on the sole count of distribution of a controlled substance alleged to have occurred on April second within the Hoover County limits, we find the defendant guilty."

I felt like I'd been punched in the chest and I had to suck in breath as though I were drowning. I gripped Teddy's hand even tighter as the judge thanked the jury for their time. Tears filled my eyes. I could barely stand; my knees felt like they might dislocate from my legs. My chest constricted like a fist.

"You fucking idiots," I shouted. "You damn fucking idiots."

"Counsel!" Roscombe bellowed. "You will apologize to this jury immediately."

I couldn't even muster the strength to yell at him. I just collapsed into my chair as Roscombe said, "Please take the defendant into custody and remove him from the courtroom. Counsel, I'm setting a sentencing date to give Adult Probation and Parole time to prepare a presentence report. I'm also scheduling a contempt hearing for Ms. Rollins immediately following the jury's removal from this courtroom . . ."

He kept talking, but I didn't hear what he was saying. I just watched, numb, as a bailiff lifted Teddy by the arm and Teddy kept looking back at me. His fingers slipped out of mine and he said, "Danielle, are we going home?"

Another bailiff grabbed him and they pulled him along. He kept trying to look at me even as they shouted at him to look forward. I couldn't meet his eyes.

"Danielle? Danielle are we going home?"

Just before he disappeared through a door, I heard him yell, "Danielle!" one more time, and then there was silence.

Once the jury left, Roscombe held a contempt hearing. He asked whether I admitted or denied the allegations. I said I admitted that he was a prick.

Back in the cell, I sat on the cot and watched the light glimmer off the linoleum in waves; it would puddle in one spot, only to move away as the motion sensors turned lights off and on. At one point, I sat completely in the dark and felt warm tears slide down my cheeks. The stuff I had said in closing about the color of Teddy's skin being the most aggravating circumstance was to make the jury feel guilty. Now I realized it was the truth.

One of the guards walked by and the lights came on. He looked at me and chuckled. When he was gone, and I was left in darkness again, I buried my face in my hands and wept.

54

Under Utah's contempt laws, Roscombe could only hold me at most for five days. He kept me that night and most of the next morning before letting me go and giving me the date for Teddy's sentencing. There was no reason to be anxious about it; Roscombe would give him the maximum sentence of five to life. The parole board would probably let Teddy out at the five-year mark, but five years in prison for a mentally disabled boy . . . I didn't know how he would survive.

When I stepped outside of the courthouse, I had to squint. The holding cells were in a dark hallway, and the lights had been off more than on.

Parked in front, leaning against his car, was Stefan. He smiled at me. "Will told me you called him and said you'd be here. I thought you could use a ride. They towed your Jeep."

"I'll just take a Lyft. Thanks, though."

"It's really no problem."

I grinned as I placed my hand gently on his cheek and then leaned in and kissed him. His lips tasted like fruity lip balm and they were soft, as soft as I remembered them being.

"You've done enough for me," I said. "You have a soon-to-be wife to take care of. You should go and take care of her."

He held my hands as he looked down at the pavement. "Dani . . ."

"You don't owe me a damn thing. I screwed it up. Over nothing. That's what really pisses me off. It was over nothing." I hesitated. "You know why I slept with that guy? I wanted you to leave me. We were getting so comfortable. So . . . normal that I couldn't stand it. I needed that drama in my life, pain and pleasure and the huge ups and down. It felt like I was dying when everything was going well with no turbulence."

"That's not a good trait."

"You're telling me. That's probably why I'll be the crazy cat lady in twenty years." I slipped my hands out of his. "Go be with your wife, Stefan."

He looked as though he wanted to say something, but he didn't. He just got into his car and drove away. When he was gone, I sat down on the curb and cried some more.

As I sat staring at the gutter, I knew I had screwed up everything in my life. My marriage, this case, my career . . . Everything had been destroyed because I couldn't be honest with myself. What I'd told Stefan was true: the mundane terrified me, and all marriages seemed to get mundane eventually. But only now did I see that maybe the mundane was where the beauty was: That you could be with another person and hold them, and the rest of the world didn't matter. That you didn't have to be doing or saying anything. Only now that I'd lost everything did I realize what it was I had lost.

My phone rang. It was Jack. I wiped away my tears and took a deep breath.

"Hey, baby."

"Hey, Mom."

"What're you doing?" I said, trying to keep it together so he couldn't tell I'd been crying.

"Dad said I should call you."

"You don't have to, baby. I'm fine."

He hesitated. "I looked up who Jim Morrison was."

I grinned through the tears. "Oh, yeah? What did you think?"

"I kinda like a few of their songs. He's pretty cool. He seems like a dude who doesn't care what anybody else thinks of him. I thought he was like you. Just like . . . doing his own thing and not caring what everybody else does."

I put my other hand to my head, staring down at the pavement. "Your mama's a screwup, baby. I wish that was me, but it's not. I've ruined everything in my life."

"I don't know. Dad said you're at your best when you're at your lowest. I don't really know what that means, but he said you always win when you want to." He paused. "Anyway, I gotta go. Love you, Mom."

"I love you, baby."

When I hung up, there was only one person I wanted to call. Will answered on the first ring.

"Where are you?" he said. "Are you out? Stefan said he wanted to pick you up, is he there?"

"I'm sitting outside the courthouse. No, he's not here. I told him to go home."

"Be there in a jiff."

"You don't have to."

"Like hell I don't."

I moved aside the strand of hair in my face and decided I would be getting drunk. I looked back at the courthouse. Teddy was completely unaware he was about to get a life sentence. He was a kid lost in a jungle. It made me want to vomit. I had to look away.

Will showed up half an hour later and I got into the passenger seat of his Mercedes. He sat looking at me awhile and said, "So? What do you want to do?"

"The nearest bar, please."

55

I couldn't remember the name of the bar, and Will went shot for shot with me. He called one of his assistants to pick up his car, and when evening came we walked to a karaoke bar across the street. It was packed, and someone was at the piano singing Billy Joel. The entire crowd sang along. We got a table in the back and ordered shots. I had now been drinking for five hours straight, but it didn't seem like enough. I guzzled a couple of fruity cocktails after the shots.

"You sure that's a good idea?" Will shouted over the din of the song.

"No, it's definitely not."

The shots came and, again, he took them with me. It was like marching to a firing squad and having a loyal friend with you. I sang at the top of my lungs and Will joined in. We held hands across the table.

When I was thoroughly trashed, Will summoned an Uber and we waited outside. I had my arm around his neck, and he had his around my waist. I rested my head against his. He smelled good, the same old cologne.

I rubbed his chest and tried to kiss him. He pushed me away. "No, not while you're drunk. It wouldn't be right."

Without any warning, the tears came. I didn't recognize them at first and had to touch my face to realize it was wet. Will asked me what was wrong, and that's when I couldn't hold it back anymore. I put my arms around him and cried on his chest. He held me tightly and didn't let go, even when the car came. Not until I was done.

"You all right?" he said softly as I pulled away and wiped my eyes.

"No, no I'm not all right. He's going to be in prison, Will. He's going to be in there with monsters and he's just a kid. He's so damn innocent he won't know what they're doing to him. The thought of it makes me want to die."

"Don't talk like that."

"What's the point? What's the fucking point, when the government can do things like this? When they can treat people as things? When they can spy on us and put us in prison whenever they want and kill us like we're nothing? Why keep moving forward when we're not human to them?"

He looked at me with his soft eyes and said, "I have never, not once, seen you back away from a fight. And you won't back away from this either."

"It's over. I lost."

He shrugged. "I haven't seen losing stop you before." He kissed my forehead and wiped away a few more tears. "Tonight, we're gonna go crash at my place. And then tomorrow, we'll think about what to do. Okay?"

I nodded, taking a deep breath. He took my hand, and we got into the waiting car.

56

I woke up in Will's soft, luxurious bed with silk sheets. It smelled faintly of lavender. Too girly for me, but I could see the appeal.

I rolled out and realized I was wearing one of his T-shirts and nothing else. I found my clothes on the floor and slipped them on before heading out to the living room. Will was asleep on the couch.

His condo was in one of the tallest buildings in Salt Lake. One wall was entirely glass and overlooked the city. The sun coming up tinted the glass on the buildings gold and cast shadows from the blinds. I stood in front of the windows and looked down over the city. I wondered what view Teddy had this morning when he woke up.

"Pancakes?" Will asked as he opened his eyes and rubbed them.

"Please. And thanks for letting me crash here."

"Anytime, woman."

He went into the kitchen for a minute and came out with two cups of tea and handed me one. I took a sip. "It's beautiful up here. Must've cost a fortune."

He shrugged as he looked out over the streets below. "What's money for if not to enjoy things?" He looked at me. "You doing okay?"

I shook my head and stared out in silence for a while. "I still can't believe it. It's surreal that Teddy's going to prison."

"You know, and I'm just playing devil's advocate here, the evidence is pretty good. It's possible he did this himself. I mean, granted, he had to have been working for somebody, but it's totally possible he knew what he was doing."

I shook my head. "It doesn't matter that he's guilty. That's what people don't understand about our system: guilt or innocence doesn't matter. It's the process that matters. The process has to be fair, otherwise we're just the Soviet Union with better robes for our judges. This process was rigged from the beginning. From the time he was arrested to the time the jury found him guilty, nothing about this process was fair."

He took a deep breath and sat down on the couch. In front of him, on the massive glass coffee table, was my Teddy Thorne file. I hadn't even noticed it, but he had spread out all the documents and photographs.

"What are you doing?" I asked.

"There's something in here. Something that can help this thing on appeal. We are appealing it, right?"

"Not me, but I'll try to get someone. Will, I've been through that file more times than I can count. There's nothing in there."

"You went through it looking for trial tactics, not appellate strategies. Right?"

"Yeah, I guess."

"So let's get to work."

We pored through the file. An hour went by. We ate pancakes with blueberry syrup while we read every line, listened to every bit of audio, and reflected on the testimony in court. The big question: Where did Teddy get the drugs? He couldn't have gotten them on his own, so that meant he got them from Kevin or someone else.

"I don't know," I said. "Kevin seemed pretty sincere to me. It's rare for someone to be that good at lying."

"He kinda did to me, too. So let's start with that assumption: it wasn't Kevin who set him up. Then who? One of the other boys?"

I shook my head as I flipped through the photos. Will, as part of his investigation, had gone to the evidence holding room and taken his own photos of everything. You never knew what photos the police would include in what they gave you, so every good defense attorney sent their own investigator. I carefully looked through Will's photos and the ones the State had introduced at trial. "If we assume Kevin is telling the truth, then he cares about Teddy. He wouldn't have let one of the other boys do that to him."

"Then who?"

I flipped through photos of the cocaine, and then saw the gym bag Teddy had carried the coke in, the FHY symbol prominent near the zipper. A photo Will had taken that I hadn't noticed before.

"Remember the bag?" I said.

"Yeah," he said with a mouthful of pancake. "What about it?"

"It's his father's bag, right? He works at FHY. You think Teddy just grabbed it and left the house? Wouldn't his father notice?"

"Not necessarily. I keep my gym bags in the hall closet and wouldn't have a clue if someone took one. If Teddy got the coke from Kevin or someone else, he'd have to put it somewhere. Maybe whoever got him the coke made him grab a bag from his father to make it look like it was his. That's what I would do if I was trying to screw somebody. And Kevin's dad and Teddy's dad might be golfing buddies, who knows? Totally possible Thorne gave that bag to Kevin's father and Kevin had Teddy use it."

"His mom did say in her written statement to the police that Teddy must've sneaked out, and I guess he could've grabbed the bag then, but if there's one thing Teddy's not good at, it's being stealthy. He can't."

"I don't know. I guess we could go ask the dad about the gym bag. Maybe talk to Kevin's dad, too."

I shook my head, staring at the photo. "What is FHY anyway?"

"I don't know, some medical supply company or something."

I took out my phone and googled it. The home page was a nice mix of blue and white, very upscale with stock photos of beautiful models in lab coats. I scrolled through the various testing outsourced to the company: blood testing, genetic testing, forensic testing, drug-therapy testing . . .

"Drug-therapy testing," I said.

"Yeah? So?"

"Don't companies like this have an exception with the DEA and US Justice Department to use illegal narcotics in laboratory testing?"

He looked down at my phone. "Holy shit, woman."

57

Will and I sat outside the office of Michael Bowman, Robert Thorne's supervisor. I paced as Will sat in one of the chairs and read a *Sports Illustrated* that had been on the coffee table.

"You need to relax, lady," he said without looking up.

"I can't believe I didn't see it before. I mean, I saw it—I saw Robert wearing an FHY logo on a jacket and a polo—but I just never put it together. Even when Zamora said on the stand that he thought he'd met Teddy through a friend who worked in a lab, I didn't put it together."

"Could be a coincidence; don't get too excited."

"No way, Will. No way this kid came up with all this himself."

The door finally opened and a bearded man greeted us. He wore jeans and a sports coat and shook my hand. We introduced ourselves, and he asked us to come back and sit in his office.

Will and I sat down, and Michael took his place behind his desk. He closed a window on his computer and crossed his legs before turning to us.

"So," he said, "you told me this was an emergency on the phone. What exactly is going on?"

"It's about one of your employees. Robert Thorne," I said.

"What about him?"

"It's my understanding he's a lab technician, is that right?"

"Yeah, he is. Robert's been with us almost eleven years. What exactly is this pertaining to again, Officer?"

"Oh, I'm not a cop. I'm a lawyer."

"Really? You gave the impression on the phone that—"

"My investigator here found that FHY does extensive studies using narcotics, is that true?" I interrupted.

He looked from one of us to the other. "Yes, that's true."

"Cocaine?"

He leaned back in his chair. "I'm afraid I'm going to have to ask you to speak to our—"

"Michael, this pertains to an ongoing felony case. I can go ask the judge for a warrant, and we can deal with your in-house counsel and jump through all the hoops. I promise though, if you just answer two minutes of questions you will save yourself and us days and days of pain-in-the-ass work. I'd have to subpoena you to testify in court and the whole enchilada. Or we can just talk now."

He hesitated a second. "What is it you want to know?"

"You work with cocaine, right?"

"Yes, we have various ongoing studies using it in the treatment of Alzheimer's. It's all been permitted by the FDA and our shipments are delivered sealed with DEA approval. Everything's aboveboard."

"I'm sure it is. That's not what we're here for. We're here because I'm willing to bet you're missing some of that cocaine."

"Missing? Missing how?"

"As in it's not there anymore."

He grinned. "I don't know who told you that, but we have a strict procedure in place that prevents any type of—"

"I bet Robert Thorne has access to the cocaine, and I'll just bet if you have a look-see you'll find that what's there and what he logged as being there don't match. He'll probably have forged a few things so you'll have to physically weigh the drugs."

He laughed. "Robert? Robert doesn't even jaywalk because he's scared of getting a ticket. There's no way he would do anything like that."

"It'll take ten minutes to go down to your labs and have a look. What'dya say?"

"I think it's best if I now refer you to our in-house counsel."

I glanced at Will. He cleared his throat. "I used to be a narcs detective, Michael," he lied. Will could no more be a narcs detective than Pee-wee Herman could. "You know, if we're right, then Robert stole cocaine from you and sold it out there in the streets. Your cocaine that the DEA entrusted you with. And I can tell you, Michael—I know these guys. The first thing they're gonna be thinking is who else was involved. That means you'll be investigated. And maybe FHY will have your back and maybe they won't. Who knows? But you help us now, you get in front of this thing. No one will even suspect you because you're the guy who uncovered it. That's if we're right. If we're wrong, then you just wasted ten minutes. I know what I'd choose."

He sighed. "Let me call down to the lab first."

58

I pounded on the door with the back of my fist. It took a good minute for someone to answer. It was Riley Thorne. She looked surprised to see me.

"Mind if I come in?"

"I don't think that's a good idea, Ms. Rollins."

"Oh, you're gonna want to hear what I have to say."

Will ran up behind me from the car after finishing a phone call. "I'm here, I'm here; you ladies can relax."

We both glared at him, and he cleared his throat and adjusted his tie.

"Let us in," I said, turning to Riley. "You'll want to talk to me."

She hesitated and then opened the door. I walked in and took a seat at her dining room table. She stood quietly for a moment, waiting for me to begin. I stayed silent until she sat down. Will stood against the wall near the fridge, taking in the décor.

I took the printout Michael had gotten me and slid it over to her. She looked down at it for a second. "What's this?"

"An inventory report from FHY. Your husband's boss, Michael, was nice enough to provide it to us."

She looked up, her eyes wide with fear. A sound came out of her mouth, but she didn't finish the word, if it was a word—it sounded more like a quiet gasp. She closed her mouth and pushed the sheet of paper back to me.

"I don't know what any of that means."

"Oh, it's really interesting. See, FHY is authorized to do experimentation with controlled substances. The DEA provides various narcotics to them for testing for things like Alzheimer's, autism, all sorts of stuff. They do a lot of experiments with cocaine, or at least they have been the last few years. They're interested, according to Michael, in how cocaine affects metabolism and brain function. Just studies in rats so far." I pushed the sheet of paper back toward her. "We asked Michael about it and he said Robert, your husband, is in charge of the inventory. So we had him go back and look through the logs, and it turns out all the books matched up in the computer. Until you actually weighed the cocaine. *Then* they didn't match up. Apparently the company's been receiving more cocaine than it has in its stock. The last time it was short, it was by eight kilos. The same amount Teddy gave to Zamora that night. Weird coincidence, don't you think? Oh and the guy Teddy gave the coke to, apparently a friend of his is a janitor at FHY. Weird, right?"

I leaned forward, staring into her eyes, which had the same expression as those of an animal stuck in a trap.

"You knew what your husband was doing, and you let Teddy go down for it anyway. You were forcing him to sell."

She shook her head. "No . . . no, I would never do that."

"Michael's pulling the security videos right now. Doesn't have all of them yet, but we did find a nice one of Robert putting multiple wrapped squares of cocaine into a gym bag at the end of March. Imagine that. He was on camera stealing cocaine at the end of March and Teddy got busted on April second."

She swallowed and looked down at the paper. "I didn't want him to do it," she said softly. "Because he was disabled and underage, Robert thought that nothing would happen even if he did get caught."

"How many times did he make Teddy do it?"

She swallowed. "Five or six I think. He would have Teddy call to set things up and Robert would tell him what to say. Teddy just . . . he wasn't supposed to ask Kevin for a ride. He was supposed to wait for an Uber like he did all those other times. It wouldn't have changed anything but at least those other boys wouldn't have gotten in trouble. I think Teddy wanted to spend time with the boys because he thought they were his friends."

Her eyes were wet with tears now.

"You don't know what it's like. We've spent all our savings on his care. Special schools, therapists, psychologists, psychiatrists . . . it never ends. The government programs don't pay for much. We did everything we could. I tried to stop it from happening, but Robert said it was risk free, that the cocaine was untraceable and no one but some drug addicts would be getting harmed."

I gave a sad little grin. "Pretty stupid to use a bag with his company logo on it then, isn't it?"

"Robert never was good at breaking the rules." She wiped the tears away from her eyes. "He said nothing would happen to Teddy because he was young and disabled. I knew that wasn't true. That's why I forced him out of the house at eighteen. I knew that Robert would make him keep selling and I didn't want to risk it. I did that for him."

"Yeah, you're a real mother of the year." I folded my arms. "Where is Robert? He wasn't at work today."

"He's fishing."

"Get him back here. I don't care how. Some agents from the DEA field office are on their way down here and they want to have a little chat."

Tears welled up in her eyes. "I didn't want any of this. It was just . . . we were going to lose our house. Robert thought that this would be an easy way to . . ."

"Riley, your son is going to go to prison. Do you understand that? He was convicted yesterday. He's in there for something your husband forced him to do. It's called duress. It's a defense for the type of crime he was convicted of. I think if you come forward, I can file—or someone else can file—an appeal and have him retried. The Hoover County attorneys might even just dismiss the case." I paused and watched her. "They don't actually need you. The discrepancies and the videos will be enough. But if you cooperate, maybe they'll consider not filing charges against you, too."

It was true; her cooperation wasn't required. We already had enough to get the verdict nullified on appeal and at the very least get Teddy a new trial. If nothing else, the appellate attorney could run this up to the federal courts away from Utah and list all the violations Roscombe committed and the new evidence. The Tenth Circuit Court of Appeals might just overturn the verdict without a retrial. I could also present the new evidence to Roscombe before sentencing and ask for a judgment notwithstanding the verdict, which meant that he could overrule the jury and find Teddy not guilty. Given the new evidence and the media attention I was about to bring to the case through Clay from the *Salt Lake Tribune*—who was flabbergasted at the verdict—Roscombe might just crack.

But I wanted to make sure it would happen. *Absolutely* sure. And if Riley cooperated and gave a full confession of how Teddy had been forced to engage in drug dealing because he didn't understand what was occurring, I knew I could get him out.

She sat still a long time before speaking. "Okay . . . okay. For Teddy, I'll help you. I owe him that much."

"You owe him a helluva lot more than that, but it's a start." Her cell phone was on the table and I slid it across to her. "Call your husband and get him back here."

———

While Riley called, with Will making sure she said what she was supposed to say, I sat out on the porch. I couldn't help but think of my own mother. Had she forced me out of the house for what she thought was a similar reason? To protect me? I didn't remember much about my mother. Maybe she was a drug addict who knew she didn't want that life for me. Maybe she was lazy—it was hard raising a child and she just wasn't woman enough to do it. She was wrong; Riley was wrong—but I felt sorry for them both.

I rose and went back inside.

59

I didn't think it'd be proper for me to stick around for the arrest. I didn't want any sort of impropriety on this. So Will and I parked down the block and watched. It was late in the evening when Robert got home. The two DEA agents were already inside the house waiting for him. About twenty minutes after he got home, he came out with his head down, each agent holding an arm. They got into the black SUV the agents had shown up in and drove away.

"Holy shit," Will said. "I can't believe you did that. Your client was convicted and you still might get him off."

"I can't believe his parents did that *to* him."

"I told you, you don't know what anyone is capable of. Not really. I don't know, though. I feel for the parents, too. Can you imagine raising a kid like Teddy? How much effort and time and money it would take? Maybe they just felt like they were owed a little something, too."

"If they had paid attention to him, they would have seen that they got more than they put in." I started the Jeep. "I need to draft a motion for a judgment notwithstanding the verdict. Roscombe might deny it, but you never know. If he denies, I'm going to give this to an appellate attorney I trust. There's so much evidence now I think any appellate judges Sandy had in her pocket won't want any part of this."

"Hey," he said, placing his hand on my arm before I put the car in drive. "Nice work. I mean that. No other lawyer would've gone through all this shit for that kid. I think it's really cool that you did this."

We watched each other a second, and then I leaned in and gave him a quick kiss.

"Wow," he said.

"I know. Don't let it go to your head."

He removed his hand and put on his sunglasses. "All right, drop me off at the Lizard. I'm going to start the celebrations while I wait for you."

"Thought you were heading to Fiji today."

"I cancelled my flight for now. Thought maybe I should stick around a little longer. You know, make sure you're okay. I can always reschedule."

"I'm, um . . . I'm glad. I mean, I'm glad that you're staying for now."

He smiled. "I'm glad, too."

60

As I had expected, Roscombe denied the judgment notwithstanding the verdict. It was basically a motion that said the jury got it wrong and it needed fixing. The day he denied it, I filed an interlocutory appeal and asked for an expedited review because my client was in custody and a susceptible inmate, meaning he could be hurt if the court of appeals didn't hurry.

The appeal included a sworn affidavit from Riley, Robert's confession to the DEA, and a letter from the US Attorney's Office indicating they would be pursuing charges against Robert ranging from distribution of a controlled substance, theft, fraud, and burglary to exploitation of a vulnerable minor. They would not pursue any charges against Teddy.

I sent a copy of the appeal to Sandy. I wished I could've been there when she saw it. Expletives must've flown, and at least one or two pens were thrown, I was sure.

I also called every media outlet I could and gave interviews. The story of the father using his disabled child to sell drugs became the talk of Utah and was even on a few national outlets. One night, I saw a picture of Sandy on a news website as she pushed past reporters to get into a courthouse. Apparently the Utah State Bar had opened an investigation into her for inappropriate conduct. Someone had sent them an audio recording of Sandy discussing getting more blacks and Latinos convicted of felonies to prevent them from voting. The other female voice on the recording couldn't be identified, according to the *Salt Lake Tribune*.

Within ten days, the court of appeals had granted my interlocutory appeal. At that point, I gave the case to David Isaacson, an attorney I trusted, and he ran with it. It would've been improper for the trial attorney to appeal, since one of the claims would also have to be ineffective assistance of counsel. It was a standard claim filed on any appeal, saying the lawyer could've done more.

Four days after I had handed the case off, they reversed the jury verdict and arranged for a new trial based on unethical prosecutorial conduct and judicial misconduct. Rather than try Teddy again, the State dismissed. Anywhere else, Sandy would have been removed from office, but that never happened in Hoover County. She was kept on as the district attorney. The only hope of removal was if the Bar suspended or disbarred her. I didn't care about that, though. Right then, the only thing I cared about was that Teddy would be freed.

When he was released from jail, I was the only one there to greet him. He came out in the clothes he had gone in with, and when he saw me, he grinned and ran up to me. I thought he would hug me but instead he went into a detailed account of the latest episode of *Lost* that they had let him watch through the cell door. I waited until he finished before I hugged him, and he hugged me back. We got into my Jeep.

"Where we going, Danielle?"

"We're going the hell away from here, buddy. And we are never coming back."

61

Kelly and I sat on her porch with beers in our hands. She had the radio on inside, something by Adele playing, and guys kept texting her.

"You are the popular one, aren't you?" I said.

"Yeah, it's kinda boring though. One date after another. It just gets old. And guys now don't want to commit to anything. It's like they're all fifteen years old and just looking to get laid as many times as they can. It's annoying being out on the dating scene. I just wish I had something like you and Will."

"Me and Will? We're just friends."

She chuckled. "You are so brutally honest with everyone but yourself, aren't you?" She took a sip of beer. "You remember that first day we met at my former firm? You walked in by yourself to a deposition that had ten attorneys on the other side. They thought they were going to intimidate you, but you scared the shit out of all of them. I thought you were a superhero. But even superheroes can only be alone for so long. You need someone, Dani. Will is crazy in love with you, and I think you love him, too."

I looked out into the road. "I don't even know what love is anymore. The one guy in my life I loved, I broke his heart. Maybe it wasn't love at all? Maybe you don't do that to people you love."

"Or maybe you're a human being and you make mistakes."

I sighed and looked her up and down. "You're pretty wise for someone that still has stuffed animals on her bed."

We tapped beers and my phone buzzed. It was a text from Will that just said: *Did I mention already how proud I am of you?*

I smiled and took another sip of beer.

62

Jack looked me over. He adjusted something on my dress, pulling it down farther over my stockings. He eyed me like a sculptor looking at a piece of marble as we stood in front of the mirror in my bedroom.

"Jack, maybe I shouldn't go to this."

"I think you should, Mom."

"I mean, neither of them want me at this thing."

"Yeah, but I want you there."

I exhaled loudly. "Fine. I'll stay for the vows and leave after that."

"Stay for the party, too."

"I don't think I have that in me, pal. Sorry."

"Okay, just the vows."

I checked myself in the mirror one more time. I had butterflies in my stomach and that tightening feeling in my chest. I thought about maybe checking on Teddy one last time. It had taken several weeks to arrange, but he was now set up in an apartment with another kid from his class. I'd helped them move in. They had a giant whiteboard with all the dates written on it of the bills to be paid and the chores that needed to be done. They took turns washing dishes and cooking and cleaning. They did everything on their own. Something almost no one, certainly not Teddy's parents and not even me, thought they could do. Kelly had been right: he just needed a chance to grow.

Teddy's schoolwork was going well, and his teacher even said in a year or two he could go to the community college. When I asked what he wanted to do, he said, "I want to be a lawyer."

I didn't talk him out of it.

"We're gonna be late, Mom."

"I'm coming."

———

Peyton and Stefan's wedding took place on the top of a cliff overlooking Big Cottonwood Canyon. It was about as serene and picturesque as anyone could imagine. Peyton's family was there, seemingly hundreds of them, and Stefan's parents had flown in as well. They didn't say hello to me.

Stefan wore a black tux. When we had gotten married, we had no money for anything. He'd worn an old suit he'd bought at a secondhand store. Seeing him here, like this, I was reminded that those were the best times we might ever have—when we were dirt-poor and happy.

The wedding began. Jack and I sat in front. My heart pounded away as Stefan stood at the altar. For a moment, we held each other's gaze. Then the music started playing and Peyton came out. She strode down the aisle with a wide smile, her father next to her. She stood before Stefan and they stared into each other's eyes. My chest tightened as the priest spoke. The magic words came and I saw Stefan look at me . . .

"Do you take her to be your lawfully wedded wife, to have and to hold, through sickness and in health, as long as you both shall live?"

He hesitated and I couldn't breathe. He looked at me again . . . and I knew I had to let him go. This wasn't my happily ever after; this was his. And I wasn't going to ruin it for him. I smiled at him and nodded.

He didn't make a gesture or say anything, but he didn't have to. I knew he understood me.

"I do."

The priest continued and said the same thing to her.

"I do," she said.

I grinned. I loved him, and I wanted him to be happy. Even if it wasn't with me.

Everyone cheered and they kissed. I put my arm around Jack, and he kissed me on the cheek. Will sat next to me and he put his hand over mine and gave it a squeeze. We looked at each other and he said, "You're much prettier than her, you know."

I chuckled.

After the ceremony, I took the tiger's head out of the trunk of my car, and waited until Stefan was alone before I went up to him. I handed it to him. "It's Peyton's. I'm sure she wants it back."

"Thanks."

I nodded and looked down at his buffed and polished shoes. "It was nice. This whole thing was just . . . nice. I'm glad you're happy, Stefan."

"I know." He hesitated. "You still moving to Los Angeles?"

"Um . . ." I glanced back to Will. "You know, someone told me that the system needs people like me to fight. We have a lot of people like me in LA. Not as many here. Maybe I'll stick around a little longer."

"I know Jack will be happy to hear it."

"Thanks."

He swallowed and looked out over the people. "I'm sorry about my parents."

"Oh, don't be. Your mom always hated me anyway."

"That's not true."

"The first time she met me, she asked if I'd ever been to prison."

"I mean . . . you were hungover."

"Yeah," I said with a chuckle. "That's what hungover means. You just got out of San Quentin."

"She's old-school. Don't hate her for that."

I inhaled deeply. "You take care of yourself, Stefan."

"You, too."

I turned and he said, "Hey."

"Yeah?"

"Don't be a stranger."

63

I was sitting by myself when Michelle came in to the Lizard. It was evening and I guessed that Stefan and Peyton were well on their way to their honeymoon in the Bahamas. They had opted to take Jack and I didn't object. I was sure he'd have a blast.

Michelle sat on the bar stool next to me and said, "Beer?"

"This Sprite's fine, thanks."

"Really? Is Dani Rollins trying to cut back on her drinking?"

"About time, I figure. I missed you at the wedding. I'm sure Stefan invited you."

She shook her head. "Couldn't care less. You're my compadre, and anyone that hurts you hurts me."

I chuckled. "You are a loyal compadre."

She held up her hand to signal the bartender. "So, what now?"

I took a sip of my drink. "Kelly thinks I'm in love with Will."

"Are you?"

"I don't know . . . I think so. But I'm terrified. If I'm ever bored, how do I know I won't get self-destructive again and cheat?"

"I think you cheated on Stefan because you didn't want to be married to him anymore and you were looking for a way out."

"Then why do I miss him so much?"

She guzzled half her beer in one gulp. "You remember Robert Pierce? That kid with the goofy haircut who was on the chess team?"

I grinned. "Oh yeah. Robert. He would follow me around in the halls and try to find some way to talk to me."

"He was obsessed with you and you never even noticed him. Not until Laney Peterson began dating him. Then, suddenly, you noticed him and started following him around. You're one of those people that wants what they can't have." She finished the rest of her beer and belched. "You're not in love with Stefan. That shit ended a long time ago. Go be a Jim Morrison, take that son of a bitch Will in your arms, and give him the wettest, longest kiss he's ever had."

And that's exactly what I did.

EPILOGUE

I don't think I had ever felt so sick in my life. I couldn't catch my breath. Jack gripped my hand tighter. The sun beat down on us and warmed my face, and I tried to focus on that sensation and push all the other thoughts out of my head.

"We don't have to do this, Mom."

"Yes we do."

"We can come back and try it another time."

I shook my head. "No, we're here. We've paid, and I don't know if I can get here again. It's gotta be now."

He looked at the front entrance and back to me. "You sure?"

I nodded. "Yeah."

Will held my other hand. Since I'd moved into his condo, he seemed to always have this boyish grin on his face. Like he was exactly where he wanted to be.

He looked from Jack to me and said, "The kid's right. This isn't necessary."

"It's necessary," I said, my eyes never leaving the entrance.

They both gripped my hands tighter. Teddy stood next to us licking an ice cream cone and said, "It'll be fun, Danielle."

"Okay. Let's do it, lady," Will said.

Slowly, Will and Jack led me forward, Teddy walking in front of us, almost skipping. Mickey Mouse sat over the entranceway, and we handed over our tickets. I looked down at my son, my boy who had stuck with his mother when she thought no one in the world gave a crap about her. I leaned down and kissed him on the head. And then we pushed through the turnstile, and into the one place in the world I dreaded more than any other.

"Mom?" he said, as we walked casually inside.

"Yeah?"

"Thanks for bringing me here."

I put my arm around his shoulders. "I'll always be here for you, Jacky. Always. Your mom's not going anywhere."

"I know." He looked around. "So you wanna go on a ride first?"

I nodded. "Yeah. The teacups. I've always wanted to do the teacups."

He put his arm around my waist, and we headed there together, the four of us, and I knew that I was wrong when I'd thought that the best moments in my life were with Stefan. This moment, right now, was the best it had ever been, and I looked forward with wonder to what else would be coming my way.

I smiled, and decided Disneyland wasn't so bad.

AUTHOR'S NOTE

The most surprising thing about writing legal novels is the amount of email I get from fans saying they loved the books, but that would never happen in real life. "The legal system doesn't work that way," they'll say.

I've been a criminal attorney for over a decade, first as a prosecutor and then a defense attorney, and you know what I've learned over those years? Reality doesn't have to make sense.

Every legal novel I've written is based on a case I actually had. Sure, I've changed names, locations, dates, details of the case, defendants' genders and ages; I've sped up or slowed down the procedure that actually took place, or left out legal details for convenience of the reader. But the core stories are the same: the weak and the helpless against a system set up to crush them. We don't like to face those facts—facing injustice is hard—but there they are for everyone to see in all their horror.

Our system is the best in the world, but there's a long way to go before we find true justice. When a judge tells me in private, "You're right about the law, but I don't care about the law—I'm going to do what I think is right," or when a police chief tells me, "You follow a black person around until they commit a traffic violation and pull them over, nine times out of ten they're gonna have drugs," I lose hope. And then every once in a while I get a case where the innocent really are vindicated, where juries and judges really do their jobs and weigh the evidence without letting their prejudice get in the way, and I think that our system still has hope.

It's only truly hopeless if good people see injustice and do nothing.

VM, Bear Lake, Idaho, 2016

ABOUT THE AUTHOR

 Victor Methos has been fighting for the rights of individuals against the government as a criminal-defense and civil-rights lawyer for more than a decade. He has conducted more than one hundred trials and has been named one of the most reputable attorneys in the Mountain West by *Utah Business* magazine. He is the author of more than forty novels, including the Neon Lawyer series and the Jon Stanton mysteries.

He currently splits his time between Las Vegas and Utah, and is on a quest to climb the Seven Summits.